Visiting Miss Austen

ANGELA PEARSE

Set in Halsey and Sabon.
Cover art by My Lan Khuc Valle.

ISBN 978-1-914531-79-8 Paperback (IngramSpark)

Catherine had nothing to oppose against such reasoning; and therefore, to show the independence of Miss Thorpe, and her resolution of humbling the sex, they set off immediately as fast as they could walk, in pursuit of the two young men.

(Jane Austen, *Northanger Abbey*)

PART ONE

An Invitation

Chapter 1

Steventon Rectory

3 May 1799

Dear Flissy,

I trust you have recovered from your nasty cold? The weather here in Steventon has been atrocious, and we have not escaped illness ourselves. Cassie has a sore throat that has lasted for three days! As you know, she hates being ill and insists on being up and about but then will complain about feeling poorly. She will not gargle, and short of tying her to the bed with strong ropes, I am not sure what else I can do. But she will recover soon enough, I hope.

But on to brighter news! I have just this morning received a letter from my brother Edward telling me he and Elizabeth are going to Bath in the middle of the month. They will stay in 13 Queen Square and reside there for six weeks. The reason for the visit is not purely pleasure—he has gout and plans to take the waters often. They know I enjoyed my visit to Bath two years past (indeed I talked about it to Elizabeth incessantly), so they have generously said I can join them. But that is not the most exciting part—brace yourself, dear—Edward has said there is room enough for me to invite a friend!!! Of course, my dearest Flissy, I immediately thought of you ...

My stomach leapfrogged as I read further down the page where the dates and logistics of the trip had been outlined in detail. Jane had ended her letter urging me to write soonest with my decision and that she hoped I would think of it as an 'adventure rather than a burden to be endured'.

Oh yes, very funny indeed. I was sure she was laughing to herself writing that! She knew I would be squirming with delight upon reading her words; and I had to admit, her invitation had come at a most opportune time, though it was naughty of me to think that.

My sister-in-law, Seraphina Fitzroy, had taken it upon herself to visit us from York for a month; and I was longing for a respite. It was a visit that had been foisted upon Max and I, and neither of us had had any say in the matter.

With her tall imposing figure, jet-black hair, and determined chin, Seraphina was a force from the north to be reckoned with. Max always joked that Seraphina had 'whipped' his eldest brother, Tobias, into shape; and I would not have been surprised if she had taken a literal whip to him.

Both Seraphina and Tobias scared me. But at least this time, she had left her irascible husband at home and brought along her eldest daughter, Lucinda—a quiet dark-haired girl of eighteen whom I liked a lot. She called me Aunty Fliss even though I was but four years older.

Seraphina's latest visit to Derbyshire—I had surmised from her various comments—was to escape Tobias's *vigour* in the bedroom as she was nearing forty, already had five children, and had no wish to become pregnant again. That was something I was glad I didn't have to worry about— Max and I were happily childless. But it was a state I knew Seraphina thought should be rectified forthwith, if her remarks were anything to go by—remarks such as 'These big rooms could do with the pitter-patter of little feet', 'Max is so good with his nieces and nephews—he would make such a wonderful father', and so on were par for the course whenever she stayed.

At first, I let my feelings of guilt overwhelm me, but now I followed Max's lead and ignored her. Or if that was not possible and she expected a reply, I said something noncommittal and then changed the subject. As Max said, it was our marriage and our choice not to spawn child after child, as was the custom; and frankly, it was none of her business what we did or didn't do in the bedroom.

But Seraphina was one of those women who liked to make other people's business her own. And Jane's letter now fell under her scrutiny as we were having breakfast.

'I am curious to know who your letter is from, Felicity. Why, you have read it at least ten times in the space of five minutes.'

I folded the letter and placed it on the table, reluctant to say anything. But as she was looking at me pointedly, I had to say something.

'It is from my friend Jane Austen, who lives in Steventon,' I said, returning to my uneaten toast, now cold since I had been perusing the letter.

'Ah, yes. Clever Miss Austen whom I have heard so much about. What on earth could she have written that has engaged your attention so entirely?' Seraphina smirked to herself, and I knew what she was really thinking: *Whatever could happen in Steventon that would be deemed remotely interesting?*

With this comment, she managed to annoy me immensely. Though I had been settled in Derbyshire for over two years now, I was still a Hampshire girl at heart, and I hated it when people looked down their noses at my small village. Steventon was where Max and I had met and fallen in love, after all; and if *he* could now appreciate the delights of the countryside, anyone could. Besides, Papa lived there; and with my sister, Harriet, now settled in London, I liked to visit him as often as possible. Suffice to say, it was a failing in me, but I couldn't help divulging the letter's contents to make her jealous.

'Actually, it is quite exciting news. Jane is to take a trip to Bath with her brother and his wife in a couple of weeks' time. And she has invited me to join their party,' I said, quelling the urge to add 'so there'.

The rustle of a lowering newspaper and Max's piercing blue eyes appearing over the top told me he'd heard what I'd said.

Blast! I'd hoped to talk to him about going to Bath in private, not under the watchful gaze of his sister-in-law. My heart sank, and Lucinda gave me a sympathetic grimace. She and Max were very similar in temperament: quiet, introspective, and sensitive. At first, I had thought Max arrogant and cold, but now I knew better. He was, as Jane had correctly surmised, painfully shy in the company of people he didn't know well. Lucinda too sometimes came across as aloof as she bore the same affliction as her uncle and had needed time to become acquainted with me. But with my natural inclination to make friends, I had brought her out of herself, like I had with Max. However, as he was also stubborn, getting him to agree to this trip to Bath would likely take all my powers of persuasion.

'How long for?' he asked.

'Six weeks,' I replied carefully, knowing instantly from his tone that he didn't like the idea. He hated me going away, and I from him. But sometimes it was a necessity, like when my sister was about to give birth. She'd needed me to stay for a few weeks to manage her husband because he was in a flap and making her feel anxious. Everything had gone smoothly for Harriet, much to our relief. But Evan had needed much hand chafing and wine to get through it.

As expected, Max's eyebrows now shot up. '*Six weeks*,' he echoed, looking aghast.

'I may not stay that long, dearest. That is just the length of time Jane said they are going for.'

He did not look happy about me going for any length of time.

Seraphina had been in thoughtful silence during our exchange, which should have alerted me that her mind was working overtime.

'Bath,' she murmured. 'Such a wonderfully lively place and so full of opportunities, especially for young ladies of a marriageable age.'

'Yes. Well, I hardly need to worry about that,' I told her. 'I am already happily married.' I took Max's hand and squeezed it, and he smiled at me, albeit in a pained way.

'And your friend Jane, will she be looking for a husband?' continued Seraphina.

I laughed a little at the thought of Jane scouring the streets of Bath, looking for a suitor. 'Perhaps. But knowing Jane, she will more likely be on the lookout for material for her next novel.'

'Oh, of course. She likes to write, like that awful Ann Radcliffe.' Seraphina wrinkled her nose slightly. 'Let us hope her novels are better than that woman's!'

'I have read one of Jane's novels, and it was wonderful,' I said defensively, glancing at Max, who still didn't know that he was Mr Darcy. Jane and I had decided it was better not to say anything unless the novel got published as he might not like what she'd written about him. But if it did get published and was popular, he might be more amenable to seeing himself portrayed as a proud, haughty gentleman who did not care to dance.

'I like Mrs Radcliffe's novels, Mama,' said Lucinda quietly. 'They are evocative and wonderfully imaginative.'

I smiled at her and nodded. 'Harriet loves them too.'

'I see I am outnumbered,' said Seraphina huffily.

As Lucinda smoothed her mother's feathers, I excused myself from the table, thinking I might peruse Jane's letter again in private and formulate a way to present it more agreeably to Max.

Before I could walk off, he said, 'We'll talk about this later, Fliss.' Then he gave me a look. What he meant was 'Mark my words, we will certainly be discussing it because I do not want you to go to Bath'.

But I was determined that I *would* go. Although I was content in my marriage, I had been feeling restless of late and was too excited by the prospect of a change of scenery to pass up the opportunity. A trip to vibrant Bath was just what I needed to blow my cobwebs away!

***

By bedtime, I was in a state of high anxiety and more than ready to go into battle with Max. I had endured his terse silence during lunch and supper and a strained game of whist in the parlour (which I let him win in an effort to make him more agreeable). We were both so strong-willed that I didn't know how this conversation was going to play out.

Max was already in bed, reading by candlelight, as I completed my ablutions at the nightstand and began plaiting my hair by the mirror, going over my opening argument in my head: *Max dearest, I will miss you so much, but it is imperative that I go to Bath.*

Finishing with my hair, I took the candle over to the

bedside table and sat on the counterpane beside him, smoothing the material of my chemise nervously.

'Max dearest—' I began.

But he didn't let me complete my sentence. 'You can go, Fliss,' he said gruffly. 'On one condition. I expect a steady stream of letters from Bath telling me what you've been doing and how much you miss me.'

I let out a squeal. 'Oh! I love you! I love you! Of course I'll write. I'll write every day—morning *and* afternoon!' I bounced up and down on the bed excitedly.

Max chuckled. 'There is no need to go to that extreme. Every second day will suffice.'

'All right!'

Placing his book on the bedside table, he held out his arms; and I launched myself at him, covering his face with kisses, making him laugh. When the kissing frenzy had died down, I snuggled against him, feeling like I had won a great prize, though I hadn't had to do anything much.

'What is all this about?' he asked, stroking my back. 'Why this sudden desire to take off to Bath? You were perfectly happy before Jane's letter arrived.'

'Well, maybe not *perfectly* happy,' I muttered, my head nestled in the crook of his neck. 'Lately, I have been a little—' I bit my lip, not wanting to say the word for fear of offending him.

'A little?' he prompted and waited for me to finish.

Oh, I may as well say it, I thought. *It is best to be honest with him.* 'I have been a little bored,' I said flatly.

Max didn't say anything in reply, but his hand stopped stroking my back and rested heavily on my shoulder blade.

'Not with you!' I added hastily.

He let out a breath. 'Well, that is good to hear. So just bored in general?'

I nodded, feeling awful. 'I'm sorry. I don't want to sound like an ungrateful wife. The house and grounds—*this place*, it is incredible! And of course our home, I *love* living here with you. But you have the estate business to occupy you and your fishing. Apart from riding George and going for walks, I have nothing to do all day ...'

'The library is well stocked,' said Max instantly.

'There are only so many books I can read,' I replied. 'I'm not like Harriet, who would be quite happy to spend all day with her nose in a book. I have no friends nearby to visit, and with Jane in Steventon and Harriet in London ...' I said, trailing off and feeling terribly ashamed of myself. *How dare I not be satisfied with my good fortune! I had secured a handsome husband who loved me dearly, and I lived on a thousand-acre estate. I wanted for nothing.* I knew other women would kill to be in my position and would keep their mouths firmly shut in case it was all taken away from them.

'I'm sorry,' I repeated. 'I am just trying to be honest about how I feel.'

To my relief, Max resumed stroking my back. 'You have nothing to be sorry about, Fliss. I am not totally oblivious to your moods and feelings. I know you have been out of sorts.' He sighed. 'It is partly my fault, I suppose. I had hoped you would be happy enough with my company and occasional visits from my family, but I know it isn't enough for you. Missing your friend and sister isn't a crime, and that is why I think you should go on this trip to Bath.'

'I love you,' I said solemnly, lifting my head to gaze at him. 'You know I never want to be parted from you.'

Max kissed my forehead. 'Nor I you. But absence makes the heart grow fonder, so they say, though my heart already feels as fond of you as it possibly ever could.'

'Oh, Max!' Tears welled in my eyes now that I was facing the reality of actually having to be without him for six whole weeks.

I stared at his beloved face and traced my finger along his cheekbone. Emotion threatened to overwhelm me, and I choked back a sob.

Max's countenance grew sympathetic. 'Don't cry, my love. Six weeks is not so long, and we will write to each other, no? Remember when we were engaged, and we wrote to each other to arrange our secret meetings? It will be like that, but without the actual meeting part.'

I giggled and wiped my eyes on his nightshirt sleeve, and he touched my cheek. 'Yes, it will be a little hard to meet when we are at opposite ends of the country, a hundred or so miles apart,' I said.

Max's gaze met mine, and his fingers that had been on my cheek lowered to undo the tie of my chemise. 'Perhaps we should make the most of the time we have left then?' he suggested huskily.

Indeed, I was feeling rather amorous too after our emotional discussion. So with that, I leaned over and blew out my candle.

Chapter 2

Two weeks later, I was in a carriage barrelling down the road towards Steventon. Outside, the day was bright and sunny, and we were making good time. Inside the carriage, everything was not quite as cheery. There had been a slight hitch in the Bath plan—Lucinda was with me. The girl had been apologising nonstop and had ceased only when we paused at Leicester for luncheon. But she started up as soon as we set off again.

'I am so sorry, Aunty Fliss. Mama is awfully persuasive when she wants something, and only Papa can stand up to her, and sometimes not even him.'

'It is perfectly fine,' I said for the umpteenth time, trying to keep my patience in the swaying carriage—travelling so fast always made me feel nauseous, but our footman wished to make haste while the roads were dry and the weather clear.

'But I hate to be a burden,' replied Lucinda tearfully.

'Do not fret,' I said, closing my eyes and tightening my grip on the door handle as we rounded a sharp bend. 'It is done. You are here, and we will make the best of it.'

'We will make the best of it' was actually borrowed from Jane's most recent letter. She'd written a hasty reply when I'd informed her that Lucinda was coming too as her mother had emotionally blackmailed me.

To give her credit, Seraphina had argued her point eloquently and with heartfelt emotion. 'There is', she had said, having cornered me in the parlour the week before I left, 'simply no one suitable in York for Lucy to marry. I have exhausted all the available options—there is a Mr Fothergill, whom she quite likes. But he is approaching thirty and has the most terrible buck teeth. I do not want my grandchildren inheriting that particular feature.' She shuddered. 'Lucy needs to widen her circle and form new acquaintances. London would be best, but I cannot be spared with four other children at home needing their mother, so you must take her to Bath while the Season is still in session.'

I was surprised that she'd assumed Lucinda could join us that easily. 'But the accommodation has been booked by Jane's brother. I cannot very well turn up with Lucy in tow for that length of time as I myself am a tagalong. Besides, it is an extra expense that they would have to incur—'

'Well, then you must quickly write to Jane and tell her that your niece is accompanying you and that her relations need not worry as they will be paid handsomely for her stay.'

I gulped. That sounded remarkably forward.

'I do not think I can.'

Seraphina shook her head at me and tsked.

'Come now, Felicity. Think of Lucy. Would you have her marry someone unsuitable? Someone with *buck teeth*?'

'Well, if she likes him—'

'No, I have decided. She must go to Bath. It is teeming with eligible young men.'

I raised an eyebrow at that, wondering from where or whom she had obtained her information. Bath was indeed a lively city, but I was not sure that the young men who visited it had marriage on their minds.

'What if there is not enough room?'

Seraphina waved a hand airily. 'Oh, there is no need to cause any fuss. Lucy is small and slim and can make do with a child's cot or a roomy cupboard if there is no cot.'

I had almost laughed out loud at that! Poor Lucinda, being forced to sleep on a cot or shoved into a cupboard!

When I'd told Max about Seraphina's interference, I was confident he'd side with me. But he'd said it was a good idea as I would have company on the journey down and added that Lucy was a good girl and wouldn't be any bother. She'd probably have her nose in a book for most of the time.

Fortunately, Jane's reply about the business had been reassuring. She had told me not to worry and that friends often turned up unexpectedly when these sorts of trips were arranged, so Edward tended to book accommodation with more rooms than were strictly necessary. She'd also informed me that Elizabeth was known for saying 'the more the merrier!' whenever someone was to join their party. So they would not mind if Lucinda came with me. She'd ended her note with 'We will make the best of it!', which I had been saying to myself as a sort of mantra. Somehow, thanks to Seraphina, my carefree escape had morphed into chaperoning my niece and finding her a husband.

And I'd severely underestimated quite how much I would miss my own. My heart had begun to ache quite palpably at the thought of not seeing Max tonight or the next night or the night after that, and I'd only kissed him goodbye this morning!

We had several days of travel before we reached Steventon, where we would spend a few days at Papa's to break up the journey. Lucinda and I would then continue on to Bath via stagecoach, which would take another day, depending on the weather. It had been dry as a bone up until now, so I had high hopes of reaching Bath speedily.

Jane had already left home with her relations and was no doubt settling into the apartment in Queen Square plus scoping out the social scene. I wondered what juicy gossip she would have to impart when we arrived.

* * *

We reached Steventon late in the afternoon on the fourth day. Our footman had deposited us in Oxford, and we had caught a stagecoach from there. When we arrived at my house after a short walk from town with our carpet bags, the sun was dipping in the sky, and the shadows were lengthening in the lanes.

As soon as I unlatched the front gate, Papa immediately flung open the door (he had been watching for me) and strode outside. He was dressed smartly in a fawn suit with a matching waistcoat and white linen shirt.

'Welcome home, my dear.' Papa's smiling countenance was familiar, but also not, and I stared in shock—he had grown a dapper moustache! But it looked well on him, and so overcome was I at seeing him after all this time that I couldn't help bursting into tears.

Papa enveloped me into a firm hug as he teased, 'What's all these tears for ... hmm? Is it that terrible to see me?' Then he kindly lent me his handkerchief, and I mopped my cheeks.

'Who's this you've brought with you?' he asked, and I turned to see Lucinda by the gate, quietly waiting to be introduced. I had forgotten all about her!

'Papa, this is Lucinda Fitzroy, my niece who is accompanying me to Bath. Lucinda, my father, Mr Blackburn.'

'Pleased to meet you, Mr Blackburn,' said Lucinda, giving him a little curtsy.

'Pleased to meet you too, Lucinda,' he said, nodding and smiling at her.

'Oh, do call me Lucy. Everyone at home does,' she replied, a faint blush colouring her porcelain cheeks.

She really is a lovely young woman, I thought. And patient too, having had to listen to me complaining nonstop about my aching bones yesterday.

'Very well. And you must call me Uncle Charles or Uncle, if you prefer. Mr Blackburn is much too formal since we are all family now.'

Lucinda smiled and bobbed again.

'Come in, come in. Both of you must be tired and hungry,' said Papa, taking up our bags.

'Exhausted!' I replied. 'We stayed in a sketchy coaching inn last night with awful damp sheets. I was sure I felt bugs crawling over my legs during the night. I didn't sleep a wink.'

Papa laughed. 'Well, you'll find no bugs here. Mary has spring-cleaned your room ready for you.'

'Dear Mary! And Sue, is she still here?'

'Yes, she is preparing a special welcome-home supper for you.'

My mouth started watering at the thought of our cook's tasty treats, and my stomach gurgled loudly, making Lucinda giggle.

Yes, it was definitely time for supper!

***

It was strange seeing my old room sparsely furnished with only the bed, dresser, and a rug. My clothes, books, and other personal effects had been sent to Derbyshire after the wedding. Being in here brought back a flood of nostalgia, memories of when Harriet and I were single and dreaming about finding handsome husbands of good fortune—little did we know our dreams would come true! I had a sudden pang of nostalgia remembering our night-time chats. *Wonderful, now I was missing my sister as well as Max!* I would endeavour to find time to write them both when I was in Bath.

Supper was served as soon as we had changed into fresh dresses, washed our hands and faces, and tidied our hair. Our travelling trunks were stored at the stagecoach office in town, so we had only what we needed in the way of clothing and accessories for a two-day stay.

'I trust Harriet's room is to your liking, Lucy?' asked Papa when we were seated and starting on the soup course.

'It is very comfortable. Thank you, Uncle.' I smiled at hearing her call him so.

Papa and Lucinda chatted away politely about various things, but I was hungry and concentrated my attention on the corned beef and vegetable broth, which was saltily delicious.

I had just finished my last mouthful when there was a bustle at the door, and Aunt Snelling appeared, beaming. 'Felicity, welcome home!'

'Aunt! How are you?'

I rose to greet her with a kiss and a hug, and she sank down next to me in a flurry of purple silk and patchouli. Aunt's timing was impeccable—she always arrived after the soup, but before the main course, which Papa would urge her to partake in.

'I'm very well. Thank you, my dear.' Her sharp eyes landed on my empty soup plate and then upon Lucinda, who was still eating hers with dainty mouthfuls.

'This is my niece, Lucinda, or Lucy, as she prefers,' I said, nodding across to her. 'She is accompanying me to Bath. It was a last-minute arrangement,' I added when Aunt raised her eyebrows.

'Nice to meet you Mrs ... uh ...' said Lucinda, not

knowing who she was.

'Mrs Snelling. I live next door, but you can call me Aunt, if you like, as the girls do.'

She glanced at Papa, and a look passed between them that I could not fathom. Apart from nodding to her when she had come into the room, he had not spoken.

It was then that I noticed Mama's portrait was not in its usual spot on the wall. First Papa growing a moustache, now Mama's portrait being moved ... What was going on?

'Where's Mama?' I asked, feeling a bit shocked.

Papa lowered his soup spoon. 'She's in the parlour,' he said, not meeting my eyes.

'Is she poorly?' enquired Lucinda. 'Is that why she does not join us for supper?'

There was an awkward silence. I didn't speak about Mama around Max's family, and as they had not attended our hastily arranged wedding, Lucinda was clueless about her.

'My mother is ... not with us anymore,' I said. 'I was referring to her portrait, which has always hung in the dining room for as long as I can remember.' I gave Papa an accusing look.

'It wasn't your father's idea. It was mine,' said Aunt. 'So you can blame me. I suggested she might be more comfortable there, just for a change.'

'Prudence,' said Papa, shaking his head at her.

Another shock wave passed through me. He had never, in all the time I had known Aunt, called her by her first name.

'I see,' I said, wondering if Harriet knew about all these goings-on. If she did, she had not written to me about them. Then again, she was busy with Evie, who was starting to crawl.

Mary came to serve us our main course. So I was distracted by slices of glazed ham, asparagus swimming in lemon butter, and minted new potatoes and did not comment further.

Aunt seemed to detect I was thinking about Harriet in that intuitive way of hers, and she changed the subject neatly. 'Felicity, did you know that Harriet and Evan are staying at Ashbury Manor next month?'

'Yes, she did mention it, but I had not heard that things were confirmed. So they are definitely coming?'

Aunt nodded. 'Yes, you could visit them when you return from Bath perhaps? You haven't seen much of Evie, have you?'

It was true, but I wasn't good with babies—even ones that were related. 'I could, I suppose, though I do not want to be in the way.' *Or have to change nappies or babysit ...*

'Oh, they have a nanny now,' said Aunt approvingly. 'So

you wouldn't be.'

I ate the rest of my ham silently, trying not to feel irritated. Not only had I been coerced into chaperoning one niece, but now it was being suggested I spend time with another who was barely out of her cradle and did not care who I was.

Why did I have to? I supposed it was because I was a woman, and women were meant to have maternal instincts. But I did not, and that made me selfish and strange in society's eyes.

I was still mulling over these thoughts when we turned in for the night. Mary had placed a bed warmer between my sheets some hours ago, and I stuck my cold feet on it to thaw them out. Max was my usual source of heat, but in his absence, I would have to make do with a copper pan.

It had been lovely to dine with Papa and Aunt, like old times. But when we retired to the parlour and I spied Mama's portrait hanging in its new position above the pianoforte, I could not help but feel disconcerted that there were changes happening beyond my control. If I had been living here, would Papa have grown a moustache and consented to Mama's portrait being moved? I think not!

Another thing I was pondering was Aunt's parting remark in the hallway when I saw her out. 'Enjoy your time in Bath, Felicity,' she had said, pulling on her gloves. 'But stay vigilant where Lucinda is concerned.'

'What do you mean?'

'I mean, as her chaperone, you will need to make sure she is not led astray. She is too young and impressionable to be going to such a place.'

I felt like saying, 'It's only Bath, not Sodom and Gomorrah.' But I held my tongue.

'I will do my best, Aunt,' I said dutifully.

She shook her head. 'Pray, what is her mother thinking, sending her there?'

'She wants her to find a husband.'

'Yes, but what kind of husband will she find?'

'A fun one?'

Aunt had tutted, but I didn't think I should be too concerned about Lucinda attracting the wrong kind of man. As Max had said, she was a good girl—a quiet bookworm with too much good sense to be 'led astray'.

Chapter 3

Breaking up our journey at Papa's had been an excellent plan. After partaking of Sue's nourishing meals and having a couple of good night's sleep, I recovered my natural optimism. But all too soon, it was time to leave for Bath; and on that morning, Lucinda and I were up bright and early.

Saying goodbye to Papa was not easy. But he reassured me that he was content and looking forward to Harriet, Evan, and little Evie coming to Ashbury. And that Mrs Snelling was always popping over with news and keeping him entertained—I tried not to dwell on that! A letter to Harriet asking if she knew anything about the nature of their relationship was definitely well overdue!

Meanwhile, we had a day of stagecoach travel to endure. Being packed in with other passengers, and Lucinda's elbow poking into my ribs whenever she moved, could have been trying. But I did not let it temper my excitement. Soon, we would reach Bath and, of course, Jane!

When the coach made an unscheduled stop on a high ridgeline to drop off a passenger who lived in a nearby farm,

Lucinda and I took the opportunity to stretch our legs while their luggage was offloaded. A thin-faced woman had insisted on the window being raised for much of the journey, so I was feeling nauseous again.

I breathed in lungfuls of cool fresh air and delighted in the glorious view. All around were green rolling meadows, and way down in the valley, I saw a church spire rising from a cluster of honey-coloured buildings.

One of the drivers, a middle-aged man with a neatly clipped beard, had joined us for a smoke. 'Excuse me, but is that Bath?' I asked him. He nodded.

'When will we reach it?'

He sucked on his cheroot and blew a stream of smoke out of the side of his mouth downwind.

'Not long, madam, an hour at best,' he replied, flicking something from beneath a fingernail. He glanced at Lucinda, who had wandered off a short way to peer at some grazing cows. 'She your daughter?'

What impertinence! How old does he think I am? 'No, she is not. She is my sister-in-law's daughter. I am but four years older.' I pursed my lips in annoyance.

He saw that I had taken offence and doffed his hat. 'Apologies, madam. It was an easy mistake to make, what with such attractive ladies as yourselves being so similar in appearance.'

I humphed, partly mollified, and he grinned.

He ground out his cheroot stub with his boot heel and said, 'Right, madam, we best be off if you and your *niece* want to arrive in Bath before nightfall.'

I went to collect Lucinda forthwith. Hopefully, it was a one-off occurrence because he had poor eyesight—I did not want to be mistaken for her mother when we were socialising!

Whether the driver urged the horses to gallop faster to make up for his faux pas, I did not know, but the last leg of the journey passed rapidly. Before we knew it, we were standing with our trunks on the front stoop of 13 Queen Square, our home for the next six weeks.

Lucinda's hand rested on my arm, and I could feel it quivering.

'Do not be anxious. The Austens are very friendly and welcoming,' I said and raised my hand to rap the brass knocker smartly on the cobalt-blue door.

We waited, but the door did not open.

'Perhaps they didn't hear it,' whispered Lucinda. So I rapped again, and we waited some more.

Eventually, a maid wearing a white cap with a frilled edge poked her head out.

'Can I help you?' she enquired, somewhat tartly.

'Yes. I am Felicity Fitzroy, and this is my niece, Lucinda. We are staying with the Austens. Are they in?'

'No, ma'am, but they should be back shortly.'

'Did they say we would be arriving?'

The girl shook her head. 'Not to me, ma'am, but I come only in the afternoon to help cook.'

We were ushered into an entranceway, and I felt rather disgruntled by Jane and her relations being out—in my head, I had been expecting a joyous welcoming party! But I quickly adjusted my frame of mind. Something must have occurred, a last-minute engagement or some such.

Lucinda fiddled with the pearl button on her glove and peered down the narrow hallway. 'It is strange they are not here to greet us,' she said, sounding nervous.

'There is nothing to worry about,' I replied, removing my hat and its pin with some relief. 'They probably had an afternoon engagement and were kept later than expected. They are no doubt hastening back to greet us as we speak.'

Because they *were* expecting us on this date and *hadn't* forgotten about us, surely?

The maid showed Lucinda and me to a bright and airy drawing room with a picturesque view of Queen Square. 'I'll let Mrs Bromley know you are here,' she said and went off. I assumed Mrs Bromley was the housekeeper.

Restless and wanting Jane to materialise, I paced about

the room while Lucinda perched on a high-backed floral sofa.

Mrs Bromley came in momentarily. She was a stout woman dressed entirely in black and most apologetic, saying that we had been expected tomorrow and not today. But of course, we should make ourselves comfortable and that the Austens were expected back very shortly. She would ask Alice (presumably the maid we had met) to bring us tea and refreshments forthwith.

Indeed, as soon as she stepped out of the room, I heard a man's voice in the hall greeting her; and a few seconds later, a handsome sandy-haired gentleman entered the drawing room. He was of medium height, rosy complexioned, and dressed in a light-brown tailcoat, embroidered waistcoat, and olive-green breeches.

He started upon seeing that the room was occupied by us and looked momentarily confused.

I smiled at him, recognising Jane's third brother. He had been adopted out to rich relations at a young age, but I had met him once or twice in Steventon when he had come to visit. And I had heard much of Godmersham Park from Jane and Cassie, which he had inherited five years past.

'Hello, Edward!'

He blinked at me. 'By Jove, Felicity? I hardly recognised you. You look quite the lady of the manor.'

I stared down at my light-blue travelling pelisse, which I was still wearing, the room being rather chilly. My attire had been upgraded, I supposed, as Max provided me with a generous allowance; and I had my own personal dressmaker, who was skilled in creating the latest fashions from Paris. Thanks to her, I had brought with me to Bath several dresses for dancing and not just two, as I had despaired of having in Steventon.

Edward went back into the hallway and called out, 'Hie up, Jane, your friends are here!'

Jane came running into the room, carrying her pelisse and reticule. Her mouth dropped open when she clapped eyes on me.

'Flissy! But we were expecting you tomorrow, the twenty-fifth!'

I shook my head. 'It was the twenty-fourth, dear. But it is no matter, as long as you did not forget we were coming at all.'

Quickly, she deposited her items on a chair and crossed the floor to grasp my hands and kiss my cheeks in greeting.

'Of course not! I am sorry I wasn't here to welcome you. If I had known, I wouldn't have gone out.'

'It is quite all right. We were kindly welcomed by your housekeeper and made comfortable. We have not been kept waiting but a quarter of an hour, so it is of no consequence.

I have been admiring the view, and Lucinda has been resting.'

I gestured to the girl to stand and meet my friend, and she did so and gave a curtsy. She did have such nice manners and was always obliging in that respect. There was no sulkiness or scowling to put up with, which was a relief.

'How do you do, Miss Austen?'

'Very well, thank you, Lucinda,' said Jane, nodding to her.

'Oh please, do call me Lucy.'

'All right, Lucy. And you must call me Jane.'

While this was going on, I was distracted by the sound of Elizabeth's tinkling tones in the hallway. Jane's sister-in-law had waylaid Alice as she was bringing our tea, and the door was ajar so I could hear her saying things such as 'much less salt' and 'please trim the fat'—Edward's diet being obviously of some concern to his wife since he had gout.

Their conversation finished, Alice appeared with a tray of tea-things; and Elizabeth followed, wearing a businesslike expression. I had met her once a few years ago on one of the occasions Edward had visited the rectory and thought she had a pleasing confidence. Now in her mid-twenties, she had not changed much in manner or appearance and was still fair-haired, slim, and elegant despite having borne five children under the age of six. From what Jane had told me about her sister-in-law's firm hand in taking charge of her unruly brood, it was safe to say that Elizabeth Austen was used to being listened to.

'Hello, Felicity. Edward told me you had arrived,' she said warmly, and we bowed to each other.

'Elizabeth, thank you so much for having us,' I replied.

'It is our pleasure. And this must be Lucinda. How lovely! Welcome, my dear! Oh no, no need to curtsy. Come and sit by me on the sofa and tell me all about yourself.'

Lucinda glanced at me, and I nodded reassuringly. The poor thing looked a bit overwhelmed at being drawn into this instant friendship, but Elizabeth was our host and not to be deterred. I had a feeling that Jane must have mentioned Lucinda was on the marriage circuit. Elizabeth was a compulsive matchmaker and had caused Jane much amusement over the years in her attempts to introduce friends (and even Jane herself) to what she deemed 'eligible suitors'. So far, none of her pairings had worked out.

It looked like Lucinda was about to be taken under her wing as her next project.

As her official chaperone, I felt a bit mean leaving Lucinda in Elizabeth's clutches. However, as Jane and I were chatting on the opposite sofa, I could easily cut in if I felt it was needed.

I took the cup of tea Jane handed me and sank back into

the tasselled cushions with a sigh. I could relax now that order had been restored!

'Where is Edward?' I asked. 'Does he want some tea?'

'He is resting before supper as taking the waters always tires him out,' said Jane. She told me she and Elizabeth had been at the pump room while he was bathing next door.

'What do you do at the pump room?' I asked.

'Oh, promenade around and make new acquaintances, as one does in Bath,' said Jane airily.

I sipped my tea. 'And did you meet anyone?'

'An older lady and her husband. They were respectable enough, but quite dull.'

She squinted and pretended to look at me through a pair of pince-nez, and I giggled.

'Now tell me about your trip. Was it terribly taxing?'

I rolled my eyes. 'Very much so. I thought we would never arrive. The inns were awful, and the carriage ride uncomfortable. The only good thing is that it didn't rain. Otherwise, it would have taken twice as long.'

'I hope you are not missing Max too much?' Jane teased.

The memory of his dear face swam before my eyes, and my heart pinched. I bit my lip and did not trust myself to speak.

'Ah, I am sorry. I should not have said that. Of course you are.' She patted my hand gently.

I pushed down the lump in my throat with another swallow of tea and took a steadying breath.

'I must write to him and tell him of our arrival so he can inform Seraphina that Lucy hasn't been accosted by highwaymen. Thank you again for allowing her to stay. I know it was very last minute.'

'Not at all. As Elizabeth said, it is our pleasure. And I fully intend to help you with your chaperoning duties and rescue her from any nefarious gentlemen.'

We looked across at where Elizabeth was questioning (read: interrogating) a blank-faced Lucinda about her dowry.

'I think Lucy might need rescuing right now.'

'Shall I suggest that she attends to her toilette before supper?'

'Yes, thank you,' I said, relieved.

Jane extracted Lucinda from Elizabeth, saying that she needed to show us to our rooms and that 'there was time enough for talking about dull matrimonial things later'.

Elizabeth laughed gaily, and I saw she was used to Jane's remarks and did not mind them. In fact, she found them amusing (luckily for Jane!).

Our rooms were at the top of the house, up a double flight of stairs.

'Elizabeth and Edward have the apartment off the drawing room,' Jane said as we ascended. 'She said I could have it, but I preferred to be upstairs. There are two rooms, one a good size and the other smaller. But both have a nice aspect across the park.'

'Oh, only two?' I asked, confused about the sleeping arrangements.

We stopped on the landing for Jane to explain further.

'I thought you could share with me, Flissy, as it has a double bed. The other only has a single. I hope you will not mind?'

I shrugged. 'It suits me well.' I had hoped for a room of my own, but needs must, and it made sense for us to share as we were friends.

'Are you sure, Aunty Fliss?' asked Lucinda worriedly. 'I can bed down on the floor on some cushions or—'

'Don't be silly, Lucy. You will do no such thing,' I said sharply before she could mention going into a cupboard. 'I'm sure Jane and I will be perfectly content—as long as she does not kick.'

'I don't kick, but Cassie told me I once recited a poem in my sleep,' said Jane, leaning against the stair banister with a grin.

'Which poem?' I asked curiously.

'John Donne's "The Flea". That morning, we had

changed the bedding for washday and discovered several dead flies on the mattress. Insects were obviously on my mind.'

I gave a snigger that came out through my nose.

'See, Lucy? You are lucky to be in by yourself. Otherwise, Flissy may disturb you with her snorting,' joked Jane.

'Very amusing,' I said, pretending to be haughty. 'Now are we going to stand about here all day, or shall we see these rooms?'

We left Lucinda to sort herself out in the smaller room, which had an interesting, and not altogether pleasing, beige tint to the walls but was quite comfortable and contained a window seat overlooking the park—something Lucinda seemed delighted with.

'I can watch people walking by rather than having to converse with them,' she said earnestly. I was again reminded of Max as they both had the same shyness of nature, and another yearning pang shot through me. Lord, hopefully, his letters would ease my heart's suffering. Otherwise, this was going to be six weeks of emotional endurance!

In the larger room next door, there was a sizeable bed, a chest of drawers, and a closet full of shelves. Jane declared that this was more of a *cupboard* than a closet as it was useless for hanging anything up. Indeed, due to the lack of storage in the room, I resigned myself to living out of my trunk for the duration of the stay.

I noticed she had set up her writing slope on the table by the window. There were no papers to be seen lying around, but I knew there was at least one manuscript lurking inside it.

'Have you been doing any writing?' I enquired.

'No, not really. I am still working on *Elinor and Marianne* and refining *your* story. To be honest, my brain has been rather befuddled since arriving as we have been so busy. That is why I mistook the date of your arrival. I should have checked your letter,' she scolded herself.

'There is no harm done,' I reiterated, not wanting her to feel bad about her mistake. 'I can understand that being in Bath would cause one to be at sixes and sevens. Tell me again what we shall do.'

Jane counted off on her fingers. 'Well, there is the pump room, which we shall see tomorrow. Then there is the theatre, concerts, balls, teas, walks in the park, and, my personal favourite, the circulating library in Milsom Street, which has an excellent supply of the latest novels.'

I wrinkled my nose slightly, and Jane noticed. 'Do not worry. We will be spending infinitely more time dancing and socialising, and I can always go on my own if you are disinclined to.'

'Thank goodness!' I said. 'I did not come to Bath to be stuck browsing books in a dusty library, though I am sure Lucinda will go with you—she loves reading.'

'A girl after my own heart,' said Jane with a smile. 'Though if her mother wants her to marry, we should introduce her to society as soon as possible. Who knows, if she meets someone thrilling, she may give me an idea for a new novel.'

Hmm, I was not so sure about *that* since my romance with Max was the subject of Jane's latest manuscript. In that case, it would be better for Lucinda to spend time at the library improving her mind rather than giving Jane fodder for her stories!

Chapter 4

Directly after breakfast the next morning, a flurry of letter writing ensued in the drawing room. For myself, I penned a hasty (but heartfelt) note to Max and a somewhat longer one to Harriet, asking her if she had deduced anything untoward happening with Papa and Aunt, and if so, why had she not said anything to me?

Lucinda wrote a 'we have arrived safely in Bath' letter to her mother, who was now back in York tending to the needs of her husband and other children. Jane said she was writing to Cassie (who was currently in Godmersham helping with the Austens' children). But when I glanced over, she had finished her letter and was writing something else that was making her lips quirk every so often and obviously amusing her. It was some scenario or conversation that she had witnessed or overheard no doubt. Perhaps the dull old couple from the pump room were, at this very moment, being immortalised by the pen of Miss Austen.

Letters written and ready for Mrs Bromley to take to the post office in Milsom Street, our party prepared ourselves

(Lucinda and I in great excitement) for our excursion to the pump room. Edward would take the waters in King's Bath, and we ladies would promenade. Apparently, the pool allowed women's bathing, but Elizabeth said that we could do so another time. For now, we should 'kill three birds with one stone in the pump room'. I assumed she meant we could take our exercise, meet new people, and introduce Lucinda to eligible young gentlemen.

The situation of 13 Queen Square was such that it was a mere five-minute walk south to the pump room, which was adjacent to the Roman bathhouse and the abbey. It was also a mere five-or-so-minute walk north to the Upper Assembly Rooms, where balls were held twice weekly.

Elizabeth pointed out this fact as we strolled to the former and commended her husband on his choice of accommodation. Indeed, as he was hobbling slowly along with crutches, I thought Edward would be better off carried to the bathhouse in a sedan chair. But he insisted on escorting us and said that he could feel the healing effects of the water, which he had both drunk and bathed in, working its magic and would be 'as right as rain and promenading with you all in no time in the pump room'.

When I queried why the place was named so, Edward said it was because the water from King's Bath was pumped into the adjoining room so that people could drink glasses of it as it was full of health-giving minerals.

'But surely not the water that people have been bathing in?' I asked.

'Of course not,' he said, turning his head and giving me a look (he was walking ahead of us with Elizabeth). 'The water is drawn from a different source.' He sounded knowledgeable, so I gathered he knew what he was talking about.

Our destination was a grand collection of buildings of light-coloured stone, impressive to look at with their columns and windowed archways. One was the King's Bath, which Edward headed to using a dedicated entrance for bathers.

Further along, a steady stream of elegant-looking people were heading through a portico, so we joined the tail end and were swept along with the chattering crowd.

Inside, Elizabeth observed the various personages heading into the salon and said to Lucinda, 'Come along with me, dear. Jane, why don't you go with Felicity to the fountain and take the waters?'

'Oh, but ...' I said, thinking as head chaperone, I should be looking after my charge. But Elizabeth obviously had other ideas.

'Do not worry. She will be safe with me,' she said, tucking Lucinda's arm into her own and whisking her off into the main salon before I could protest.

Jane said that it was a rite of passage when in Bath to drink the waters, though she did warn me it was 'an acquired taste'. We made our way to the side of the room where a large Grecian urn spouted a steady stream of water into the mouths of four jumping fishes.

A counter had glasses of water set up, which were being collected at the fountain by an attendant. People were standing around, drinking the water and conversing. It seemed to be the thing to do.

The aroma of the water resembled rotten eggs, so I was reluctant to drink it. But maybe it tasted better than it smelled? However, this was not the case. 'Urgh,' I said after a sip. 'It tastes like it's been strained through dirty stockings. How can anything that tastes so foul be considered a healing elixir?'

I said this rather loudly. A couple of young blonde ladies, a little older than Lucinda, were standing nearby with their mother. The prettiest of the two overheard me and tittered. She pointed to her mouth with a gloved finger and mimed gagging, and I smiled at her, delighted that someone else shared my opinion.

Jane had drained hers with her fingers pinching her nose, which I gathered was the way to do it.

'Well done, you're brave,' I said. 'Now that we've had

our magical water, shall we go and find Elizabeth and Lucinda?'

Jane nodded, and eager to leave, I deposited the remnants of my glass in a potted plant without anyone noticing. I hoped it would not kill it.

The main salon was humming with people, a twisting throng that had a life of its own, and I could not spy Elizabeth and Lucinda within it. Jane linked arms with me. 'Come on, we're sure to find them soon enough.'

I was not one for parading around indoors. The green meadows of our estate and the woods surrounding it were far more to my taste than tramping up and down on floorboards. But the room itself was lovely, with high arched windows along the side and a raised balcony at one end. Presiding over everyone was an enormous tiered chandelier dripping with crystals. There were far worse ways to spend a morning than being amidst such grandeur.

I wondered how Edward was faring in the bath and if he was stomaching the smell of rotten eggs. Perhaps it was like all bad smells: the longer you smelt them, the more your nose became accustomed to them.

As Jane and I walked around the room, we passed couples of varying ages and pairs of single men and women who had stopped to converse and look each other over. It was rather like attending the stock sales. You saw a cow you liked the look of, so you enquired of its breeding and made an offer to the farmer for a good price.

I was musing along these lines as we paused at the far end of the room for a breather, and I caught sight of Lucinda and Elizabeth. They were over by the window talking to a gentleman in his early twenties. As I gazed at him, taking in his countenance and stature, veritable sparks flew out of my eyes.

I leaned into Jane. 'Who is *that*?' I whispered.

'I am not sure,' she whispered back. 'But whoever he is, Lucy certainly seems captivated—she cannot take her eyes off him.'

Indeed! I thought. For he was tall and lithe, wearing a dark-blue tailcoat and breeches, his snowy cravat impeccably tied. His hair was slightly longer than fashionable, but it was a rich dark brown, groomed and parted in the middle—the glossy locks framing a superbly handsome face. He tilted it now, smiling at something Lucinda said, and my stomach tingled—it was a smile that could ruin a woman's good intentions.

'Well, he *is* very good-looking. I do not blame her,' I murmured.

Jane glanced at me. 'Quite, but he is still a stranger. We should go over and make his acquaintance before Elizabeth agrees to anything on Lucinda's behalf.'

I shook myself out of my trance. Jane was talking sense as usual. You should not judge a book by its cover, especially when it came to men. I, of all people, should know that, having misjudged Max poorly when we first met and deemed him 'dour' and 'unfriendly'.

Speaking of Max, I was a happily married woman and should not be getting distracted by such an attractive male specimen!

As we walked over, I felt rather jittery but composed myself and was ready to make his acquaintance in a calm(ish) manner. But the gentleman had finished his conversation and strode away on long legs, the tails of his coat flicking behind him, before we had the chance. I let out a breath that was tinged with rotten eggs. It was a good thing he had gone, for in truth, I did not think I could remain composed in his presence. Yet part of me was disappointed that I had been denied the opportunity to meet him.

It seemed I was not the only one who had been fascinated by the gentleman. My niece was all aflutter when we reached her.

'Aunty Fliss!' breathed Lucinda. Her throat and cheeks were flushed pink, and her rosy skin complemented her soft dark hair becomingly. She clutched at my hands, and I could feel the heat of her palms through her thin gloves. 'Oh, you have just missed the most *amiable* gentleman!'

'Oh, believe me, we saw him,' I assured her. 'From across the room. Did you have a nice conversation? Was his manner pleasing?'

'It was! I do not know how I managed a single word as I was so impressed by him, but he was easy to talk to, and I did not feel too awkward. How strange that such a handsome gentleman should want to talk to me!'

'Not at all, Lucy,' said Elizabeth indulgently. 'He has a pair of fine eyes in his head, and you are a pretty young thing. Your mama should be well pleased if *he* becomes her son-in-law.'

She threw Jane and me a self-congratulatory smile, as if to imply that if this occurred, *she* should be the one to get the credit for instigating the match.

'We should learn more about this man before we start planning Lucinda's wedding,' Jane said, frowning. 'What is his name to begin with?'

'Mr Dorian Hart,' supplied Elizabeth.

'Isn't it sublime?' said Lucinda dreamily. 'He sounds like a poet.'

Elizabeth and I agreed that it was a very poet-like name. Jane didn't pass comment.

'And does he stay in Bath or ...?' I enquired.

'He is visiting for the Season but is a resident of the

county, though he did not say where exactly,' Elizabeth said.

'Why was he here alone?' asked Jane, sounding suspicious. I noted that she did not seem quite as taken with Mr Hart as we all were.

'He was promenading with his friend from Eton, a Mr Smith-Withers. But Mr Hart lingered for so long talking to Lucinda that his friend excused himself as he had an appointment.'

'But why did he speak to you in the first place?' Jane pressed. 'It was very forward that he should make your acquaintance without being introduced, at least by the master of ceremonies.' She did not look impressed about Mr Hart having an Eton education, but to me, it signified he was at least intelligent and possibly wealthy.

'It was only because he bumped my shoulder rather hard that his attention turned to us,' explained Elizabeth. 'After he apologised most profusely and hoped that I was not injured, he noticed Lucinda and immediately enquired as to our situation here in Bath. Of course, I happily told him as I saw he was quite struck with her. My shoulder is now a little sore and may in fact be bruised, but I do not mind as it brought about this meeting. In fact, I see it as a happy accident!' She clapped her hands excitedly despite Jane shaking her head at her.

'And was there any talk of a future meeting?' I asked Lucinda, hardly daring to enquire in case the man had not said anything of that nature.

'He said he hopes to see me at the ball tonight and become better acquainted,' Lucinda murmured, blushing furiously and looking as if she might melt into a puddle on the floor.

'Gracious,' I said. 'So I suppose we will be attending too?'

'Upon my word, we shall not miss it for the world,' said Elizabeth firmly. 'Even if I have to drag Edward there on his crutches.'

Speaking of her husband, the man had availed himself of a sedan chair and was resting on the sofa when we returned from the pump room.

'Ladies! How was your outing?' he enquired. The baths must have been hot as his shirt was half unbuttoned, and he was perspiring heavily and mopping his forehead with a small white towel.

'It was excellent, my dear,' said Elizabeth, patting his red sweaty cheek and then wiping her hand on her skirt. 'I have procured a suitor for Lucy, and we shall see him at the ball tonight.'

Edward began to protest that he was in no fit state for a

ball, but Elizabeth would hear none of it.

'We shall be taking Lucy to the ball. Sometimes, my dear, we must sacrifice our own comfort for the happiness of others.' She touched her right shoulder gingerly and winced. 'Excuse me, I shall ask the cook to fix me a poultice to ease my bruising and see about luncheon.'

The rest of us removed our pelisses and bonnets and flopped down on the other sofa when she'd left. Lucinda looked as deflated as I felt. After the excitement of meeting Mr Hart, the afternoon was sure to be a dreary one. But Jane suggested that we could visit the circulating library, so that was better than nothing.

Elizabeth came back soon after and said luncheon would be served in half an hour, so my spirits lifted upon hearing that. I was starving after all the walking around in the pump room, and I wanted to rid my mouth of the taste of the water.

'Felicity, you have a letter. Mrs Bromley brought it back from the post office,' said Elizabeth, taking it out of her skirt pocket and handing it over. I recognised the handwriting on the front instantly, and my heart leapt.

'It's from Max!' I said joyfully, all thoughts of Mr Hart instantly forgotten (indeed they had never really taken root as the words of my husband were the true emotional nourishment I desired).

Wanting privacy, I said I would read it in my room and flew up the double flight, my feet pounding on the stairs so loudly it was like an elephant ascending. *How lovely of Max to write before receiving mine*, I thought, jumping onto the bed. *But now he shall get my letter from this morning, and I won't have replied to anything he has written in his!*

Breaking open the red wax seal, I eagerly scanned the contents of the letter.

My darling Fliss,

You will be in Bath by now, so I wanted to write a short note for you to receive on your arrival. How was your trip, dearest? I trust you did not suffer too much. I know how much you detest long carriage journeys. Have you been out in society already with Jane and met some nice people? Has Lucinda been a help or a hindrance? Only time will tell perhaps!

It is evening here, and you have been away for three days, and I know not what to do with myself. I miss you more than I can say, and any words I write here will not do my emotions justice. I have taken a little red wine as solace these past nights, and I may take a little more tonight. But do not worry. It is only to soothe the ache around my heart, and I will not fall victim to dependency. I will write again when I have received your first letter (or perhaps your second as our letters may now have crossed).

Love your Max x

PS: George sends his best whinny. The stable boy took him for a ride yesterday, but he refused to go any farther than the second paddock. He is no doubt missing you as much as I!

I frowned in concern when I read that Max had 'taken a little red wine'. Oh dear, that did not bode well. I hoped it *was* only a little as I knew exactly what happened when Max partook of red wine in excess. The servants would not be impressed if he stumbled around the grounds singing badly.

Oh, Max! His angst at my absence was loud and clear from his letter, and I wished I was with him right this second—my husband needed me, Bath and its balls be damned!

But short of packing up my trunk and leaping into the next passing carriage to head north, there was nothing I could do about it. And I could not leave Lucinda now that she had attracted attention from an eligible young gentleman—my duties as a chaperone were more pressing than ever. All I could do was pray Max would receive my letter shortly and that it would put him back on an even keel.

Chapter 5

Luncheon was served promptly at one o'clock; and I helped myself to the selection of meat tart, cheese, thinly sliced bread and butter, and dressed salad from the sideboard. Everyone else at the table was tucking in too, and for a time, no one spoke as they were too busy eating.

Then Lucinda enquired politely, 'How is Uncle Max, Aunty Fliss? Is he well?'

I took a sip from my glass of lemonade and deliberated. Taking up my cutlery again, I said 'Quite well. Thank you for asking, Lucy.'

I decided it best not to mention his wine tipple.

'And missing you, no doubt,' said Jane, smiling at me from the other side of the table.

'Perhaps. But it is understandable. We have not been apart for this many weeks since we were married.'

'You won't be able to go off on jaunts so easily when you begin having children, Felicity,' remarked Elizabeth with a laugh. 'At least not until they have grown somewhat or you have a trustworthy nanny, like Edward and me. Of course, we also have Jane's dear sister, Cassandra, who has kindly offered to lend a hand while we are in Bath. You should write back to Max and remind him that he should relish his freedom while he can!'

Edward nodded in agreement. 'Yes, I love our children dearly, but being away from them is a tonic for my ears.' He smiled at his wife knowingly as only a father with a number of small children under six could.

Jane and I looked at each other. I had told her of Max and my decision to remain childless, and she approved wholeheartedly and did not judge me. It was not a secret as such, and she had undoubtedly told Cassie, but neither of them had let it slip to Elizabeth. For that, I was grateful. But now it was awkward, and I felt obliged to say something. But I had a feeling Elizabeth might choke on the cherry tomato she had just popped into her mouth if I told her the true state of our situation.

Fortunately, Lucinda, who was not privy to the information either, had been sitting quietly and now offered her own solution. 'Should I write to Mama and suggest that Papa visit Uncle Max for a time? He does so love to go fishing with him.'

'That is sweet of you to think of it, Lucy,' I replied. 'Yes, please do. I am sure Max would be glad of his brother's company.'

It was a good idea. Tobias was pragmatic and would

keep Max from brooding.

Lucinda smiled happily and said she was glad to be able to help. Jane suggested then that we visit the circulating library after luncheon. Elizabeth was neatly distracted with the thought of getting a romance novel for herself and something for Edward. 'Oh yes, he does so enjoy comic novels. Don't you, dear?'

Jane winked at me, and I sighed in relief.

The day was fair and perfect for an afternoon stroll. Queen Square was most pleasing to the eye, and the streets were busy, but not so much that we were jostled. Passers-by smiled and nodded, and one young man even doffed his hat to us.

We strolled two abreast—Elizabeth and Lucinda in front, the former chattering and looking in shop windows and the latter listening quietly but offering decisive opinions when asked for them.

I was glad my young niece had been accepted so readily by Jane's relations and was proving to be a help and not a hindrance, as Max had wondered in his letter.

'Lucy is most agreeable,' whispered Jane. 'I can see why your sister-in-law thinks she should marry.'

'But quite so soon?' I replied. 'She is only eighteen and barely out of pigtails.'

'You yourself married at twenty,' countered Jane. 'It is not so much older than Lucy is now, and she is mature for her age.'

'That was an exceptional circumstance,' I said.

'By "exceptional circumstance", do you mean you fell in love with Mr Stonyface?' teased Jane.

'I think you'll find that Mr Stonyface fell in love with *me* and proposed forthwith,' I corrected.

'Yes, the circumstances surrounding that event are still rather shady, but I shall get the truth of it one day.'

Not if I can help it, I thought, remembering Max's drunken proposal in the field behind our house. *That* was a story best left untold, especially to an aspiring author.

After a short walk from Queen Square, we turned left at the end of the road and reached our destination: Milsom Street. It was the most fashionable street in Bath and where the wealthy came to shop, if the number of ladies in richly coloured silks and feathered hats was anything to go by.

The circulating library was located about halfway along, in a narrow honey-coloured limestone building. It had six windows, three small on top and three larger on the bottom, and was sandwiched between a bank and a bookseller—the prices of whose books Jane pronounced 'extortionate'.

'Why', she asked, 'would we bother buying a book for two pounds when we could borrow multiple books for a monthly subscription of five shillings?'

I agreed that it was a much more sensible arrangement.

Elizabeth wanted to stop in at a milliner's across the street, but Jane was itching to go to the library, and so was Lucinda. In the end, we said that we would meet Elizabeth inside and order a book for Edward. 'Anything that's comical or adventurous—Jane knows what he likes.'

I was not sure of the protocol, but Jane said it was a matter of perusing the library catalogue and choosing a title. The clerk would then retrieve it for us. We could also take light refreshments in the reading room if we so desired.

'How civilised,' I said, wondering if there was any proper food like cake to be had. I could definitely get used to visiting the library if there was cake.

I myself was not interested in scouring the catalogue. So I waited, feeling a bit bored, while Jane and Lucinda pored over it, discussing various titles. I went over to the other side of the room to look out the window and saw Elizabeth crossing the street, clutching a hatbox, which made me smile. She seemed to have ventured out more with the aim of shopping than visiting the library.

When I returned to the counter, Jane was checking out a book for Edward and already had one for herself sitting on the counter.

'What's that?' I asked, peering at the brown leather

cover.

'Volume two of *The Monk* by Matthew Lewis. It's just been returned,' she said, sounding pleased.

'What's it about?'

Jane motioned me away from the counter and said in a low voice, 'I will tell you later. It's rather scandalous. The clerk warned me it was not for young ladies and was reluctant to let me have it. But I insisted, saying that I had read volume one and had not been overly shocked.'

'Gracious,' I said, intrigued.

Jane grinned. 'Shall we see if there's anything to eat in the reading room? Lucinda has already gone in.'

'Ooh, yes.'

I had high hopes. But in the reading room, there were only a few hard-looking biscuits and tiny fish paste sandwiches, neither of which appealed, and cups of fruit-flavoured cordial that was bright orange. It was most disappointing.

Elizabeth joined us presently and agreed, saying it was not edible, so we decided to take our leave and have afternoon tea at home. Lucinda and Jane strolled off together discussing their books, so Elizabeth fell into step with me.

'I hope you don't mind,' she said conversationally. 'But I took the liberty of picking up this from the library. I thought you might find it helpful.'

Reaching into the pocket of her striped skirt, she drew out a pamphlet. She handed it to me, and I sighed inwardly when I saw the title: *The Mother's Companion: A Guide to Pregnancy and Child-Rearing*.

I promptly handed it back to her. 'That was kind of you, but I won't need to read it.'

There was an awkward silence as she put the pamphlet back in her pocket, and we continued walking. But the subject was obviously still uppermost in her mind as she said, 'How long have you been married now, Felicity?'

'Two and a half years,' I replied warily, having a notion of where this was going.

'Forgive me for asking, but is there a problem?'

'A problem?' I echoed.

'Yes, I feel for you as I myself was pregnant almost immediately. In truth, I believe I conceived on our wedding night. But *two a half years*—that is a long time to wait.'

She leaned in closer to me. 'Can he not?' she whispered, then lifted her little finger into the air along with an eyebrow.

I inhaled sharply. That was going too far!

'It is a common issue and nothing Max need be ashamed of,' continued Elizabeth blithely. 'Edward was the same for a while between our second and third. But the doctor prescribed a daily tablespoon of ginseng and a cold bath once a week, and he was ready to go once again—'

'I assure you, Max has no problems in that department,' I interrupted hastily, not wanting further details of Edward's marital prowess.

'Oh, then why have you not ...?'

Lord, she was not going to let it alone.

'It is simple enough,' I said tightly. 'I have decided not to have children, and Max supports my decision. I thank you for your concern, but we are both perfectly happy, and there is no problem or anything else that needs discussing.'

Elizabeth seemed not to know what to say to this except to mutter 'extraordinary' under her breath and was content to be silent for the remainder of the walk until we reached the house.

* * *

I mentioned the conversation to Jane later on when we were getting ready for the ball, and she was shocked at Elizabeth's gumption.

'I am sorry she interrogated you so. She should not have made enquiries of that nature,' she said, smoothing her white muslin down over her pink silk slip. I gestured she should turn around so I could do up the small ivory buttons.

'It is only because she is popping them out left, right, and centre that she thinks every other woman must do so as well.' She shrugged her shoulders in indignation, and the button I was struggling to do up slipped out of my grasp.

'Speaking of popping out, stand still. These buttons are fiddly.'

'Sorry.'

'Well, I told her the truth, and she barely managed to disguise her shock. I am only mentioning it to you because she may want to discuss it, so be warned.'

'If she does, I will say that she needs to keep her nose out of your affairs!'

'All right, but perhaps word it more gently. I do not want to offend my host when I have only just arrived.'

I knew Jane could be snippy when she decided to voice her opinions.

Her buttons done, I turned my attention to my own white gown. It was the nicest and most expensive one I owned. The muslin was shot through with gold silk thread, and it had a small train. My dressmaker had assured me it was the height of fashion in Paris. Not that I'd had any chance to wear it yet living in Derbyshire—balls were few and far between in our part of the country.

Once we had affixed our white ostrich-feather headdresses, we were ready.

'Good enough for first bench material I should think,' Jane declared, looking at her reflection in the mirror.

'First bench?'

'Yes, the first bench is closest to the dancing and where the eligible young men can take their pick of a partner. Elder ladies and children are on the second bench.'

'I should be on that one then since I am an old married woman,' I said. 'Look, I have crow's feet.' I scrunched up my eyes, causing faint wrinkles to fan out.

Jane giggled. 'Don't be ridiculous. You will be on the first bench with Lucy and me. I expect you to be in high demand since you look so beautiful.'

'You have to say that as you are my friend, but thank you.'

There was a light knock at the door, and Lucinda called out, 'Are you ready? Can I come in?'

'Speak of the devil,' I murmured, and Jane giggled.

'Yes, come in, Lucy!' she called back.

I had been buoyed up by Jane's compliment, but seeing Lucinda looking pretty as a picture in a flower-sprigged muslin made me deflate a little.

'Aunt Elizabeth arranged my hair,' she said, patting her updo self-consciously. Soft dark ringlets framed her heart-shaped face, and her pert bosom swelled propitiously above the low rounded neckline of her dress. In short, she was a peach ripe for the plucking. Mr Hart might have competition once the other young gentlemen clapped eyes on her.

If so, then he might be free to ask me to dance, I thought but quickly pushed the notion out of my head. I should not expect to be the object of his attention, not with my being married and delectable Lucinda on the scene. But there was nothing wrong with observing him from a distance, was there?

'You look simply delicious!' said Jane approvingly, and I nodded.

'Lovely!' I contributed.

But Lucinda looked anxious rather than pleased.

'Is everything all right, dear?' I enquired.

'I confess I am nervous about attending the ball. I want so much to speak with Mr Hart again, but what if he does not come over?'

I let Jane do the reassuring while I filled my small green velvet reticule with a clean handkerchief, my fan, a tin of lip salve, a pot of rouge, a vial of scent, and some spare pins in case of a hair emergency. It rather bulged at the seams with all these items, but I deemed them all completely necessary.

'He has said he wishes to become better acquainted, so I do not think you have anything to worry about,' Jane soothed. 'If he does not stand up with you at least once, I will be most surprised.'

'Perhaps you should let Aunt Jane dance with him first to determine if he is a man of consequence,' I interjected, pulling on my gloves. 'She is an excellent judge of character.'

I wiggled my brows at Jane, and she smirked.

Oh yes, both of us were eager to discover more about Mr Hart (on Lucinda's behalf, of course!).

Even though the Upper Assembly Rooms—or 'the rooms', as Jane and Elizabeth referred to them—were situated not far from the house, a hackney was called for regardless. Edward did not want to walk the distance on crutches, and Elizabeth did not want to dirty the hem of her dress.

So just before seven o'clock, one gent in an evening suit and four ladies in muslins, full of excited anticipation of the evening ahead, were transported and deposited at our destination barely three minutes later. The driver commented with a laugh that his horse had hardly broken a sweat, but he obligingly helped us alight and was tipped for his trouble.

The exterior of the rooms was unassuming, a squat building of golden stone with a triangular portico. But I soon discovered it was not the case once inside. What a glorious and elegant sight met my eyes!

I found myself in an enormous rectangular dance room, painted eggshell blue with Grecian columns inset around the walls along with artworks and gilt-edged mirrors. I counted not one or two, but five crystal chandeliers lit with candles, and Jane told me there was space for at least 500 people. On this night, there were fewer than that number in attendance, but it was still crowded.

The first dance was about to take place; and with the swelling noise of the orchestra, the loud chatter of the throng, and the cloying heat, I felt a little dazed by the spectacle and wished I'd added smelling salts to my reticule.

When we had entered, Elizabeth had escorted Edward through to the octagon as he'd said he was quite happy to spend the evening playing cards, and she said she would see him settled but find us presently.

'Quick, let us secure a spot on the first bench for the next dance while it is mostly unoccupied,' urged Jane now.

An excellent plan, I thought and we pushed past the onlookers and sank onto the 'bench'. It was a long high-backed settee with armrests and curved wooden legs. Upholstered in red velvet, it was placed at the front of the ballroom, giving us a clear view of the dance floor. It was also rather hard on one's behind, being stuffed with horsehair or some such, but I supposed sitting in such a prime position was worth the discomfort.

I noticed we were gaining sharp looks from some of the other young ladies standing around the room, and there was whispering and peeking at us from behind fans going on. 'Are you sure we can sit here?' I hissed to Jane.

She shrugged. 'You and Lucinda are high-ranking enough to warrant it, and Elizabeth mentioned she had informed the master of ceremonies of your presence in Bath. So do not worry about that. If anyone is likely to be turfed off the first bench, it is me.'

'Let us pray that does not happen,' I said. 'At least before you have had one dance with an eligible gentleman.'

Speaking of eligible gentlemen, I surreptitiously scanned the groups of white-muslined ladies and tailcoated gentlemen who were performing a lively cotillion.

My heart skipped a beat when I caught sight of a certain someone.

I nudged Lucinda. 'There is your Mr Hart,' I said in a low voice.

'Where?' she said eagerly.

'Over there, to the right.'

'Ah, yes, I see. Oh, he is an elegant dancer,' she whispered, a note of enthralment entering her tone.

Indeed he was, and though I attempted to watch other people, my eyes kept being drawn back to him. As well as being an elegant dancer, he also was not hiding the fact he was having a thoroughly good time, which I thought was capital. I approved of men who enjoyed dancing.

The dance ended, and the participants took their bows.

When Mr Hart straightened, he must have felt our collective gaze upon him as his eyes immediately roved over us ladies, as if he were at the butcher's determining which was the choicest cut of beef.

Hastily, I averted my eyes and stared at the chandelier overhead. But it was too late.

'Lord, have mercy,' murmured Lucinda, who had started fluttering her fan at a great rate. 'I can't breathe. He's coming over.'

Chapter 6

Mr Hart strolled directly to us after bidding his mousy-haired partner a polite, but disinterested nod after the cotillion. The young woman looked none too pleased to be dismissed so soon and scurried across to her two friends, the ones who had been whispering and peeking at us from behind their fans.

'How lovely to see you again, Miss Fitzroy,' said Mr Hart, directing his full attention to Lucinda, who stiffened under his intense gaze. Indeed, as well as being extremely handsome, he possessed a commanding presence that was difficult to ignore.

'Good evening, Mr Hart,' replied Lucinda, continuing to fan herself. But the poor girl's cheeks were fiery, and the fan wielding was doing nothing whatsoever to cool them.

'Who are your friends?' he enquired with a tilt of his head. 'I did not have the pleasure of meeting them at the pump room this morning.'

'This is my aunt, Mrs Felicity Fitzroy, and her friend Miss Jane Austen.'

'Charmed, I'm sure,' said Mr Hart, bowing to Jane and

me. When his eyes met mine, a small bird fluttered in my chest, and my own cheeks heated imperceptibly. But I refused to simper and gave him a polite nod. He was sightly to behold and had pretty manners, but we still did not know anything about him.

'Would you care to stand up with me for the next dance, Miss Fitzroy? I believe it is a minuet,' he said to Lucinda, smiling amiably and waiting for her reply.

Lucinda agreed but seemed unable to stand, being struck by something like stage fright.

'Go on, dear,' I whispered encouragingly. 'Everyone is taking their places.'

Slowly, Lucinda rose and took Mr Hart's arm, and he led her to the dance floor. She looked like a doll next to him.

'Gracious,' I said to Jane when they were out of earshot. 'I hope she manages to dance all right.'

'He seems to be giving her words of encouragement,' said Jane.

We watched as Lucinda stood a little taller and seemed more at ease. By the second promenade, her face had relaxed, and she even smiled as Mr Hart spoke to her, and she replied with a comment.

'What are they saying? Can you tell?' I asked Jane (she was good at reading people's lips).

'I am not entirely sure, but I think that he asked about her day, and she said, "We went to the library."'

I warmed to him then. It was kind that he was conversing with her and making her feel comfortable. I could not stand men who refused to talk while dancing. It always made things so awkward. What was the point if you could not get to know your partner?

I'd enjoyed the conversation Max and I had on our first dance at Ashbury, even though we mostly spoke about him collecting his hat. But it was then that I realised I had feelings for him as he had looked so vulnerable when he'd asked to call on me and was awaiting my reply. He'd looked terrified that I would say no!

In thinking of it, I began to miss him terribly and wished he was here to dance with me. Max was an excellent dancer and would not have hesitated to whisk me onto the floor (well, he would do so as soon as I had given him encouragement). I would be up there doing the minuet myself rather than sitting here, getting a sore bottom.

And Jane, being single, should really be up dancing! I looked around, attempting to subtly catch the eye of an agreeable gentleman for her.

But in doing so, I was surprised to see Elizabeth conversing with a woman who seemed to have waylaid her. She looked familiar, and I realised it was the mother of the pretty blonde girl at the pump room, the one who had made the gagging motion. Whatever it was the woman was saying, Elizabeth did not seem to be pleased by it as she made several attempts to leave and join us but was prevented from doing so by the woman holding tightly on to her arm and talking intently.

Eventually, Elizabeth extracted herself from the woman's grip and came over, looking very stern.

'What was that all about?' asked Jane, who had seen the performance as well as I.

Elizabeth sat down, breathing heavily and looking disconcerted. 'Well, I never!' she said. 'I did not expect to be accosted at a ball, but there is a first time for everything.'

She told us how the woman had introduced herself as Mrs Spencer and that their conversation had at first been of the usual 'Who are you here with?' kind. But when Elizabeth had indicated Jane and me and then pointed out Lucinda on the dance floor with Mr Hart, the woman's lips had tightened, and she had remarked that Elizabeth should pay heed to the company Lucinda was keeping.

'I said, "Whatever do you mean, Mrs Spencer? Lucinda is dancing with that nice gentleman, Mr Hart, and having a splendid time by the looks of it." But the woman said that he was not a nice gentleman at all. She then proceeded to tell me about how Mr Hart had made the acquaintance of her elder daughter, Cecilia, at the Season last year, and ...' Elizabeth paused and lowered her voice. 'She said she could not reveal exactly what he did as we were in the midst of polite society, but that his conduct was very bad. She strongly recommended that we sever Lucinda's acquaintance with him immediately and pronounced him—and, my dears, this is distressing—a most appalling *scoundrel*.'

'Oh no,' said Jane worriedly. 'We must rescue her at once when they have finished dancing.'

We looked over at Lucinda and Mr Hart. They looked to be getting along wonderfully, with much talking and smiling taking place.

'But look at how happy she is,' said Elizabeth mournfully. 'Should we really be so hasty to separate them? What if Mrs Spencer is a spiteful mama whose daughter had gained, then lost Mr Hart's attention, but through no fault of his own? She may be trying to interfere for her own gain. What do you say, Felicity?'

I took a deep breath, not knowing what to think. 'Painting him as a reprobate is quite harsh, and we only have her opinion to go by. Still, perhaps it is better to err on the side of caution until we have more information about his character.'

'Then it is settled,' Jane said firmly. 'Elizabeth and I will escort Lucinda to the tea room. And, Flissy, you can make sure that Mr Hart does not follow us.'

'An excellent plan,' I said. 'But how am I supposed to carry out my part?'

'Distract him by talking about the weather or some such. He'll get bored soon enough and find someone else to dance with. Look out, here they come.'

Sure enough, the pair had finished the dance and were coming over to us, cheerfully ignorant of all that we had been planning to break up their acquaintance.

'Here she is, safe and sound,' said Mr Hart, presenting Lucinda to us with a flourish.

Before Lucinda knew what was happening, she was told that tea was now on the agenda. Jane and Elizabeth firmly grasped an elbow each, and she was whisked off, leaving me alone on the bench to deal with a surprised-looking Mr Hart.

'Ah, dancing is thirsty work,' I said hastily. 'They thought Lucinda would be parched.'

He narrowed his eyes. 'How discerning of them. But I take it you are not parched since you are still here?'

'No, I am well ... hydrated,' I said ineffectually.

'In that case', he said, flashing me a smile, 'you can dance the next with me since I am now without a partner.'

'Oh no, I cannot ... I am married.'

Mr Hart looked around. 'Pray, where is your husband? Hiding in the tea room?'

'He is in Derbyshire,' I said, stifling a giggle. Max *would* very likely be hiding in the tea room if he was here.

Mr Hart raised an eyebrow. 'Derbyshire! Then he will not mind if I steal you for one dance. If he is not here to witness it, there is no impropriety.'

I swallowed. What Mr Hart was saying made logical sense. But still, I knew I shouldn't.

'Thank you, but I can't leave my ... er ... belongings.'

Mr Hart eyed my bulging reticule. 'I should think it should be quite safe, unless you have brought a kitten to the ball? If so, it might be best in the cloakroom as it may get squashed.'

I laughed at that. 'A kitten?'

'You may be surprised at the things the young ladies of Bath stow in their reticules.'

'Well, if I had been silly enough to do so, I'm sure it would be quite suffocated by now.'

'Indeed. So there is no need to stay here and look after an expired kitten. You may as well dance with me,' he said with a grin.

I got the impression from this ridiculous conversation that he was determined to persuade me and would not take no for an answer.

'All right,' I said, giving in.

Well, I was itching to dance.

And it was just one.

Plus I could be of use to Lucinda because I did have some skills in discerning men's characters.

Satisfied that I was doing the right thing, I took his arm, and he led me to the floor.

'Which dance is this one?' I asked.

'If I remember correctly from the programme, it is the waltz,' Mr Hart replied. 'Are you familiar with it?'

I gulped. I had never waltzed with anyone, not even Max. But I knew it involved more proximity to one's partner than the minuet. 'I am afraid not. Perhaps I should sit …'

Mr Hart stepped into the space between us and grasped my gloved hands. 'It is very easy. I will show you the steps quickly now before it starts. See, your hands go on my shoulders, here.' He placed them so. 'And mine go on your waist.' He settled his hands, and I felt the heat of them sear through my muslin and onto my flesh. He was directly in front of me, and I would have no choice but to look at him and be held by him. Oh Lord. I glanced at the doorway, praying that the others did not choose that moment to reappear.

'Now we move in a circle. One, two, three. One, two, three. Then we greet the partner of the couple next to us, and ladies do an underarm turn. Then we all join hands and meet in the middle. Then we are back to each other for more waltzing. See? Simple.'

'I suppose so,' I replied hesitantly.

'I think you'll find it an excellent dance for getting to know one's partner. That is, if you like to converse while dancing?'

A friendly smile played on Mr Hart's lips, and I softened.

'I do, indeed,' I replied.

'Then we shall have a pleasant time of it, for I do as well.'

The music began, and it was as he had said. The dance itself was not hard, and Mr Hart was a strong partner, so all I had to do was follow his lead.

The only difficulty lay in the intimacy the dance required. As we were facing each other, I had ample time to look at him and him at me. And the experience was distracting, to say the least.

Mr Hart was even more striking up close. He possessed deep brown eyes, high cheekbones, along with a superior nose and an appealing pair of lips. He also had the most impossibly perfect complexion—apart from one tiny mole underneath his left eye, which acted like a beauty spot, drawing one's attention fully to his countenance.

Feeling a bit overcome by him, I decided the best thing to do was to imagine that I was dancing with Max. Conjuring up his dear gruff face, I plopped it on top of Mr Hart's own visage. Then I was free to glance at him now and then without feeling uncomfortable.

But he, of course, noticed this.

'Do I have something on my nose, Mrs Fitzroy?' he enquired.

'P-pardon?'

'You keep looking at me most intently. I can only assume

that it is because I have inadvertently smeared myself with jam or perhaps honey?'

A blush hit my cheeks. *Blast, he was too perceptive for his own good.*

'N-not at all,' I stuttered. 'I was simply imagining you as my husband.'

He arched an eyebrow. 'After only half a waltz? That is quick work. Most of the ladies here would not be thinking of me like that after so short an acquaintance. And didn't you mention you already had a husband?'

'I do!' I exclaimed, annoyed that I had been flustered and not clearly explained myself. 'What I meant is that I had replaced your head with my husband's own for the sake of propriety ... Oh, I see. You are making fun of me.'

His lips were pressed together, as if trying hard not to laugh. Mr Hart's propensity for teasing and his enjoyment in doing so were becoming quite apparent.

'Let us talk about something else,' I said hastily, not wanting to give him the chance to tease me again. 'Do you reside in Bath?'

He glanced over at the other dancers as we waltzed. 'Yes, for the present.'

'Where do you usually reside?'

He looked back at me and said with apparent seriousness, 'In a castle.'

I laughed at that. 'I can see you like to joke, Mr Hart ...'

He shrugged his shoulders under my hands. 'I'm telling you the truth, Mrs Fitzroy. I live in Hartmoor Castle when I am not in Bath or London for the Season. It is a hulking draughty pile of stones, but it is home.'

'Gracious,' I said, a bit awestruck in spite of myself. 'I've never met anyone who lived in a castle before.'

We transitioned into circling then, so he could not reply but did so when we were back together.

'And how long are you staying in Bath for, Mrs Fitzroy?' he enquired.

I had wished to hear more about the castle, but it seemed he did not wish to speak of that any longer. Very well.

'Six weeks,' I replied.

'Marvellous. Then I hope we will meet again.'

I gave a polite nod, unsure if I should agree to this or not.

The dance ended. Mr Hart removed his hands from my waist, and I from his shoulders, and we clapped politely. I thought he would bow as was expected, but he held out his hand for me to shake.

Bemused, I placed my gloved hand in his own.

'It was most enjoyable to meet you, Mrs Fitzroy,' he murmured, gazing at me.

Before I knew what was happening, he drew my hand up to his lips and placed a quick kiss on my fingers. It was unexpected, and I snatched my hand out of his grasp immediately. Even though his lips had not touched my skin, a thrum of traitorous desire reverberated in my stomach.

'Good evening, Mr Hart.' Without looking at him, I hurried to the bench, collected my reticule, and headed in the direction of the tea room. I resisted the temptation to look round as I was sure the man would be watching me with laughter in his eyes.

Oh, Mr Hart was trouble with a capital *T*, and Lucinda was not the only one who should stay away from him!

Feeling hot and flustered, I entered the tea room, which was situated next door to where the dancing was held. This room was cooler, and the array of tables neatly laid with white linen tablecloths and the people decorously drinking tea calmed me considerably.

In saying that, there was no tea drinking at the table Elizabeth, Jane, and Lucinda were ensconced at, although there was a teapot and cups. They all looked rather disgruntled, in fact.

'Flissy, there you are,' said Jane upon seeing me. I pulled out a chair and sat down. 'Is everything all right?' she enquired curiously when I extracted my scented handkerchief from my reticule to dab my perspiring forehead. I considered using my fan to cool down as well, but that might look suspicious.

'Yes, quite,' I said. 'It was rather warm in the dance

room. What is happening here?'

'We were discussing if we should collect Edward and leave shortly as we are all rather tired. It has been a busy day.'

'I am not tired, though,' said Lucinda somewhat petulantly, folding her arms.

'We have been explaining to Lucy about Mr Hart,' said Elizabeth carefully. 'And that it may not be wise to associate with him based on what Mrs Spencer has said.'

'Forgive me, but I think that is most unfair,' said Lucinda stiffly. 'Mr Hart has been a perfect gentleman to me, both at the pump room and just now when I was dancing with him. You have taken one spiteful mother's opinion and believed it wholly without even giving him the chance to defend himself!'

Elizabeth and Jane looked at me expectantly, and I knew that they had tried their best to make her see reason, but she was resisting it because she liked him a lot and did not want to hear a bad word said about him. So now I had to try.

'That is true, Lucy,' I said gently. 'But in this case, where there is smoke, there is usually fire.' (Heat was still emanating from where his hands had touched my waist, so I certainly knew what I was talking about.) 'I am sure there are numerous other young gentlemen who would be more than happy to make your acquaintance. Besides, your mama would want you to get to know as many gentlemen as possible in the time we are here rather than narrow your focus to one so soon in the piece, as then you will be able to compare them more objectively. Someone who appears to be a perfect match on the first or second meeting may on the third show a deplorable tendency to let off wind.'

I thought this was rather a good speech and light-hearted too as Jane giggled. But Lucinda only scowled. She opened her mouth to say more on the subject. But at that moment, Edward came hobbling into the tea room on his crutches, looking for us. Elizabeth told him we were more than ready to take our leave. With that, we exited the rooms and flagged a hackney to take us the three minutes back to Queen Square, whereupon Lucinda flounced to her room in a huff. Jane and I retired to our room silently after bidding the others good night.

I was a touch concerned about Lucinda's behaviour but hoped she was just tired and would be back to her sweet self tomorrow. As for myself, I felt I had done what I had been asked to do—namely prevent Mr Hart from entering the tea room. But in doing so, I had somehow caught his attention.

All I could do was hope that he would forget our meeting and not pursue any further acquaintance with myself or any of our party.

PART TWO

The Chaperone's Dilemma

Chapter 7

I desperately wanted to talk to Jane and tell her what had occurred between Mr Hart and myself while she and the others had been in the tea room. But we went straight to bed as she was exhausted and wished to blow out the candle without chatting, so I did not have the heart to insist she prop her eyelids open and listen to me.

But I could not sleep.

My conversation with that gentleman circled around in my head, and I dwelt on the moment he kissed my hand again and again until I had convinced myself I had broken my marriage vows to Max, which distressed me no end.

Eventually, I told myself I was being silly—that one dance with a handsome stranger *did not* constitute unfaithfulness. And I was sure that Jane would agree (once I told her) that I was overreacting. Indeed, all it showed in truth was that I loved my husband and was missing him.

Feeling much better at having sorted it out in my mind, I slept deeply without dreaming and rose refreshed and ready for the day's activities.

However, when Jane and I descended for breakfast, we

discovered Elizabeth out of sorts because she had a bad headache and Lucinda looking distinctly glum.

Only Edward was in the mood for conversing, and Jane and I were subjected to an in-depth explanation about the electricity treatment he would be receiving for his gout that morning. Apparently, his physician, a certain Dr Fellowes, had not made any objection to it when Edward had suggested that, as well as taking the waters, he undergo this type of treatment.

Having live sparks directed to one's swollen big toe sounded a little barbaric (and possibly dangerous) to my mind, but I did not like to say anything when Edward was clearly putting a lot of faith in the treatment to ease his painful inflammation.

Jane, on the other hand, was not shy about stating her opinion. 'I hope it helps, Edward, but perhaps you should not expect too much from it. A restorative diet and abstaining from port will probably do you more good.'

With that being said, Edward was the only one who was making plans to leave the house after breakfast. And as Elizabeth was not well enough to accompany him, he said he would take a sedan chair to the treatment room. He suggested that Jane come along. But she declined, hastily saying she had letters to write, and went upstairs.

Elizabeth retired to her room to lie down with a cool

cloth on her forehead, and that left Lucinda and me. My reply to Max's letter was pressing, and I wanted to write it forthwith. But I needed to convey a light, cheerful tone, and I could not achieve that from sitting inside and looking at Lucinda's morose expression. No, I needed to walk around outside and get my thoughts in order so I could compose it properly.

The possibility of rousing Lucinda from her slump seemed slim, but I thought I should offer all the same.

'I might go for a stroll in Queen Square and get some fresh air,' I said to her. 'Would you care to join me? It might improve your spirits.'

But the girl looked as though she was more inclined to burst into tears and turned away, biting her lip.

Oh dear, that was evidently the wrong thing to say!

'Never mind,' I said hastily. 'I will be perfectly content walking alone. Perhaps you might like to read in your room instead?'

She let out a sigh (either of frustration or boredom, I could not tell), and off she went upstairs, dragging her feet.

At this point, I could have cheerfully strangled Mr Hart for the emotional upheaval he was causing. Why, Lucinda had been happy enough before she had made his acquaintance! Perhaps all she needed was a day of rest, quiet, and reading; and she would be back to her old self again.

It was with no small measure of relief that I escaped from the house of misery just before ten o'clock and crossed the road wearing my best bonnet and a light shawl (in case I had misjudged the temperature).

But I had not—the day was delightfully warm with nary a breeze and a deep blue sky harbouring high wispy clouds. Queen Square was the right sort of size too for stretching one's legs, and with its wide gravel pathways, one need not bump elbows with fellow strollers who were also taking the air.

I did several turns around the outside of the park, all the while composing a humorous epistle to Max. I decided I would only briefly mention that we'd had an encounter with an 'appalling scoundrel'. But I would be quick to reassure him that we had survived the ordeal, thanks to being forewarned, and that Lucinda's virtue was safe. Hopefully, it would show him that I was taking my chaperone duties seriously as well as make him laugh. Smiling to myself, I hurried back to the house to put quill to paper.

The grandfather clock in the hall was chiming eleven when I re-entered. As I had been wandering around outside for nearly an hour, I wasn't surprised to see Edward had now returned and was reclining on the sofa in the drawing room with his newly bandaged foot propped on a pillow.

Elizabeth must be resting still, and the other two are upstairs, I thought.

'Hello,' I said, removing my bonnet and flopping down on the other sofa. 'How was the treatment?'

Edward grimaced. 'Not pleasant, I have to say. But I think it has helped as the pain has eased some.'

'That's good!'

'Yes, and thankfully, I do not have to go again for another week.'

I thought I would leave him in peace and see if Jane had finished with the table upstairs so I could write my letter. But our room was empty, and so was Lucinda's.

That was most odd. Where were they?

Perplexed, I ran back down to Edward, who was reading his library book. 'Forgive me for disturbing you. But have Jane and Lucinda gone out? They are not upstairs.'

He lowered his book. 'Are they not? How strange. Elizabeth is not in her room either. I assumed she felt well enough to venture to Milsom Street. Perhaps they are all looking at hats as we speak?'

'But Elizabeth bought a hat only yesterday.' And I did not think Jane would be lured out by the milliner's alone. *They must have gone to the library again. But why did they not stop by the park and collect me?*

'Mrs Bromley may know where they are,' said Edward,

returning to his book. 'I'm sure they haven't gone far.'

I went off in search of the housekeeper down the narrow hallway, which led through to the kitchen. The cook was whisking something lumpy on the Aga, and when I enquired, she indicated the door with a frown and said Mrs Bromley was in the garden.

Indeed, the housekeeper was arranging a couple of dripping cream-coloured chemises on a washing line that had been strung up between two trees.

'Mrs Bromley? Sorry to disturb you ...' I said from the doorway.

She turned and saw me watching her. Her cheeks coloured a little, and I guessed it was her personal undergarments on display, not those of Elizabeth. 'I was just taking the chance to get these washed while the weather's fine,' she said, sounding defensive. 'I will get to the other laundry presently.'

'I did not come about the laundry,' I said.

'Oh ... Well, how can I help you, Mrs Fitzroy?'

'Do you know where everyone is? There is only Edward in the house, and no plans were made to go out during breakfast.'

Mrs Bromley's shoulders relaxed.

'Why, yes, a gentleman came calling. I let him in myself. I am not sure of the exact conversation that took place in the drawing room. But afterwards, Mrs Austen came out to see me and said they were going out, so they would not need luncheon. And then there was a mad rush for the ladies to don their gloves, pelisses, and such. Then they piled into the gentleman's carriage and took off at a great rate of knots. That's all I can tell you, I'm afraid.'

I blinked. *What on earth?*

'This young gentleman, what did he look like?' I enquired breathlessly.

Mrs Bromley sniffed and continued pegging her chemises.

'I am not in the business of describing gentlemen. But if you want to know, he was taller than most and had dark-brown hair.'

'And a mole under his left eye?'

She considered. 'I cannot say for sure, perhaps. But mole or no mole, he caused a disturbance. Cook had started preparing luncheon and is most put out.'

I thanked Mrs Bromley and, leaving her to her washing, went back inside, feeling as disgruntled as the cook. There was no other conclusion but that it was Mr Hart who had called. But what had possessed Elizabeth (who had been nursing a headache!) and Jane (who was good sense itself!) to go off with him in his carriage?

It was a mystery that could not be solved until they

returned. So I had to be patient, a trait that was not my strong point. Fortunately, I had my letter to Max to keep me occupied; and then Edward and I ate a luncheon of ham, cheese, and bread. Mrs Bromley was most apologetic as to the meagre fare but said that what had been planned for luncheon was now going to be supper due to the 'exceptional circumstances' of that morning. Edward remained as puzzled as I as to these 'exceptional circumstances' and where everyone was.

After luncheon had been cleared away, Edward went off to have a nap, and I was left to pace about in the drawing room and look out the window. At long last, a shiny black carriage drew up outside the house, and three ladies popped out. The carriage then raced off and did not linger.

Finally, they were back!

The front door opened, and the sound of excited chatter reached my ears as they removed their bonnets. Still feeling mightily put out that I had been excluded from this impromptu outing, I continued looking out the window but was unseeing of anything.

When they all came into the drawing room with smiles on their faces, I turned and said frostily, 'Hello. Have you all had a nice time?'

Jane knew me well enough to detect when I was annoyed and immediately came over.

She rubbed my poker-stiff shoulders briskly and said, 'Let us sit down, and we will explain everything.'

Reluctantly, I let her lead me to the sofa, and they all settled themselves next to me. Elizabeth looked well again, and Lucinda's cheeks were high in colour. Her gloominess from this morning had definitely dissipated.

'What happened to make you all go off like that? I came back from my walk, and no one was here but Edward,' I said peevishly.

Jane glanced at Elizabeth. 'I told you we should have done a loop around the park and picked her up.'

Elizabeth patted my arm briefly. 'We are so sorry, Felicity, but it all happened in such a rush. Mr Hart called on us!'

'I learned that from interrogating Mrs Bromley,' I said dryly. 'Go on.'

'Well, of course, no one was expecting him to call. I was indisposed, so Lucinda and Jane received him in here.'

'He said he was on his way to Sally Lunn's to meet his friend Mr Smith-Withers for luncheon and asked if we wished to join them,' piped up Lucinda.

'Lucy instantly said yes before I could stop her,' said Jane with a laugh. 'She ran into the hallway and was putting on her pelisse and bonnet before I knew it.'

'Lucy!' I said, shocked at her wilfulness.

'I am sorry, Aunty Fliss. I was just so happy that he had called. It was an impulsive, but kind gesture as he was passing by and thought we might like the outing.'

She gave me a downcast look, but her countenance did not seem that contrite.

'Of course, I could not let her go alone with him,' murmured Jane. 'Especially as he was meeting his friend. So I roused Elizabeth and explained the situation of there being two unmarried gentlemen—'

'Suffice to say, I had to play chaperone despite still having my headache,' interrupted Elizabeth. 'It was most inconvenient. But surprisingly, the outing has done me the world of good. After a cup of tea and a bun and an interesting conversation, I feel much better.'

'I am glad to hear it,' I said flatly, wondering what this 'interesting conversation' entailed. 'So why was there not time to wait for me?'

'He was in a hurry to meet his friend,' explained Elizabeth. 'And we did not know exactly where you were. We did look over at the park, but we couldn't see you walking back. And Mr Hart kept taking out his watch and glancing at it, so ...'

Humph, I thought. But I could imagine them all peering out the window worriedly to see where I was and, I supposed, mentioning me to Mr Hart. So I was not really forgotten.

'We missed you, of course,' Lucinda confirmed. 'And Mr Hart sends you his regards.' She thrust a box at me. 'He said he was sorry you had not been there when he called and bought you a bun.'

He bought me a bun? I opened the box to see an innocuous-looking brown bun sitting there.

'Well,' I said, slightly mollified by the explanation and the bun gift.

'He was going to buy Edward one too, but Aunt Elizabeth said he wasn't allowed sugar,' said Lucinda.

The bun had been cut in half, and each side was slathered in melted cinnamon butter. When I took a bite, it was still warm and tasted delicious.

'So you all had tea and buns with Mr Hart and Mr Smith-Withers and then came home?' I asked, taking another bite of my bun and leaning back on the sofa, now feeling more inclined to hear the rest of the story.

'Yes, he dropped us off but could not come in as he had another appointment,' relayed Jane.

The fact that they were all very well disposed to Mr Hart had not escaped my notice. It was as if he had waved a magic wand over them, and now they could not think highly enough of him. It couldn't have been the Sally Lunn buns that had sweetened them up, surely?

'And did you learn any new information about the gentleman?' I asked Jane and Elizabeth. 'Last night, we were all convinced he was a rake and shouldn't be let within two feet of Lucinda. Now here you both are, singing his praises!'

'Yes. Well, some things came to light when we were at the tea room,' said Elizabeth. 'I do not usually go back on my first opinion of people, having extremely good instincts, you understand. But in this case, I was so very wrong ...'

I looked enquiringly at Jane since Elizabeth seemed disinclined to say more.

'It appears our Mr Hart is not a rake but has been wrongly accused of being one by Mrs Spencer,' she said. 'Cecilia and Mr Hart were in fact very much in love ... and were cruelly separated.' Jane gave a sorrowful sigh.

'*In love?*' I said, startled. 'Are you sure? Did Mr Hart tell you this?'

'Yes,' replied Lucinda, joining in the conversation. 'And before you say anything, it was a subject that was not prompted by us. Indeed, it was his friend Mr Smith-Withers who commented that Mr Hart was looking much jollier today.

'I asked him, "Why should he not be jolly?" And he told us that his friend had had his heart broken some months back. Cecilia the girl's name was, and he had been about to propose but had been thwarted.'

'Of course, we all wanted to know what had happened,' said Jane, taking up the story. 'But Mr Hart did not reply. He just sat there, eating his bun and sipping his tea. He left it up to his friend to convey the sorry tale.'

She went on to say that Mr Smith-Withers, with sympathetic glances at his friend, had told them Mr Hart had called on Cecilia for Sunday luncheon. Mrs Spencer had left them alone for a minute to speak to the cook about the gravy. 'And when she came back, she had caught them kissing.' Jane lowered her voice dramatically. 'He was thrown out of the house and barred from seeing Cecilia ever again.'

'This must be the conduct that Mrs Spencer had deemed "very bad",' I mused. 'Did his friend say anything else?'

'Only that Mr Hart had been in despair and kept writing to her, but to no avail. He never received any reply. Her parents must have been confiscating his letters.'

'Gracious!' I said, feeling sorry for the man. 'What is a quick kiss if two people are in love? Mrs Spencer must be a very religious mama.'

Lucy nodded. 'Yes, Mr Smith-Withers said both parents are evangelical Anglicans and are bringing their daughters up to conform to the doctrine. I did not know exactly what that entails. But Mr Smith-Withers said it meant that they are deeply pious, so probably even holding hands would have had the same reaction.'

'It sounds like he would have had no hope in making a match with her then,' I remarked, thinking of how Mr Hart had taken liberties with my own hand. It had been a bit shocking even for me, and I was only slightly religious.

'No, her parents would never have agreed to it,' said Elizabeth, shaking her head sadly. 'It all makes so much more sense now. Poor Mr Hart has been hard done by. The way that woman was gripping my arm and talking so to me.' She shuddered. 'I should have known it was nothing but religious fervour. I am sorry, Lucy, that your dear Mr Hart has been through such heartache in the pursuit of true love.'

I raised my eyebrows. Now it was *dear* Mr Hart! Having not been privy to their conversation and even though the bun he had purchased for me was very tasty, I was able to maintain some semblance of objectivity on the matter. But how could I remain steadfast in thinking he was a rake when everyone else was now convinced he was not? Surely, it was safe for me to change my opinion of him too?

'And as the trouble happened last Season, he is now well over it, after having written many angsty love poems,' continued Jane eagerly.

'Oh, so he *is* a poet?'

'Apparently.'

I knew how much she liked romantic poetry, so this was another feather in his cap.

'Perhaps you can ask if he is willing to share them to see if they are of merit? He may be a budding John Donne.'

'I did ask, but he said they were awful and actually no longer exist as he flung them into the fire on New Year's Eve.'

'How cathartic,' I said deadpan, and Jane gave a huff of laughter.

Lucinda pursed her lips. 'We should not make fun of his pain.'

'Yes. Sorry, dearest. I should not have been flippant. So I suppose he is casting about for a new muse now that his heart has quite healed?'

Lucinda fidgeted with the charms on her bracelet. 'Perhaps. He did say he was feeling quite inspired after our meeting at the ball and had gone home and jotted down some lines.'

My lips twitched at the thought of this, but I could not make jokes—it would be tantamount to teasing a sweet child. And I could not blame her for being enthusiastic about a potential suitor. I remembered all too well how my encounters with Max had fired me up. But luckily for me, that had led to love and marriage—would it do so in the case of Mr Hart? Only time would tell.

As we were finishing our conversation, there was a knock on the door, and Mrs Bromley poked her head in. 'Oh, you are all back. Good. And having buns, I see.' She glanced at the box on my lap.

'I'm off to the post. Are there any more to go?' She held up the letter that Jane had written to Cassie this morning and the one I had written to Max. The story of last night was all in there. I had told Max in brief (but light-hearted) detail about how we had survived our meeting with an 'appalling scoundrel' and that we would take care to avoid him in future.

Should I rip it up? Because we had not avoided him—he had turned up again and was apparently not a scoundrel after all.

But I did not say anything, for I did not want to arouse curiosity about what I had written. Perhaps Mr Hart's bun outing was a subject best left for my next letter.

Chapter 8

After 'bun day' (as I privately referred to it), Mr Hart was a permanent fixture at 13 Queen Square. He was either calling in to see if we were free for a jaunt, sending invites about future jaunts, or popping in from jaunts of his own to join us for afternoon tea. Sometimes he lingered for so long that the afternoon turned into evening, and he stayed for supper and a game of whist. He and Edward got along famously, and Jane found him 'very witty' and 'amusing'. Elizabeth also enjoyed his company.

I had not pressed Lucinda for her thoughts and feelings, but if the day did not involve a visit or at least an invite from Mr Hart for a jaunt, then she was mightily subdued. And although he was always careful to include everyone in his invitations, we were under no illusion of why he was visiting—he was courting Miss Lucinda Fitzroy. She received his first bow when he entered the room, and she was the first to be offered his hand when boarding his carriage. It was as it should be.

Jane often begged off a walk around to the pump room if it was drizzling or a stroll on the lawn of the Royal Crescent if the weather was windy, stating that she wished to write. So it fell to me, as Lucinda's official chaperone, to accompany the pair no matter the weather. But it gave me time to closely observe Mr Hart's behaviour, and on each occasion, it was impeccable. He did not touch her, unless to help her in and out of his carriage or to proffer his arm if the cobblestones were slippery. And I began to trust, as we all did, that his intentions towards my niece were honourable, that he held an affection for her (as she did for him), and that it was deepening each day.

Whatever attention he had directed to me at the ball faded in my mind until I was wondering if it had only been in my imagination. Indeed, he was nothing but polite and friendly to me in company. There was no subtle flirtation of any kind. I was glad and relieved that I had not said anything to Jane, for it may have coloured her opinion of him; and I knew that she, along with Elizabeth and Edward, held him in the highest regard.

Mr Hart was staying in an apartment in Royal Crescent, which he said was 'but a ten-minute walk from Queen Square and on the carriage route to the pump room, so very convenient all round for visiting'. But we never saw his lodgings, as he seemed to prefer our house to his, and lamented that his place was 'rather draughty as it took in the wind coming directly off the crescent' and that he would hate for any of us to catch a chill whilst taking tea.

During this time, Max and I had resolved the timing of our correspondence; and I had fallen into a rhythm of waiting until the delivery of his letter, then writing immediately to reply. The mail delivery between Bath and Derbyshire was reliable enough that I was receiving a letter from him every two to three days. It grounded me to have regular contact with him, especially as Mr Hart was always on the scene and who, with his good looks and sparkling humour, was a wholly distracting presence at the whist table.

Writing to Max meant I had an excuse from playing, and while the others enjoyed themselves, I would sit at the desk in the corner and compose my replies.

It was no chore to do so. I enjoyed it as Max was an excellent letter writer and had a very droll sense of humour. In one letter, he wrote,

> *In your absence and in my desire to leave off the wine, I find myself gravitating to the kitchen in search of company. The cook has become rather used to me sitting at the bench, helping to prepare vegetables for supper. I can now peel a carrot in under ten seconds ...*

Whether he was actually carrying out this task or trying to make me laugh, I could not tell. But knowing Max, it was a little of both. My reply was thus:

> *Darling, I am glad that you are making new friends and learning some culinary skills in the process. Does this mean that you will next be taking up a duster and beating the rugs? I hope when I return that you will possess a range of household skills as this will make you even more desirable as my husband ...*

Often, I would chuckle away to myself; and in doing so one evening, I attracted notice from Mr Hart. 'Pray, what is so funny, Mrs Fitzroy?' he asked, looking up from his cards.

'Only my husband's letter, Mr Hart. He has a way with words that amuses me immensely.'

'Indeed,' said the man, sounding curious. 'What exactly has he written, if I may ask?'

But I shook my head and said it was a private joke, and Mr Hart nodded and did not question me further. I got the impression that he thought quite highly of his own wit and was pleased when a joke landed well, resulting in peals of mirth from his audience. So another man who could also make a woman chuckle immediately interested him.

Ah, I thought, *Mr Hart likes to be the centre of attention where ladies' amusement is concerned. I wonder what would happen if he and Max were ever in the same room.* For my husband was quite his equal in terms of looks and gentility. Perhaps Max did not have Mr Hart's ease of confidence when meeting new people, but when you got past his reserve, his natural sense of humour was quite wonderful. Besides, I loved him dearly, and to think of him peeling carrots in the kitchen because he missed me made my heart ache.

***

Perhaps Max's letter and my reaction to it had made an impression on Mr Hart. Or perhaps it was completely unrelated. All I knew was the next day, Mr Hart did not appear; and in the afternoon of the following day, Lucinda received a letter saying that he had written a poem for her, that he hoped she liked it, and that if she did, to please show everyone else.

Of course she was delighted.

Here was proof that she was his new muse.

Knowing how Mr Hart liked to talk, I was expecting it to be multiple grandiose verses declaring his undying love for her. But when she gave it to me to read, it was short and sweet: four rhyming verses about a little mouse that was running amok in his house and getting up to all sorts of mischief until he lured it into a mousetrap with a hunk of Cheddar cheese.

'Isn't he clever?' Lucinda exclaimed after I'd handed it back to her.

'Yes, it is very witty,' I replied.

She read it again and frowned a little. 'Am I the mouse? I cannot see how he is trying to convey his affection, especially as the mouse does not seem to come out of it well.'

I had not been able to detect anything of an intimate nature in it, but I didn't read poetry, so I probably wasn't the best judge. He might indeed be cleverly implying some affection ...

'I really couldn't say. Let Jane have a look.'

Jane set her novel on the side table and took the paper from Lucinda. After perusing it, she said slowly, 'As poems go, it is not half bad ... The language is descriptive. It rhymes well, and it seeks to amuse. But I do not think it conveys affection in the sense you are hoping for.'

Lucinda's expectant face fell.

'*However* ...' Jane tapped the paper with her finger. 'It is proof of his affection in a way because he has written it *for you*. Does it amuse you and please you?'

Lucinda nodded.

Jane smiled. 'Then his poem has done its job admirably.'

'I see. Thank you, Aunt Jane,' said Lucinda politely, but I could tell from her flat tone that she had been hoping for something more demonstrative than a mouse running around Mr Hart's house. I felt the urge to quip that she should write back, suggesting he get in a mouse catcher if he was having rodent issues. But I held my tongue as I knew it was a sensitive subject, and she would not find it funny.

I prayed Mr Hart's future poetic musings would be more romantic to give her the reassurance she needed.

That evening proved to have nothing much to commend it. There was no ball to attend and no Mr Hart popping in for supper and staying to play a game of whist. We all sat around in the drawing room, either reading or tending to embroidery (or, in the case of Lucinda, sitting on the window seat and looking wistfully out the window into the dark street).

Elizabeth, glancing at her, said in a low voice to Jane and me, 'We should not rely so much on Mr Hart to provide our entertainment. It is Ladies' Day at the baths tomorrow, so we should go. Having a good soak in the hot water will do Lucy the world of good and stop her moping.'

Jane wrinkled her nose and whispered, 'I am not sure I

wish to submerge myself in a stinky bath. But I will go along if everyone else is in agreement.'

'If it was good enough for the Romans, it's good enough for us,' Elizabeth muttered, turning to me. 'Felicity, what do you think?'

I nodded my agreement. 'Having witnessed my sister nearly make herself ill waiting for Evan to write or call, I think it would be a good idea to get her out of the house,' I murmured.

So it was settled. We would go to the baths at nine o'clock tomorrow morning to distract Lucinda from brooding about Mr Hart.

There were no gentlemen allowed, so she could relax amongst female company, and perhaps he would call on her later.

Speaking of gentlemen, a letter from Max had arrived at the same time as Mr Hart's poem, and I had been keeping it to peruse at bedtime. As Jane also wished to do some reading, we retired early with our candles.

Making a quick job of plaiting my hair, I hopped into bed and eagerly opened his letter. He began with general news about the estate and then told me that his brother Tobias was visiting, which made me smile. *Here was Lucinda's plan in action!* There was no further mention of preparing vegetables and rather more talk of fishing and riding, and he seemed happier from the tone of it. So my niece's idea had been a good one indeed.

However, the next part of his letter made me sit up straighter.

> *Tobias has been asking me if I know anything about some fellow called Dorian Hart. Apparently, Lucinda sent a letter to her mother announcing they were courting, and Seraphina thinks it is quite fast and wants to know more about him—namely is he kind, well mannered, and of good breeding? (And she also wishes to know what his teeth are like.) Tobias said she is a tad concerned that Lucinda is infatuated with him (this might be too strong a word, but it is what Tobias relayed from his wife rather than me!).*
>
> *I did not know what to tell him as I did not have any information, and you have not mentioned anything about him, my darling. I assume he is not the 'appalling scoundrel' that you told me about in a previous letter? I know you have better judgement than to allow Lucy to form an acquaintance with someone like that ...*

Oh Lord! What on earth had Lucinda been saying to

make Seraphina think she was infatuated? A few strolls in the pump room and a poem about a mouse did not mean that Mr Hart was going to propose! Now I would have to write to Max and tell him that Dorian Hart was indeed the scoundrel I had mentioned, but we had got the wrong end of the stick, and he wasn't one at all. *How awkward.* I let out a sigh of frustration.

'Is everything all right?' asked Jane.

'Actually, no. I told Max about our first meeting with Mr Hart and how we'd had a run-in with an "appalling scoundrel", but that we had escaped his clutches. How was I to know that you would all go off and have buns with him and discover he was perfectly sound? Apparently, Lucinda has sent an enthusiastic letter to her mother commending him. Now Tobias is visiting and pressing Max for more information on Seraphina's behalf. Of course, thanks to me, my husband now thinks the worst of Mr Hart. I will have to write back and tell him that he is in fact the gentleman that Lucinda is besotted with!'

Jane tsked sympathetically. 'Oh dear, that is a bother. But you should not blame yourself—you were only relaying the information you had at the time ...'

'Yes. And I have not had time to get him up to speed about Cecilia, her strict religious mother, and Mr Hart's being thwarted in love, et cetera.'

'Then I suppose you will be writing a long letter tomorrow afternoon after our visit to the baths?'

'I suppose so,' I grumbled.

'You have to, Flissy, for Lucinda's sake. Otherwise, her mother will get in a flap. Just tell Max we got it wrong and convey succinctly what we now know—that Mr Hart is a reputable young gentlemen, residing in Royal Crescent, who has been schooled at Eton and whose family estate is Hartmoor Castle. Tell him that you are keeping a firm eye on their courtship, and there is nothing amiss. Max will write to Lucinda's mama to dispel her fears forthwith, and she will then be at ease about her daughter. All going well, she may soon have a new son-in-law to add to her family tree.'

I raised an eyebrow. 'Are we not being too hasty in that regard ourselves? I mean, I know he wrote her a poem, but you saw it yourself—it was not in the least romantic ...'

'At least he tried to please her. It was sweet of him to do so.'

Jane shifted into a more comfortable position against the headboard, and my eye fell upon the title of the book she was reading: *The Monk: Volume II.*

'I thought you had finished that volume?'

'I have. I am reading it again as volume three isn't available until next week.'

'What's it about? You never actually said.'

'Well, speaking of scoundrels, it's about this monk who starts out devout but falls into temptation, which leads into a downward spiral of lust, murder, and a pact with the devil.'

'So it's a comedy then?' I said dryly.

Jane giggled. 'It's melodramatic enough to be one. It's actually touted as a romance.' She showed me the title page, which indeed said 'A Romance', along with a lyrical verse of what was inside:

Dreams, magic terrors, spells of mighty power,
Witches, and ghosts who rove at midnight hour

'Though by the way it is going, I have a feeling the story will not involve love nor a happy ending,' she said with a grimace. 'And I do like my stories to end in a satisfactory manner for the couples involved.'

I glanced across at her desk by the window. It was shut up tightly, with no paper lying around to indicate her writing efforts—even though she had been scurrying up here every afternoon to pen something mysterious.

'Is it inspiring you to write your own Gothic novel?' I asked.

She smirked. 'All I can say is that what I have begun

writing is more of a Gothic spoof.'

'Oooh,' I said, for I loved novels that poked fun at popular literature, and Jane's humour always tickled me. If it was anything like her previous novel (about yours truly), it was sure to be an excellent read.

'Do not get too excited,' she said, blowing out her candle. 'I have some characters in mind, but no firm plot or setting. And I need to include a spooky castle or some such.'

Mr Hart lives in a castle, I thought sleepily, folding up Max's letter and blowing out my own candle. *I wonder if she will subtly ask him to talk about it for the sake of her book. I would definitely like to hear more about this Hartmoor Castle myself.*

Chapter 9

We ate a light breakfast of toast and tea the next morning with our wraps over our chemises. Then it was time to change into the bathing gowns and caps that Mrs Bromley kept on hand for female guests. The gowns were not attractive—shapeless dun-coloured dresses made of flannel designed purely to maintain modesty.

I took one look at myself in the mirror and burst out laughing.

'Surely we are not walking to the baths in these?' I glanced over at Jane, who looked equally ridiculous. She'd tied her cap tightly round her chin to prevent her hair from getting wet and rather resembled a chestnut mushroom.

'Good Lord, no! Mrs Bromley has arranged sedan chairs to take us there.'

'Thank goodness for Mrs Bromley,' I muttered. 'What would we do without her?'

Bidding Edward goodbye, we scurried outside in our drab garb, bringing with us the necessary items for changing and drying off afterwards.

The waiting sedan chairs, to my mind, resembled tall boxes. Each had two porters to carry the poles and could fit one person. Inside, there was a padded seat and, to my relief, a curtain, which I drew immediately over the window. However, the porters were disinterested in our appearance and did not seem to care one jot, I suppose having seen much worse sights than us.

I was the end chair of our convoy, with the other three ladies in front of me; and after I got used to the bouncing movement, I have to say, I rather enjoyed the experience. The men called out to passers-by to 'wotch it!' and so called attention to us, and it did rather make one feel as though one was royalty being carried through the streets of Bath. Peeking through the curtain, I saw people glancing at us and shifting to the side to avoid our chair train.

Yes, I thought, smirking to myself. *That's it, move out of the way. Very important people coming through!*

As we came out of Princes Street and turned left into Monmouth Street, I happened to glance down the latter street and spied a tall, slim gentleman some distance away. He was heading in the direction of the pump room, and his self-assured stride and general appearance were all too familiar. I jerked back from the window, my heart beating rapidly. If my eyes had not deceived me, it was Mr Hart!

Fortunately, he had not seen me, nor was he privy to our

plans to visit the baths this morning. I cringed to think of him running after the chair and tapping on my window, wishing to say hello. I would positively *die* if he saw me in an ugly bathing gown.

After I had recovered a little from the shock, I realised that it was strange to have seen him in Monmouth Street at all as it was not the route that he usually took to the pump room. Indeed, he had made a point of mentioning that he walked from Royal Crescent down Milsom Street, on the days he was not collecting us from Queen Square, as it was quicker.

He probably wanted a change of scenery, I thought. *Stop being so suspicious, Felicity!*

It was of such little consequence that I did not say anything about it when we were deposited at the ladies' entrance to the baths. We were endeavouring to get Lucinda's mind *off* Mr Hart, so to mention that he was at the pump room while we were next door would not have helped her to relax. She was liable to go rushing in to see him, ugly bathing gown and all! No, I would keep the 'almost' encounter to myself.

The day was chilly and overcast, and the dark-green water of the bath made a striking contrast to the grey sky above. Plinths and columns lined the pool edge, and it indeed felt like we were following in the footsteps of the

Romans. However, entering the hot water was a tad painful, especially if you had cold feet.

'Ouch,' Elizabeth complained upon having dipped in a toe, but the attendant said that our bodies would get used to it and to go in slowly.

We took her advice, and after ten minutes of 'ouching' and 'aahing', we were soon fully submerged with our gowns floating around us. However, the water was very smelly, making Jane mutter, 'Pooh, it stinks.'

But to counteract that, we had small bowls hung round our necks with string that held scented handkerchiefs and nosegays of fresh lavender that Mrs Bromley had prepared for us. So the odour of the water was unpleasant, but not unbearable if you kept your bowl close to your face.

Another small group of ladies were bathing on the far side of the pool, but with the rising steam from the water, it wasn't possible to detect their faces. We did not know many people in Bath, so they were probably strangers to us anyway.

The others wanted to sit on the steps and relax in the water, but I was feeling in a sociable mood, so I said I would do a lap around the pool and perhaps make the acquaintance of the other group of ladies.

It was only when the steam parted upon my approach to them that I realised my error. I *did* know one of them:

Cecilia Spencer, the pretty object of Mr Hart's thwarted affection. She was bathing with two other young women. Her mother and sister were not there. It was too late to pretend I had not seen her and terribly rude if I did not speak to her. Besides, my dratted gown was cumbersome and would not let me change direction. So I pasted a smile on my face as I floated towards them.

'Good morning!' Cecilia said immediately, smiling back cheerfully. She was sitting a little apart from her friends, who were engaged in their own conversation. 'How do you do? I believe I have seen you in the pump room taking the waters?' She was not wearing a cap and did not seem to mind that the springy blonde ringlets at the base of her neck were damp.

'Hello. Yes, I remember.' I was now in the position of needing to introduce myself. 'I'm Mrs Felicity Fitzroy. My niece, Lucinda, and I are visiting our friends the Austens. That's her, the dark-haired girl with Jane and Elizabeth over there,' I said, pointing at them through the steam.

She nodded. 'I'm Cecilia Spencer, and these are my friends Charlotte and Susannah. But everyone calls us Ceci, Lottie, and Sukey.' I nodded politely to her and her friends, wondering if I should mention I was called Fliss since we were all sharing nicknames.

But her friends resumed their conversation, and Cecilia

was watching Lucinda with narrowed eyes.

'I believe, from what my mother observed at the ball the other night, that your niece appears to have attracted the attention of a certain gentleman—a gentleman who last year was interested in *me*,' she said pointedly, and I stiffened, not knowing what to say.

'I ... uh ...'

'Oh, do not worry. I am not cut up about it, not *now* at least.' She smiled at me genially and settled back against the edge of the pool. 'In fact, it is rather a relief *not* to have Dory's attention this Season.'

Dory? It was very intimate to call him that! I sucked in a breath that reeked of sulphur and let it out slowly, wondering if I dared to ask my question and how she should react. 'Ah, were you and Mr Hart close?' I said carefully.

Cecilia glanced at her friends and whispered to me, 'Let us leave Lottie and Sukey to their gossip and take a little swim over here.'

She breaststroked away from her friends, saying she would be back shortly, and headed to the opposite corner of the pool. I had no choice but to dog-paddle after her with my bowl banging against my chin. Besides, my curiosity was burning. Here was a chance to find out more about her relationship with Mr Hart.

'So what do you know already?' she asked in a low voice

when we were at the foot of a pillar. We were safely out of earshot of her friends, but I assumed she did not want to take any risks.

'Only two things, but each contradicts the other. Your mother told Elizabeth at the ball we attended that Mr Hart was an "appalling scoundrel" and we should have nothing to do with him. And then the day after, he called unexpectedly. And my niece, Jane, and Elizabeth went off with him to Sally Lunn's. Whilst there, they were informed that your mother cruelly separated "a couple in love". His story was backed up by his friend Mr Smith-Withers and believed entirely by my niece and my friends. Now I am confused, both to Mr Hart's nature and his intentions.'

'I do not doubt it,' said Cecilia with a rueful smile. 'But can I tell you my own side of the story? I do not wish to keep you from your party, but I promise it is not too long-winded a tale, and you look like you would lend a sympathetic ear.'

'Very well.'

She closed her large blue eyes briefly, as if gathering her thoughts, then said, 'As you may have noticed, Dory is a remarkably handsome man.'

There was no point disagreeing. 'He is indeed.'

'So you can imagine how even a small amount of attention paid by a man that handsome might be overwhelming.'

I nodded. Even the mere crumbs Mr Hart had paid me at the ball had made my brain whirl until I had regained my good senses. A young woman with far less experience than I would be caught off guard.

'I understand.'

'But he singled me out from all the other young ladies. And well, it made me feel special, and I was charmed ... No, that is not even the right word ... I was *dazzled* by him. I could think of no other but him from morning to night. And if my day did not have him in it, then, oh, it felt as if I should shrivel up and die. Until he called upon me the next day, and miracle of miracles, I was instantly restored. He was like a drug. Have you ever taken opium, Mrs Fitzroy?'

'Oh, er, no. I cannot say I have,' I said, a bit taken aback. 'But I did eat four slices of poppy seed cake at an afternoon tea party once. The next day, I felt very poorly.'

Cecilia nodded eagerly. 'Exactly. Being around him was like being presented with a delectable poppy seed cake. I could not just take one slice.'

'What are you trying to say, Miss Spencer?'

'Ceci please.'

'Very well ... Ceci.'

She leaned closer to me. 'You will think me base saying this, but my passions were inflamed by him. He is the kind of man who inflames one's passions. Don't you think, Mrs Fitzroy?'

'Please, call me Felicity,' I said, ignoring her question about Mr Hart inflaming one's passions. 'So then it is true ... that your mother happened to come across you kissing in the parlour? And as she is a strict Anglican, she banned him from seeing you?'

An expression of surprise crossed Cecilia's features. 'Is that what he's been saying?'

'Yes.'

She stared at me blankly for a moment, then let out a snort of laughter. Glancing over at her friends, she grabbed her scented handkerchief from her bowl and pressed it against her mouth and giggled into it. When she had recovered, she took a deep shuddering breath and said weakly, 'Oh, how funny, yet how *kind* of him to protect me.'

By this time, I was growing impatient and overheating in the water and tired of her talking in circles. 'Ceci, please, will you speak plainly? I am a married woman, after all.'

'Very well, Felicity, if you want the plain truth. My mother did catch Dory and me together one afternoon, but we weren't in the parlour—we were in my bed. And we were doing much more than kissing, as you might imagine,' said the girl, lowering her eyes.

Good gracious, I was not expecting that! A throb of heat raced through my body, and it was not because of the temperature of the water. A sordid image of *Dory* lying naked on top of *Ceci* had flashed into my brain.

'What on earth!' I gasped, my pruney fingers flying to my mouth.

Ceci nodded solemnly. 'It is true and why I cannot tell my friends about it as they are apt to gossip. If word gets out, I would be ruined. But I feel that I can trust you on this matter as you have your niece's best interests at heart. And you won't tell anyone, will you, Felicity?' she said beseechingly.

'Of course not,' I said before I knew what I was agreeing to. In truth, I was stunned by what she had said.

'I realise now how silly I was to let myself get so *enamoured* with him, and I *hated* my mother for separating us. But she was doing it for my own good, though at the time, I did not think so. But a year makes all the difference, and now I can see things more clearly. I could not seem to control myself when he was near me, and I did not much like that feeling. He and I are better kept at a distance. We were like shooting stars colliding. There was bound to be an explosion ... I was only lucky I did not get pregnant.'

I stood there in the pongy water, listening to her go on and on about star-crossed lovers, while I was still reeling from what she had said and getting angrier and angrier by the minute at Mr Hart's deception. *Oh, Lucinda*, I thought. *Why did you have to go and fall in love with such a rake?*

'Your niece seems much more sensible and much less inclined to let her passions run away with her,' Ceci was saying, and I brought myself back to reality with an effort. 'I am sure they will be happy together.'

Not if I have anything to do with it, I thought, bristling with indignation. *He is not fit to be in the same room as her!*

'Thank you, Ceci, for clearing up my confusion about Mr Hart,' I said politely, taking a step backwards. 'I trust the rest of your stay in Bath will be a pleasant one.'

'I hope I haven't offended you, Felicity?' she said worriedly. 'Please do not worry. Your niece will be quite safe with Dory as long as her passions are not inflamed. It is *I* who was the guilty party and *I* who flung myself at him. He did not have a choice ...'

'On the contrary', I said stiffly, 'there is always a choice, and Mr Hart chose poorly. I blame him entirely.'

'Oh no, you should not!' said the girl, sounding aggrieved. I was not sure why she had decided to blame herself for Mr Hart's despicable behaviour, but I did not need to hear more. She saw it as him protecting her reputation, but it was obvious to me that he had deliberately twisted the events to his advantage and had meant to deceive Lucinda with a sob story.

'Please excuse me, I must rejoin my party. Good day,' I said, nodding to the girl, and dog-paddled away as quickly as I could through the greenish water whilst breathing in my lavender nosegay deeply. But the sweet scent did nothing to relax me or stop me from feeling wretched. What was I going to do now?

Chapter 10

The steam from the bath had obscured my private meeting with Cecilia, so the others had not detected who I was talking to and did not question me about it. This was both a blessing and a curse: I was left alone (whilst in the pool and on the solo chair ride home) to ponder the information, but I also had no one in which to confide my suspicions.

Everyone was in thrall to Mr Hart, so I could not simply blurt out what I had learned during luncheon. It would definitely cause Lucinda pain and put Cecilia's reputation at risk. And I had stupidly said that I would not tell anyone, so it would put my good word at risk too.

Mr Hart had also done a good job of giving himself an alibi in the form of Mr Smith-Withers, so Cecilia's story could be construed as a way of trapping him to marry her. It wasn't uncommon for young girls to try such a thing if they had a rich eligible husband in their sights. Mr Hart could come out the whole thing smelling of roses and still ruin Lucinda.

No, there was only one thing for it: I had to be cleverer than that nefarious gentleman. If I gave him enough rope, he would hang himself eventually. But first, I had to find the rope.

The opportunity to do so came sooner than expected, for when we arrived back, a letter from him stating his intention to call this afternoon was waiting for Lucinda. Along with another poem. She raced upstairs, clutching the epistle to her bosom, no doubt to add it to the growing stash. For he had written a couple of other poems for her of late: one about the flowers he could see from his window in Royal Crescent and another about how walking in inclement weather had made his boots wet. Both had been exclaimed over and complimented as being 'clever' and 'witty' and 'original' by everyone when he had asked for our opinion. I myself had said nothing, which had caused him to throw several curious glances my way. But thankfully, he had not pressed me to give my opinion. I should probably comment on this current poem so he would not suspect I had any qualms about him.

'How lovely!' commented Elizabeth, removing a hairpin from her bathing cap. 'That will give Lucy something to look forward to this afternoon. I shall give her my rose water scent so she can spritz her skin before he arrives. Mr Hart will not want his bride-to-be smelling of rotten eggs!'

It was on the tip of my tongue to remark that perhaps she should not and that it would be a true test of Mr Hart's intentions if he still wished to court Lucinda even if she stank. But it was not the time nor place, so I said nothing.

'You have been very quiet since the baths. Is everything all right?' asked Jane when we had changed back into our day dresses, availed ourselves of Elizabeth's rose water scent, and were waiting in the drawing room for luncheon.

Oh, my eagle-eyed friend, if you only knew!

'I am simply a little tired from our outing. The water was hot, and I feel somewhat drained.'

'Yes, me too,' Jane agreed. 'I can see why Edward always has to have a nap afterwards. But at least we have Mr Hart calling this afternoon. He will liven things up!'

I nodded and smiled. 'Ah, yes, that is true.'

'Shall I read you a bit from *The Monk*? It is so atrocious it is funny.'

'Very well, and I will attempt to start my letter to Max.' *If I can determine what to tell him without outright lying ... Oh Lord.*

Jane picked up her book and flipped to a page. 'So in this bit, Ambrosio, the monk, is struggling with his lust for innocent Antonia and is justifying his actions.' She cleared her throat and read in a dramatic tone,

'Weak wretch! Was it for this that I renounced the world? Is this the result of eighteen years of mortification? Am I now

to yield to a passion which I have despised for so many years?' He paused, and then added in a lower voice, 'But I am now to become a slave to a passion which is so natural, so excusable!'

Jane cackled. 'Isn't it rich? In the previous chapters, he was prattling on about how he was so pious.' She rolled her eyes. 'What a hypocrite.'

I raised a brow, noting that she had turned the corners of several other pages of the book. How many times had she read it?

'You will be glad to get volume three, I suppose?'

'Ooh yes, I have put my name on the waiting list.'

'I wonder if Mr Hart has read *The Monk*,' I said dryly. 'It sounds like the sort of thing that would appeal to him.'

'I did ask. But he said he has not read it because the themes of the novel are morally corrupt, and he reads only books and poetry that uplift the soul.'

I raised both brows at this. 'Was Lucinda there at the time?'

Jane nodded. 'I believe so.'

My lips tightened. 'How appropriate.'

'He does seem a very *good* sort of person,' Jane mused. 'I don't think I have even heard him cuss, which is strange for a man. Even Edward cusses, especially when his toe is hurting. Does Max?'

'Oh, definitely. He has quite the temper, though it is usually directed at George rather than me. It is almost as if that horse knows exactly how to rile him up.'

Jane chuckled, and I myself felt cheered by thinking of Max and George. Perhaps I only needed to write a short upbeat letter, one that stated that Lucinda was in good hands and that Seraphina shouldn't worry. I would explain that Dorian Hart was a friend of the family (well, he was *now*), that there were several more suitable contenders, and that he would likely be old news by the time Lucinda next wrote to her. *Indeed, if I had my way, he would be.* I dipped my pen in the ink and began ...

Several hours later, I was sitting in exactly the same spot, looking at my sealed letter addressed to Max, and wondering if I should open it and add a postscript: *Ignore everything I wrote above. Things are NOT in good hands. Please help!*

Suffice to say, things did not go quite as I wanted them to in the afternoon. I was determined to find a crack, a flaw—something that would without a doubt reveal Mr Hart's true colours. It was supposed to be an extremely satisfying moment, one in which I would announce to everyone, 'Aha! Now you see him for the rogue he is!'

But events occurred that were completely out of my control, and the outcome was most upsetting. I hardly knew what to think or what to do next!

Mr Hart arrived promptly at three o'clock, and we were served afternoon tea in the drawing room. Having managed to finish my letter to Max beforehand, I was relieved to have it off my plate. Now I could concentrate on the business at hand—namely exposing Mr Hart.

Of course, when he entered the room and paid me the usual courtesies (enquiring after my health, saying I looked well, etc.), I was momentarily flustered. But that was par for the course with him. He sought to charm and flatter, and he did it with everyone, not just me. He was a handsome gentleman with faultless manners, to be sure, but I was certain his attentiveness was a ploy and he meant none of it.

Upon hearing that we had been to the baths that morning, he was most interested in what we thought of the experience. Settling himself on the sofa, he took the cup of tea Elizabeth handed him while Lucinda, seated alongside, told him all about it in great detail.

At one point, he leaned towards her and sniffed. 'Ah, I can still detect the aroma of the Romans.'

Lucinda looked put out. 'I spritzed with rose water ...'

'A rose by any other name,' he quipped. 'I am sure you did, my dear. But with such a concentration of sulphur, calcium, and magnesium in the water, it would be difficult to erase it completely. It does not matter to me. I like it, and you look so well after bathing.'

Lucinda smiled and looked pleased. *Point one to Mr Hart,* I thought.

'Did you yourself take the waters at the pump room this morning, Mr Hart?' I asked.

His gaze shifted to me on the opposite sofa, and I squirmed as his deep brown eyes roved over my face in a most impertinent manner. 'Why, thank you for enquiring, Mrs Fitzroy. I did indeed, just after nine o'clock,' he said at last.

'I hope you did not find Milsom Street too busy with street sweepers at that time?' I said. *Hah, now I had him.* If he alluded to Milsom Street being busy, then I could ask how come I had seen him on Monmouth Street, which was nowhere near there. I was looking forward to watching *him* squirm.

But he smiled and said without missing a beat, 'I did not notice any street sweepers, I'm afraid, Mrs Fitzroy. I was in my own little world, busy composing my latest poem for Miss Fitzroy.'

Blast, I thought, *he is as slippery as an eel.*

He nodded to me, and the talk turned to his poem, which was titled 'The Whispering Boughs of Solitude' and was about a lonesome tree. The poem was written with the utmost propriety, of course. Only I, knowing that Mr Hart had baser instincts, saw the double meaning in phrases such as 'rooted need'.

I smirked to myself but said nothing.

'What about you, Mrs Fitzroy, do you like my poem?' he asked suddenly, and I dropped the smirk.

'It is good, but not very realistic,' I said, helping myself to another slice of almond cake. 'Trees are not sentient beings. They do not have feelings, so I doubt they can feel lonely. But I liked the general tone of it and the descriptions of nature.'

'Have you written any poems yourself, Mrs Fitzroy?' asked Mr Hart frostily. 'Perhaps we can hear one.'

I swallowed my mouthful of cake abruptly. 'Ah, no, I have not.'

'Well then', he said curtly, 'you may not be the best judge of my poem's merit.' He looked away, but not before I glimpsed a flash of pain in his eyes, which were most expressive, admittedly.

Oh, I have hurt his feelings, I thought, surprised. *How strange, that he should care what I think when it is Lucinda's opinion that should matter the most, and she has told him repeatedly how much she adores it.*

Jane saw as well that my reply had wounded Mr Hart

and hurriedly changed the subject.

'Well, I thought it was a lovely poem, and I have read a fair few! Are there many lonely trees where you stay, Mr Hart?'

'Around Hartmoor Castle you mean, Miss Austen?' he asked.

'Yes. I have a clear picture in my mind of the landscape from what you have previously described. But how many turrets did you say your castle had?'

Hah, she was pressing him for information about his castle for her book as I had thought she might. It seemed we both wanted something from Mr Hart: me, truth; her, inspiration.

'Perhaps it would be easier if I drew it for you?' he said, warming to the subject.

'Ooh yes, please do!' exclaimed Jane, and Lucinda clapped her hands excitedly.

Mr Hart smiled at their enthusiasm. 'If I could acquire some paper and borrow a pencil, then I will happily draw you a quick sketch.'

'There is some paper in the desk drawer. Flissy has just been using it to write a letter,' Jane said helpfully.

'And I have a pencil,' said Elizabeth, producing one with a flourish from her dress pocket. She seemed to carry all manner of articles in there.

When he had all the implements he needed, Mr Hart retired to the desk in the corner, and we waited for about fifteen minutes or so while he sketched his castle. In truth, I was not expecting much from this drawing, but the look of amazement on Elizabeth's face when he handed it to her caused me to reconsider.

'Why, Mr Hart, you are not only a poet but an excellent artist!' she declared. 'This drawing is something that I would not hesitate to frame and hang on a wall!'

'By all means, do so if you wish to,' he said with a little bow, and Elizabeth looked pleased as punch.

I sighed inwardly. Mr Hart had obviously added another feather to his cap by proving to be a competent sketcher. I still had not seen the drawing as I was on the opposite sofa, and Jane and Lucinda were now crowding around Elizabeth. But I was itching to look at it (without revealing to Mr Hart that I was interested, of course). He was standing behind the sofa and overseeing their reactions with a chuffed look on his face.

'Ooh, lovely,' said Lucinda, wide-eyed.

'Aah, wonderful,' murmured Jane, and I could almost see the cogs turning in her brain as she thought of how it could be used in her story.

Craning my neck to see was no longer working, and my impatience could not be contained. 'Can I see it too?' I asked when the oohing and aahing had died down.

'Of course, Flissy,' said Jane and handed it over.

My eyebrows raised slightly upon seeing the sketch, for it was very professional. The castle Mr Hart had drawn was quite large as castles go, with a round crenellated turret at one end and a collection of smaller turrets at the other. They were joined in the middle by another crenellated structure, like a manor house, which had a portico over the entranceway. His pencil strokes were light, but confident, and he'd even done some shading to bring the grey stone to life.

'What do you think, Mrs Fitzroy? Is it realistic enough?' enquired Mr Hart with a touch of irony to his tone. I lifted my gaze from the sketch to discover him watching me. As he was still standing behind the sofa, I was the only one who had his full view. My cheeks coloured as he arched an eyebrow, waiting for my verdict.

I could not find fault with his sketch, and knowing I would seem petty if I did so, I had to give credit where it was due. 'You are indeed an excellent artist as Elizabeth has said, Mr Hart. Your castle looks to be most striking.'

He nodded and said, 'Thank you, I am glad you think so.' But his attention lingered on me, as if he wished to further the conversation, but I most certainly did not.

I lowered my eyes and silently handed the drawing back

to Jane. She, after peering at it again, handed it carefully to her sister-in-law.

'I shall visit the picture framers tomorrow,' said Elizabeth, turning her head to smile up at Mr Hart. 'I know the perfect spot to hang it too—in our front parlour at home, by the window.'

Jane heaved a sigh. 'A sketch, albeit a good one, is all very well. But I do wish I could see it with my own eyes,' she muttered. 'Otherwise, how can one capture the *atmosphere* of the place?'

She was talking mostly to herself, but Mr Hart had ears like a bat. 'Well, that is easily fixed,' he said smoothly. 'I am due to visit my father in a few days. You are all most welcome to join me. I will be there for around a week.'

There was a stunned silence. Then Lucinda squealed with delight, and Jane's mouth dropped open.

Oh, no no no! I thought in alarm. *Lucinda and he under the same turrets? It cannot happen! Not after what Cecilia Spencer has told me! Any number of attempts could be made by this man to ruin Lucinda in a week!*

Mr Hart's invitation caused a flurry of excited chatter, and it was difficult for me to get a word in edgeways. Lucinda was determined to go, as was Jane, but Elizabeth said she could not because of Edward. I jumped on this, appealing to Jane.

'Elizabeth is right, Jane. We cannot up and leave Edward,' I said.

'But a week is not long,' she countered.

'And he is very welcome to come too,' cut in Mr Hart, but Elizabeth shook her head.

'My husband is on a strict treatment plan for his gout and must follow it faithfully. I'm afraid skipping a week will undo all his good work.'

'And there is much we need to do in Bath,' I added. 'We have not even been to the theatre yet …'

'Pooh, the theatre!' scoffed Jane. 'Who cares about the theatre when we've been invited to a *castle*? We can go to the theatre when we get back. There is nothing exciting on anyway, only *The Taming of the Shrew*, and I saw that the *last* time I was in Bath.'

I could see I was not going to get any help from Jane— she was hell-bent on seeing the dratted castle for her book. I tried another tactic.

'Lucinda, I don't think your mother would approve of—' I started, but Mr Hart cut in again.

'My father will be there, Mrs Fitzroy, and yourself and Miss Austen. *Three* chaperones is surely plenty for Miss Fitzroy!' He chuckled softly, but I was not amused.

Lucinda was practically bouncing up and down on the sofa, and I eyed her helplessly.

'Please please *please*, Aunty Fliss!'

Everyone was looking at me as I seemed to hold the deciding vote.

'All right, very well. If Mr Hart's father will be there.'

Lucinda squealed again and leapt up to hug me, crying, 'Oh, thank you! *Thank you!*'

I glowered at Mr Hart over her shoulder, and he gave me a cherubic smile.

'An excellent decision, Mrs Fitzroy. I am sure you will find Hartmoor to be a most interesting diversion.' He winked at me, and my heart sank. I should have tried harder to extricate my niece from his company, but now she was in even more danger because of this trip to his damned castle. I was the worst chaperone ever!

PART THREE

Playing With Fire

Chapter 11

There were two good things about the journey to the castle: First, it was only three hours away. Three hours was close enough to Bath that I could organise an escape at short notice if I needed to.

Second, Mr Hart did not travel in his carriage with us for propriety's sake but rode next to it on his horse. However, I soon discovered this was not an advantage. As the afternoon grew warm, he took off his riding coat, flinging it over the pommel. This meant his backside, clearly outlined in his fitted breeches, rose up and down on the saddle as he trotted along; and the sight was somewhat distracting. Lucinda also seemed rather interested in the scenery as she kept leaning over me to peer out until I pulled the curtain across smartly, blocking both our views, saying the sun was in my eyes.

'But what if Mr Hart wishes to say something to us?' she grumbled.

'I cannot imagine what he would have to say about the fields. I'm sure if he has some pressing insight about ploughing, it can wait until we reach the castle.'

Jane snickered, and it was only after I said it that I realised the double entendre. But it stiffened my resolve further to protect Lucinda from any *ploughing* Mr Hart might have in mind.

However, after what felt like many more hours of being jolted around inside the airless carriage than just three, I finally succumbed to my nausea and knocked on the roof. There was a 'Whoa, boy!' from outside, and the carriage came to a halt.

Yanking the curtain aside, I lowered the window and spoke directly to the gentleman, with Lucinda elbowing me aside to make room for her too. 'Forgive me for asking, Mr Hart, but how much longer is it?'

He drew his watch out of his waistcoat pocket and looked at it. 'Not too much further. How do you fare?' he enquired. 'There is a copse beside the road if you need another comfort stop.'

'No, I do not—'

'Well, *I* do,' said Lucinda, opening the door before I could stop her. She jumped down to greet Mr Hart, who was descending from his horse.

'Do you want to come with us?' I asked Jane, but she declined. By the time I had put on my bonnet and alighted from the carriage, Lucinda and Mr Hart had strolled off together down the road.

Of course, that would not do as Mr Hart could not accompany her to the trees!

'Lucinda! *Lucinda!*' I called out sharply. 'Wait for me, please!'

'I have changed my mind, Aunty Fliss. But you go ahead, and I will converse with Mr Hart while we wait for you.'

I opened my mouth and shut it again. *The sneaky little minx!*

When I returned from the trees, the pair of them were nowhere in sight. Panicking, I raced back to the carriage, calling out, 'Jane! Did you see where they went? I swear, this blasted trip will be the death … Oh.'

Lucinda and Mr Hart were now ensconced in the carriage with Jane, and they had all been discussing something in an animated fashion, which ceased when I appeared.

'Never mind,' I muttered and walked off a short way to compose myself.

I turned around to find that Mr Hart had stepped down from the carriage and followed me. 'Is everything all right, Mrs Fitzroy? You seem rather agitated,' he said mildly.

I saw he had removed not only his coat but also his cravat, and his shirt was unbuttoned at the neck. This ensemble, along with his wind-blown dark hair and the light sweat bathing his upper chest, gave him a look of roguish dishevelment, which suited him since I now knew he was one.

'No, I am perfectly well,' I said tightly, removing my gaze from his with an effort. 'Are you sure we are nearly there? What is the time exactly? We seem to have been travelling all afternoon.'

Mr Hart looked at the sky, which had drifting clouds interspersed with patches of blue. 'We will be there before sundown.'

'Sundown? But that's another two hours at least,' I said, frustrated at his vague timekeeping. 'Why did you say your castle was three hours away if it was five?'

He frowned at my tone. 'It is three hours or thereabouts. It depends on the roads, and we were slow leaving Bath. Plus we would get there sooner if you ladies did not keep wanting to stop.'

Admittedly, we had required a comfort stop twice before now. But what did he expect when we had been bored and had nothing to do but repack our luggage and drink tea because he was late showing up at the house with his carriage?

I took a deep breath, trying to control my temper. He must have sensed I was doing so because his countenance softened.

'Pray, is my carriage not comfortable?'

'It is, but I succumb easily to travel sickness,' I explained. 'And if we open the window, insects fly in, so there is a lack of fresh air.'

A mischievous grin crossed Mr Hart's lips. 'Well, if it is fresh air you require, you can always ride with me on my horse.'

I drew a breath—how impudent!

Declining to reply to that invitation, I stalked past him back to the carriage, locked the door, put up the window, and abruptly pulled the curtain. That gentleman was starting to walk a fine line between humour and inappropriateness, and if he tried anything with me, he was going to get a tongue-lashing!

As we rolled off down the road, Lucinda, knowing how long carriage rides did not agree with me, tucked her arm through mine and said gently, 'I am sorry you are not feeling well, Aunty Fliss.'

Jane too looked at me with concern. 'Yes, you do look a bit pale. Poor you. Luckily, I have the constitution of an ox and do not get sick, but Cassie suffers greatly.'

The carriage lurched, and I took a deep breath to try to ease my nausea and hoped I did not vomit out the window. That would give Mr Hart something to write a poem about.

'Is there anything we can do to help? Maybe Aunt Jane can read us some of her book to take your mind off it?'

'That is a good idea, Lucy,' said Jane with a smile and a nod.

Tears welled at my niece's kindness, and I reminded myself that she did have a sensible head on her shoulders. I needed to trust that Seraphina had brought her up to know right from wrong (since Mr Hart was so very wrong!).

Jane turned to one of her marked pages and cleared her throat. 'Oh please, do not read from *The Monk*,' I said quickly, closing my eyes as the carriage lurched again. 'I don't think I can bear to hear any more of that. It will only make me feel sicker.'

'All right. I do have something else.' She opened her writing desk, which was sitting next to her on the seat and never allowed out of her sight. 'Shall I read a passage from one of my novels? It is a romance.'

'Ooh, yes please,' said Lucinda. 'I would love to hear it.'

Jane looked at me slyly. 'Do you mind?'

'Why would she mind?' asked Lucinda.

'Well ...'

The carriage swayed, and I swallowed, my mouth dry.

'It is fine. Just read it,' I said, feeling decidedly green. 'I need the distraction.'

Jane coughed delicately. 'So in this scene, our hero, Mr Darcy, proposes to our heroine, Lizzy. Keep in mind that she has taken a dislike to him because of his dour temperament and, up until this point, has had no reason to suspect his regard for her.'

Lucinda nodded enthusiastically, and I groaned inwardly. I nearly asked Jane to read a different scene but had not the strength of mind (nor stomach) to do so. And indeed, hearing Mr Darcy profess his ardent admiration for Lizzy would help to remind me of Max as it was described so well. When Jane reached Lizzy's fervent (and, some might say, rather punishing) rejection speech, I noticed with some amusement that Lucinda was captivated by the story. She was leaning forward and hanging on to every word.

From the very beginning—from the first moment, I may almost say—of my acquaintance with you, your manners, impressing me with the fullest belief of your arrogance, your conceit, and your selfish disdain of the feelings of others, were such as to form the groundwork of disapprobation on which succeeding events have built so immovable a dislike; and I had not known you a month before I felt that you were the last man in the world whom I could ever be prevailed on to marry.

Lucinda let out a whoop. 'Oh, she is so forthright in her derision! I imagine Mr Darcy does not take kindly to Lizzy saying that!'

'Indeed he does not,' said Jane with a wry smile. 'He thanks her for her time and gives her his best wishes for her health and happiness, then hastily leaves the house with his tail between his legs.'

Lucinda laughed out loud, and I could not help but smile too.

'I am glad it is only a story!' she exclaimed. 'I am sure I would not like to meet a man like Mr Darcy in the flesh. He seems so brusque and scary!'

Jane looked at me enquiringly, and I shrugged. She may as well know since she was his niece.

'You have met him, dear,' said Jane. 'He is your uncle.'

Lucinda's mouth hung open. 'What? Mr Darcy is Uncle Max? But that means ...' She turned to look at me in wonderment. 'Are you ...?'

I nodded solemnly. 'Yes, Aunt Jane has cleverly invented a story involving your uncle and me. Of course, she has taken many liberties.' I narrowed my eyes at Jane, and she laughed. 'And she has not written about the more private aspects of our story.' Aspects involving red wine that would forever remain a secret between Max and me.

As Lucinda and Jane fell into a discussion about the plot and how she had contrived to make Mr Darcy more insufferable than his counterpart, I had a strong image of Max riding his horse alone with a glum look on his face.

Suddenly, I felt a terrible longing to be with him—to leap from this wretched carriage and jump on the nearest stagecoach back to Derbyshire. Thankfully, at least he knew where to write to me, and we could still correspond. I had managed to add a postscript to my letter before Mrs Bromley took it to the post office the next morning.

> *PS: Dearest, our circumstances have changed somewhat since I wrote the above, and we are now to take a short trip to visit Mr Hart's castle. I do not particularly wish to go. But Lucinda and Jane are most excited about it, and I did not want to spoil their fun. Mr Hart's father will be in attendance, as well as Jane and I, so Lucy will have chaperones in abundance! Still, it might be best not to mention the excursion to Seraphina. I will write to you from Hartmoor Castle, Love your Fliss x*

* * *

Despite Mr Hart's assurance that we would arrive at the castle before sundown, we did not. We rolled along in pitch darkness for quite some time before the carriage finally ground to a halt. A feeling of overwhelming relief rushed through me as it felt like I had been grappling with a gloopy stomach for hours.

'At last,' I said, throwing open the carriage door. Eager to alight and breathe the air, I descended and stepped directly into a pile of fresh horse droppings.

'If only you had waited for me to assist, Mrs Fitzroy, you could have avoided that,' Mr Hart's amused voice drawled from behind me as I wiped my soiled boot on a clump of grass on the roadside.

'If only we had arrived *before* sundown, then I could have *seen* where I was stepping, Mr Hart,' I replied dryly.

He warned the others about my misfortune as he assisted them from the carriage. Lucinda emerged tired, pale-faced, and rumpled, followed by Jane, who seemed in much better spirits.

'I am so excited to see your castle, Mr Hart,' she said, peering into the darkness and pulling her shawl around her for warmth as there was a nippy chill in the air. 'But pray, where is it?'

'Just a short walk through those trees,' he said, gesturing vaguely off to the side. 'We will be using the back entrance.' He collected a lantern from his driver, who was giving the horses some oats and who, I assumed, would then be delivering our luggage. But I was quickly learning it was not wise to assume anything when it came to Mr Hart.

'Why can we not use the front entrance?' I asked warily.

'The door is locked from sundown to sunrise as my father does not like to receive visitors during that time. But Maurice knows we are coming and will have the fire lit in the parlour and a hot supper ready for us. This way, if you please, ladies.'

He held the lantern high and strode off down a narrow path into the trees, and we had no choice but to trail after him like lambs following their shepherd.

Indeed, the thought of a warm firelit parlour and hot supper did motivate me to start walking, so he had said the right thing.

'Who is Maurice?' I questioned, attempting to scrape the remnants of horse dung off the side of my boot as we went along.

'Our butler' was the reply. I had further questions, but his curt tone stopped me from asking them. Besides, I needed to comfort Lucinda, who was gasping every time she brushed by a twig. An owl hooted above us in the trees, and she almost jumped out of her skin.

'I'm scared, Aunty Fliss,' she whimpered, and I took her trembling hand in mine and held it tightly.

'It is not much farther, dear,' I said through gritted teeth, silently cursing Mr Hart, who strode on relentlessly in front of us through the thicket. We had to keep pace with him or else be left floundering in the darkness. I myself was not afraid of the trees or the darkness or the scurrying noises of small animals in the undergrowth, having grown up in the country. But I was becoming uneasy as to where he was leading us.

The 'short walk' he had described was turning into a veritable hike, and I bit my tongue in an effort to keep my complaints to myself for the sake of Lucinda and Jane. The forest was, I suspected, an ancient defence system planted around the perimeter of the castle designed to deter intruders. But Mr Hart was not an intruder nor a visitor—his family owned the castle. So it was strange that his father would not permit the opening of the front door for his own son and instead force him to use the back entrance like a servant.

We emerged from the trees a while after, and in the limited light of the lamp, I saw that I had been correct. The forest stretched away from us on either side and formed a protective barrier around the monstrosity of stone that loomed before us.

'Ladies, I give you Hartmoor Castle,' said Mr Hart theatrically. 'But you will be able to see it better without the light.' There was a 'poof' noise as he extinguished the gas lantern, which resulted in a collective gasp as darkness enveloped us. He chuckled softly to himself, and I got the impression he was enjoying our fear and uncertainty.

Lucinda and Jane huddled close to me, and I took a deep breath to steady my pounding heart. However, he was right. A gibbous moon hung in the sky directly overhead, and as my eyes adjusted, I saw the castle more clearly. It was indeed the one in his sketch. The turrets were there as depicted, but the moonlight also revealed stonework that was badly in need of repair. There were black gaps like missing teeth all over it. To my mind, it was more of a dilapidated ruin barely held together with mortar than what Mr Hart had drawn. His version was more like Hartmoor Castle in its heyday.

Jane, who had been clamouring to visit his castle, was not saying anything. As Mr Hart walked off towards the creepy-looking fortification, not waiting for our opinions or comments, I nudged her. 'A bit different to his sketch, don't you think?'

But she declined to answer, possibly grappling between the truth and politeness.

It made me think that perhaps I was being too hard on him. If this was the back entrance, perhaps the front of the castle was in a better state?

Chapter 12

We stumbled along a narrow rutted path after Mr Hart, who was making his way towards a studded wooden door. As we approached, I happened to look up and, to my consternation, spied a large stone gargoyle crouched on a ledge—its mouth stretched wide in a gaping grin. I decided not to point it out to Lucinda, who, by this stage, was scared stiff, if her fingers digging painfully into my forearm were anything to go by.

Mr Hart knocked on the massive door thrice, with the aid of a heavy door knocker bearing the head of a lion. The booming noise it made echoed through to whatever lay beyond, which, by this point in time, was anyone's guess.

In spite of my trembling knees, I was still impressed that Mr Hart's family owned a place like this. It was difficult not to be. But it did not override my annoyance that he had misled us. For if he had drawn the dilapidated castle as it truly was, I doubt Elizabeth would have wanted the sketch framed and hung in her front parlour or indeed been so encouraging of us visiting it!

The door began to creak slowly inwards, emitting a shaft

of yellow light, which illuminated our waiting party. A silhouetted figure appeared in the doorway and shuffled towards us, moving in an odd lopsided manner. It was only when it came closer did I see it was a man and that he had a hunchback. He raised a hand in what seemed a menacing fashion, causing Lucinda to hide behind me with a stifled scream.

But he was only beckoning us inside.

'Thank you, Maurice, my good fellow,' said Mr Hart blithely as we filed past the man and into a stone entranceway with a curved ceiling.

'I was expecting you hours ago, Master Dorian,' said Maurice, pushing the door shut after us and locking it with a giant iron key. He held up his lantern and perused us ladies, beady brown eyes peering out from underneath a straight fringe. I was surprised to see that he was only middle-aged and not as ancient as I had thought. He had a pleasant face, although it was rather serious.

'Yes. Well, we had a few more stops than were necessary,' said Mr Hart, looking pointedly at me.

Remembering my manners, I said, 'How do you do? I'm Mrs Felicity Fitzroy. This is my friend Miss Jane Austen and my niece. Miss Lucinda Fitzroy.' I gestured to each in turn. Jane said 'Hello' and Lucinda bobbed from behind my shoulder.

Maurice inclined his head at us.

'Welcome. Let us go through to the kitchen, where it's warm.' He shuffled off down a narrow stone hallway, and we trailed behind him, albeit slowly as he did not walk fast. There were candle sconces that had been lit on the wall, but they only served to throw out spooky shadows. It seemed a dark, cold, and gloomy old place.

But I endeavoured to keep my spirits up—in this case, by looking forward to a change of clothes and a wash. I turned my head and enquired brightly of Mr Hart, who was bringing up the rear, 'Will our luggage be delivered soon? I'd like to freshen up before dinner.'

'I'm afraid you will have to make do this evening, Mrs Fitzroy,' he said. 'My driver has retired to a nearby inn for the night. But he will bring your luggage first thing tomorrow.'

I could not believe my ears.

'That is most inconvenient,' I said tightly.

'There will be warm water and soap provided if you want to wash, and what you have on is fine for supper. As for afterwards, you sleep in your chemise, do you not? Or perhaps you don't?' he added in a lower tone.

I whipped my head to the front again, pretending not to have heard his insolence. But from the soft laughter behind my right ear, he knew I had.

'Either way', he continued when I declined to give him an answer about what I wore to bed (which was frankly none of his business), 'you will have no need of anything in your luggage until the morning.'

Jane will be so angry about this, I thought with glee. *It will put him in her bad graces, and he'll have a hard time wriggling out of them.* For she'd left her writing desk in the carriage on the assumption that it would be delivered forthwith.

When we reached the kitchen, it was much more cheerful, thanks to the numerous lanterns set around. Warmth flowed from a huge black leaded stove, which had a cast-iron pot steaming upon it. Unable to help myself, I murmured to Jane, 'We are not getting our luggage tonight. He says tomorrow morning.' I gestured to Mr Hart with my chin.

Jane's eyes darkened, and her lips pressed into a straight firm line. I chuckled to myself, looking forward to the showdown. The manuscripts she kept in her writing desk were her darling children. Woe betide him if something should happen to them. His head would be on the chopping block.

'Mr Hart!' she said sharply.

'Yes, Miss Austen? How can I be of service?' he said cheerfully, coming over to us.

'I understand our luggage is not to be delivered until tomorrow?' she said icily.

'That is correct,' he said. 'But do not fret. I took the liberty of ensuring your writing desk is held under lock and key with the innkeeper. And he has been given strict instructions to shoot anyone who tries to make off with it.'

Jane's eyebrows shot up into her curls. 'Goodness,' she said, sounding impressed. 'Thank you, Mr Hart.'

He bowed low. 'My pleasure, Miss Austen. Consider it a favour from one writer to another. Meanwhile, if you should wish to jot anything down, I have an ample supply of quills and paper to satisfy any creative urges.' Mr Hart winked at her, and she giggled. I rolled my eyes in disbelief that he had escaped reprimand once again. He seemed to have an answer for everything.

Maurice said supper was to be served in half an hour in the parlour, and we could freshen up in our rooms meanwhile. He handed each of us a new candle in a holder, and we left him in the kitchen to attend to whatever was in the pot on the stove.

Mr Hart had lit his own candle with a taper and now led us through another stone hallway to the main foyer of the castle. This was bone-chillingly cold, but very grand and hung with tapestries—it showed no signs of the disrepair of the exterior. Above us was a wooden ceiling inset with panels, and there were a multitude of candle sconces, which highlighted a wide flight of ornately carved wooden stairs. These led up to a dark landing.

'Your rooms are on the first floor. Just choose any one you like,' Mr Hart said, his voice echoing slightly in the cavernous space. 'They are all much of a muchness. But I thought you might like the pink one, Miss Fitzroy, as it matches your pretty colouring.'

Of course, Lucinda simpered at the compliment, and I fought the urge to roll my eyes again.

'Oh, will you not show us the way, Mr Hart? It looks so dark up there,' pleaded Lucinda.

'I would like to, but sadly, I cannot,' said Mr Hart, shaking his head. 'It would not be proper, and I fear your chaperone would scold me if I escorted you to your bedroom.' He shot me an amused glance, and I stared stonily back. 'But you will be quite safe. There is nothing up there more alarming than a few cobwebs.'

Gazing around at us, he said in a stately voice, 'I will see you all presently in the parlour. It is the room there to the left of the stairs. We can have a bite to eat, a glass of wine and relax after our long journey.'

Jane breathed a sigh of relief at his words. 'That sounds wonderful,' she said, peering at the woodland scenes on the tapestries and obviously thrilled at the prospect of sleeping in a real-life castle.

Lucinda was still reluctant to leave Mr Hart's side, but he smiled kindly when lighting her candle and murmured further words of encouragement to put her at ease. He did have a knack for saying the right thing, I had to admit, and was playing the role of host perfectly.

After he'd lit Jane's candle, she took Lucinda's arm, and they started up the stairs. Mr Hart came over to me, and I held up my candle to be lit from his, but my hand was shaking a little—whether from nerves, the cold, or being so near to him, I could not say. He didn't pass comment but covered my hand with his own to hold the candle steady while he lit it. His fingers were warm, and his touch made my stomach dance along with the guttering flame that appeared between us.

'Everything to your liking, Mrs Fitzroy?' he asked, his dark eyes boring into mine, soft candlelight flickering over the planes of his handsome face. I nodded, not knowing what to say, and I gently extricated my hand from his. It felt very much like Mr Hart was asking if *he* was to my liking.

However much I mistrusted him and even though I was happily married, I could not deny his presence affected me. And the castle seemed to magnify it even more. The sooner this visit was over and we were back in Bath, the better!

As Lucinda and Jane had gone up the stairs before me, they had first pick of the rooms. Lucinda chose the one farthest away from mine with rose damask curtains and a four-poster bed. As Mr Hart had intimated, it did suit her colouring, being all pink and cream decor.

Jane had chosen the one next door to me, which had light-blue-painted walls and white furniture. That left me with a comfortable, but sombre room with dark-green velvet curtains, a heavy oak bedstead, and several disconcerting portraits. Were the unsmiling figures in the paintings of Hart lineage? I did not know, but one young gentleman posing with a sword and a hound looked a lot like Mr Hart. In fact, the resemblance was quite striking. He had the same dark-brown eyes, aristocratic cheekbones, and sensual lips. But if he had dark hair, I could not tell as it was hidden under a white powdered wig.

The painting was hung in the middle of the room, the effect being that wherever I stood, that gentleman's eyes landed upon my person. I had resolved to have a short nap before dinner but could not close my eyes under his arrogant stare. Perhaps Jane would swap rooms? The only painting she had in hers was a poodle with a blue ribbon tied around its neck. But as blue was her favourite colour, I did not like my chances.

A jug of lukewarm water, plus a bar of oatmeal soap and

flannel, had been placed in a bowl on top of a dresser and were rudimentary toiletries indeed, but better than nothing. Indeed, after a cursory wash and repinning my hair, I felt somewhat restored. The last thing I wanted to do was go back downstairs and make polite conversation with Mr Hart, but my stomach was rumbling. So back down the stairwell I went, gripping the stair banister tightly.

Pushing open a similar studded door to the one we had entered the castle, I stepped into a cosy, well-furnished parlour to find a party of four in residence. An unfamiliar sandy-haired gentleman with whiskers was standing by the crackling fire speaking with Jane while Mr Hart and Lucinda were seated on a leather sofa conversing.

For a moment, I stood in the doorway, too surprised to say anything. Then Jane beckoned me over. 'Flissy, come and meet Mr Smith-Withers. He's Mr Hart's good friend from Eton and the family's lawyer.'

Mr Smith-Withers! I knew he was Mr Hart's friend, but I had never met him as I had not been invited to 'bun day', and he had never accompanied us on any other outing. Now here he was—and without a mention by our dear Mr Hart, who had had ample opportunity to do so throughout the course of the day!

But I held my suspicions in check, pasted on a pleasant smile, and went to greet him.

'Mr Smith-Withers, this is my dear friend Felicity Fitzroy, who I told you was staying with us in Bath.'

'Mrs Fitzroy, we meet at last,' said Mr Smith-Withers, bowing. 'I was sorry not to make your acquaintance at Sally Lunn's.'

'And I yours,' I said smoothly. I was not sorry in the slightest, but it was the polite thing to say.

He was perfectly cordial, and his plummy accent suggested education and good breeding. But for some reason, I did not take to him. It may have been his eyes. They were slightly bloodshot and set too close together. Along with his whiskers and thin lips, it gave him a weaselly appearance.

'Mr Hart did not say you would be joining us,' I said.

'Oh, it was a last-minute decision. Dory told me you were all taking a jaunt and invited me along, but I was unsure I could make it. But my plans fell through at the last minute, so here I am. I arrived this afternoon to surprise you all.' He gave a short bark of laughter.

'And his father doesn't mind so many of us being here?' Jane asked.

That gentleman we had yet to meet, and I was growing unsure that he even existed. By now, my mind was throwing up all sorts of scenarios. *Had they done away with him? Were they going to do away with us?*

Mr Smith-Withers looked over at Mr Hart and said in sotto voce, 'It is a large castle, and Dory and his father keep on opposite sides of it—a turret each if you will.'

'Oh,' said Jane, frowning. 'Of course, I see.'

No more was said on the matter, but from that, I assumed Mr Hart and his father did not have a good relationship. Mr Smith-Withers changed the subject to a book he was reading, and Jane was happy to comply as she had read it too.

I listened to them with half an ear until I saw Maurice enter the room through a servant's door at the back of the room. He was struggling to hold a soup tureen aloft. Alarmed that he would drop it, I excused myself from Jane and Mr Smith-Withers and went over to help him place it on the table.

'Thank you, Mrs Fitzroy. It was heavier than I expected.' He mopped his forehead with a handkerchief. 'I shall fetch the bread and cheese.'

'Please, let me assist you,' I said, feeling sorry for him.

He blinked at my request but did not stop me as I followed him out the servant's door.

'Do you not have a cook or a maid?' I asked conversationally as we made our way down the narrow passage to the kitchen, which, from its direction, seemed to go around the back of the staircase. He obviously used it frequently as there were half-burnt candles set in sconces and blobs of wax dripped down the wall. The pungent smell of tallow in the close space was overpowering, and the smoke made my eyes sting.

'No, Mrs Fitzroy. There is only me, though I did poach a maid from the inn to help me with the setting up of your rooms.'

Gracious, I thought. *Maurice is a one-man band. I suppose there is no point having a full retinue of servants with only Mr Hart's father to look after*. But still, it seemed like a lot of work for one person to run a castle all on their own, especially as he could not move around that easily. I felt a bit guilty that our party had turned up and created extra duties for him. It was another black mark against Mr Hart in my mind. Looking after our servants, namely making sure they were well provided for and not overworked, was important to Max and me.

When we returned to the parlour with a board of bread, cheese, and a few other condiments for the meal, I found everyone seated at the rectangular oak dining table. Jane was playing mother and ladling meat broth into bowls from the soup tureen.

The only spare seat on the bench was on the end next to Mr Hart, so I reluctantly took it. He did not move over for me as an agreeable gentleman would have but stayed put. I had to squeeze in beside him, which meant our bodies were touching from the shoulders all the way down to the knees. It was most improper!

Being forced to sit this close to him, I could clearly feel his hard thigh muscle and smell the spicy cologne he had applied while freshening up. It was distracting enough that I had difficulty concentrating on spooning broth into my mouth. And by the way that uncivil man kept flexing his leg against mine under the table, I could tell he was rejoicing in causing me to squirm. I elbowed him sharply in the ribs to make him stop, and he let out a huff of quiet laughter.

As I was engaged in a private battle with Mr Hart under the table, I was not taking much notice of the polite supper conversation, and it was only after a comment from Mr Smith-Withers that it came to my attention that I had been blatantly ignoring Lucinda.

'Mrs Fitzroy, your niece has been attempting to speak to you for the last five minutes, and you have been in a world of your own,' he said, giving me a stern look, as if I were a naughty child.

I collected my senses immediately and nodded to him.

'Thank you, Mr Smith-Withers. I must be more tired than I realised. My apologies, Lucy. What were you saying?'

'I was only curious to know where you went, Aunty Fliss. I saw you disappearing with the butler.'

By this time, Maurice had retreated to the kitchen, so he was not privy to our conversation. So I did not mind replying to her.

'Yes, I thought he might need some help since he is the only servant here,' I said, directing my remark somewhat pointedly to Mr Hart to make him feel bad about it.

'That is a lot of work for one person indeed,' said Lucinda. 'Mr Hart, we must rally round and lighten his load. I was a little frightened of him at first, but he seems like a kind soul. I would hate to think he is tired out because of us.'

Good for you, Lucy, I thought, pleased with her.

'Well, Miss Fitzroy', said Mr Hart in a mock peeved tone, 'if you wish to don an apron and spend your time with Maurice in the kitchen rather than with me, then you must do so.'

'Oh, I did not mean ...' began Lucinda, her face falling.

'It is all right. I am just teasing you. I know our butler has a certain je ne sais quoi.' Mr Hart dipped a piece of bread in his soup. 'It is his deformity. All the ladies want to mollycoddle him, but in truth, he is perfectly capable.'

During this discourse, I was wholly aware that Mr Hart's other hand had strayed beneath the table and now rested lightly on his thigh. I willed him to keep it to himself, but his fingers moved to pat my leg every now and again while he was talking. But was he doing it idly? Or deliberately? Whichever it was, it was causing a strange sensation in my spine. Drawing in a breath, I attempted to shift away from him, but there was nowhere to go but the floor.

'All the ladies?' I queried, determined to make him do some squirming himself. 'Pray, exactly how many ladies has Maurice had the pleasure of meeting?'

Mr Smith-Withers sniggered, and the patting fingers beneath the table stilled, then withdrew. Mr Hart seemed disinclined to answer my question—making a big show of asking if anyone wanted more broth, ladling two spoonfuls into his own bowl, and cutting further slices of cheese that were not really needed.

'Ah. Well, I can always ask Maurice, I suppose. He seems like a conversant-enough fellow,' I threatened softly but loud enough for Mr Hart to hear.

A moment later, his thigh began juddering against mine under the table, as if he were mightily disturbed by my comment; and I smothered the urge to laugh.

Yes, I thought, *you dastardly rake. Indeed, you should be worried!*

Chapter 13

The supper had been light, but nutritious, and I silently commended Maurice on his cooking. But thanks to exhaustion and the warmth of the room, Jane and Lucinda were on the verge of nodding off into the dregs of their soup.

'I believe it might be time to retire,' I said, rising abruptly before I myself fell asleep on Mr Hart's shoulder. I began to stack the bowls, but he placed a hand on my arm.

'Leave them for now, Felicity. Maurice will clear them,' he said. Before I could protest (at the dishes being left, him touching me, and him using my first name without permission), he added, 'By the way, you are right to point out my shortcomings as an employer. Maurice does need more help while we are here. I will hire a cook and a maid from the village to assist him.'

I nodded, too tired to scold him further. 'Good. I am glad to hear it.'

'We used to have more staff,' Mr Hart continued as we all left the parlour, the gentlemen escorting us ladies to the foot of the stairs. 'But Father has seen fit to let them go.

Maurice is the only one he trusts completely.'

'Where exactly is your father? When will we meet him?' I asked. Now that Mr Smith-Withers was here, there were an equal number of unmarried men to women, so it would be more appropriate to have another chaperone. I could not be expected to be everywhere at once. But would Mr Hart's father even be a suitable chaperone if he was responsible for bestowing his son with such a loose nature?

'So many questions, Felicity,' Mr Hart said playfully, and I bristled at him being overly familiar again. But I could not request that he call me Mrs Fitzroy now as I had not corrected him previously. 'All in good time. You will meet him tomorrow. He gets tired easily and takes supper in his room. And with that, I bid you good night.'

He bowed, cutting off our conversation, and took his leave to say good night to Lucinda and Jane. It was then that I realised that the shroud of mystery he was creating around his father wasn't for dramatic effect. There was something he wished to keep hidden. But what? A wave of weariness rolled over me, and I decided not to try to unpick the knot that was Mr Hart this late at night—I was only going to give myself a bad headache.

Mr Hart had given us a stub of one of the foyer candles by which to see, but it was still darker than sin, so Lucinda wished us to accompany her to her room. With both of them huddled on either side of me, I held the candle aloft, and we set off down the hallway. A faint creaking noise sounded overhead like someone was walking around.

'What's that?' hissed Jane, and we all stopped to listen, but it did not come again. Lucinda made a whimpering sound in my ear.

'It is nothing but the wind,' I told her firmly. 'There is no such thing as ghosts.'

'Ghosts!' she moaned. 'I had not been thinking of them until now ...'

To get her mind off apparitions, I spoke cheerily of what we might do after breakfast the next day if the weather was fine. 'We could explore the grounds, see what the castle looks like from the *front*, and it might have a library.'

'Oh yes, it does have one,' said Lucinda, loosening her grip on my arm so the blood could flow freely again. 'Mr Hart said it contains quite an extensive collection of books. He told me he spent practically every waking moment of his teenage years in there when he was not at Eton.'

'Ah! Well, then you will sleep like the dead having that to look forward to.'

Lucinda's grip tightened on my arm again, and I sighed.

I really had to watch what I said around her.

In my room, I had another cursory wash (as I felt sullied

after Mr Hart's proximity under the table), removed my dress, and slipped between the cool sheets wearing my chemise. But that man's sly words, wondering if I wore a chemise to bed or not, kept mocking me. And I fancied I could still feel the warm touch of his leg against mine. Oh, he was insidious! And his counterpart on the wall was not much better. His eyes seemed to search for me even in the darkness. It was a state of affairs not conducive to sleep even though I was dog-tired.

Frustrated, I threw back the covers, grabbed my shawl, and went next door to Jane's. I knocked softly and poked my head around the door. She was in her nightdress and shawl hunched over a piece of paper on the nightstand. The candle had burnt low, so her proximity to what she was writing was such that she was nearly singeing her plait, and there were a fair few ink splotches on the page.

Jane lowered her quill and glanced round at me. 'Can't you sleep?' she whispered.

I shook my head.

She sighed. 'Neither can I. There are a thousand words in my brain clamouring for escape. I cannot wait to have my desk back tomorrow. This set-up is throwing me off my plot.'

I came in and sat on the edge of her bed, curling my feet under me for warmth.

'Do you not think it strange that Mr Hart's father has the door locked so promptly at night? Our luggage could surely have been delivered.'

Jane shrugged. 'Perhaps. But it is a bit of a strange household altogether.'

Thank goodness I was not the only one who thought so!

Encouraged by this admission, I said, 'Which part of the castle do you think Mr Hart is staying in? He did not mention it.'

'Perhaps in one of the turrets ... Does it matter where he stays?'

For some reason, it did. I felt the need to know that gentleman's whereabouts so I could keep tabs on him. But I did not want *him* to know that I was asking where his room was.

'As Lucy's chaperone, it is only proper that I make sure that he is well away from her room.'

Jane frowned and lowered her quill. 'But he would not even accompany her upstairs. He is more decorous than you give him credit for.'

'Hmm.'

'Do you not trust him at all?'

This was the moment when I should share what I knew about Mr Hart's relationship with Cecilia, but Jane was likely to say we should leave immediately, and I quailed at the thought of having to tell Lucinda the reason why. Then there were the transport arrangements that would have to be made by Mr Hart, and he would want to know why we were leaving when we had only just arrived. And the thought of that confrontation made me quail even more, not to mention having to bring up the sordid details of the affair with Mr Smith-Withers in attendance. The two of them were likely to deny the whole thing, and I would look like a fool.

No, it was easier to cling to the hope that Mr Hart had changed his ways and was courting Lucinda with the intention to marry. Of course, to believe the fable I was telling myself, I had to ignore his flirtatious behaviour towards me, which I was sure I was not imagining. It was all quite confusing.

'I trust him to some extent,' I said slowly. 'And I suppose everything is above board. But I worry he is overly vivacious.'

Jane giggled. 'Overly vivacious? Surely, vivacity of any kind is welcome in a young man. Would you have Lucy marry a boring toad like Mr Humbleton?'

I wrinkled my nose. 'Definitely not.'

'Well then, you should let nature take its course, and it will work out fine. Yes, the castle is a bit more "crumbly" than we expected, but that is actually perfect as it adds to the atmosphere I want to depict in my novel. A pristine castle would not do at all.'

Jane placed the page upon which she had been writing on top of the stack of blank paper Mr Hart had given her, and I realised he had won her over because he had proven he was a 'writer' and an 'artist'. She had claimed him as a kindred spirit because of those professions. It would be hard work to convince her he was not a worthy gentleman unless I had solid proof of his duplicity. I needed more evidence than the testimony of a young girl whom he had supposedly corrupted.

I pulled my shawl tighter around my shoulders. 'I am getting cold. I should let you get some sleep.'

'All right, Flissy. Good night. I'll see you at breakfast.'

She waited until I had reached the door and blew out her candle and then dived under the bedcovers.

Feeling conflicted, I tiptoed down the dark hallway back to my room. But when I got there, the painting was still disturbing me—so much so that, in desperation, I threw my shawl over it. Covering up that charismatic gentleman was the only way I would get any sleep!

***

Breakfast was served in the dining hall, situated at the rear of the castle at the end of another dark passageway. In any other house, it would have been a relatively cosy affair, like our dinner the night before in the parlour. But the castle's dining hall was the size of a small church with a wooden vaulted ceiling and a table that could seat at least thirty running down the middle.

'This room is absurdly large,' whispered Jane.

'I know!' I whispered back.

Wide-eyed, we helped ourselves from the numerous silver serving dishes on the long sideboard that contained bacon, eggs, tomatoes, and mushrooms. There were also several racks of toast. *Maurice must have been up since dawn frying all this*, I thought. *Unless the assistant cook has already arrived.*

Mr Hart was seated opposite me, next to Lucinda, and the two of them were chattering away much too brightly for so early in the morning. Mr Smith-Withers was also interjecting with pithy observations and comments, making Jane giggle. I myself was still half-asleep after my restless night and concentrated solely on eating my breakfast despite Mr Hart attempting to draw me into their conversation. I felt it best to stare at my bacon and eggs rather than his jaw, which was glowing pink from being freshly shaved, or his eyes, which, when directed my way, caused a sensation of discomfort rather like the gentleman in the painting.

But after I had eaten my fill and drank a cup of strong tea, I felt rather more perky and in control of myself. Maurice came in near the end of the meal to tell us that our luggage (along with Jane's writing desk) had been delivered, which was pleasing news.

'Thank goodness for that,' whispered Jane in my ear, and I felt glad for her. Now she could really get stuck into her story.

Maurice paused by my seat.

'A letter for you, Mrs Fitzroy. My apologies. It arrived yesterday, but I forgot about it until this morning.'

He placed it next to my plate, and when I saw Max's handwriting, I felt my spirits lift even further. This was turning out to be a most excellent day.

'Receiving mail already!' remarked Mr Hart, buttering his umpteenth piece of toast. 'And who might be writing to you?'

'It is from my husband, Mr Hart.'

'Ah, he must be an astute man to discover your whereabouts so quickly.'

'He is astute, but I wrote to him before we left telling him we had been invited to visit Hartmoor Castle. So it is not as much of a surprise to me as it may be to you.'

I did not speak with the intent to wound, but maybe he felt slighted as Mr Hart inclined his head without comment.

Then after a brief pause, he changed the subject entirely. 'Miss Fitzroy has requested a tour of the castle and the grounds this morning. How does that suit everyone?'

The rest of us murmured our assent.

'Will the tour include the library too?' Lucinda asked anxiously.

'Yes, of course. The library is on the list of highlights, along with the dungeon ...'

'Dungeon!' said Jane, sounding awestruck. 'How thrilling!'

I left them to it, saying I would ready myself for the tour now that my luggage was here. But really, I wanted to read Max's letter privately in my room.

Dearest Fliss,

Forgive me for writing before you have sent your promised letter, but I wanted to send a note forthwith. In truth, I am surprised and a tad worried to hear of your castle excursion because it involves this Hart fellow again. It seems odd that he was initially described as a 'scoundrel', but an invite to visit his residence suggests he has lately risen in everyone's esteem. Has Lucinda rejected her other suitors and now singularly focused upon him?

I know I may be worrying out of turn, and I do not mean to suggest that you do not have good insight into men's characters—only that if you have any concerns about this gentleman yourself and need advice on how to proceed, please let me know, and I will do my best to help from here. And if you require it, I will come down in the carriage and defend Lucinda's honour (I am quite serious). Besides, Tobias left yesterday, so I now find myself at a loose end without his company.

Write soonest,
Love your Max xx

PS: George wants to know when you are coming home as he misses you terribly. He has quite gone off his oats.

I took a deep breath to stem my tears. As much as I wanted to see my dear Max, him travelling hundreds of miles to defend his niece's honour was a bit ludicrous. For really, there was nothing to report when it came to Lucinda. The actual issue was Mr Hart being overly attentive and possibly showing a lack of propriety when it came to me! But how could I ask Max for advice about that? He would lose his mind, leap into his carriage, and come storming into the castle with a face like thunder, demanding a duel. I could imagine the amused look on Mr Hart's face if he did that!

I ran to Jane's room, swiped a piece of her paper and a quill, and hurriedly penned a reply.

Dear Max,

It was lovely to receive your letter at breakfast this morning. I have come upstairs immediately to write back! Darling, I appreciate your concern, but I hope I can set your mind at ease by saying you need not worry about anything. We arrived last night, and Mr Hart is being the most cordial and respectful host. In fact, he is going to give us a tour of the castle and grounds this morning. Apparently there is a library so Lucy is most eager to see that, as you can imagine.

I need to get ready for the tour now, but I will write more soon once I have something remotely interesting to share. Are you interested in medieval architecture at all, or does it bore you to tears?

Love your Fliss xx

PS: I miss George terribly too and hope he recovers his appetite soon—perhaps you could give him a few carrots now that you are so good at peeling them?

***

The first stop on the Hartmoor tour was the dungeon, accessed by a narrow flight of stone stairs from the kitchen. It was a small stale-smelling dark room strewn with straw.

'We use it as a storage cellar now,' said Mr Hart.

Indeed, when he held his candle up to show us the space, there were several sacks of potatoes piled up in one corner and a wooden rack of dusty wine in another. But he also pointed out some iron rings set into the far wall and said that was where the prisoners had been tied up.

'How awful!' said Lucinda. 'Imagine being a prisoner trapped down here in the dark for weeks or maybe months.'

'Oh, I don't know,' said Mr Hart airily, leading the way back up the stairs. 'I'm sure they made friends with one another. And it is dry at least and near the kitchen, so they were probably well fed. The cook could stand at the top and toss them down some bread and meat.'

He stood on the top step and mimed bowling a cricket

ball. It was designed to amuse, but no one laughed. He pouted when we were back in the kitchen, saying we were 'a difficult audience'.

'If we do not respond to your liking, Mr Hart, it is because you joke about men's suffering. And it is in rather poor taste to do so,' I said primly.

'My apologies, Mrs Fitzroy. I did not mean to offend any delicate sensibilities. But the prisoners *have* been dead for hundreds of years ...'

'Still,' I said, determined to press home my point, 'it would be decent of you to show the dead some respect, even if on behalf of your forebears.'

He bowed politely and with an uppish smile said that he was glad that I had pointed out his error and that he would be far more considerate when showing guests the dungeon in future. I felt like rebuking him some more for mocking me but feared it would only encourage him, so I bit my tongue and let the others go on ahead.

Drawing my letter to Max out of my pocket (carefully folded, addressed, and sealed with one of the wafers I'd brought with me), I approached Maurice, who was cleaning some mud-caked potatoes in the sink.

'Maurice, would it be possible to have my letter sent as soon as possible please? It is a reply to the one you brought me during breakfast.'

The man smiled at me, and his brown eyes twinkled, which quite transformed his face. I thought my offer to help him last night had gone some way to softening his reserve and also trusting me as he seemed a lot friendlier.

'Of course, Mrs Fitzroy,' he said, wiping his dirty hands on his apron and taking the letter from me. 'A mail coach passes by in the morning and afternoon on the way to the inn, and the driver always stops to collect any letters—not that we usually have any, so it will be a nice change to actually give him one.'

'Excellent, thank you,' I said, feeling glad that Max would soon have my comforting reply and be at ease. I looked at the mound of potatoes before him. 'Did Mr Hart mention that he would hire a cook to help you with meals for the duration of our stay?'

'Yes, he told me he had done so this morning.'

'When will they be arriving?'

'Tomorrow, I believe.'

'All right. Until then, I hope you do not mind if I offer to assist you as I often do so in my own household when we have guests,' I said, taking a leaf out of Max's book. If he could peel vegetables, so could I!

'Thank you, madam. I appreciate the offer,' he said.

Feeling quite pleased with my cleverness, I walked away to follow behind the others, who had headed down the stone hallway to access the grounds. My plan was not only to help Maurice, but to find out more about our mysterious host and his reclusive father—but in a subtle way so as not to be detected.

Chapter 14

The tour continued outside as we followed an overgrown path around to the front of the castle. Broken branches blocked our way at points, so we had to keep stopping for the gentlemen to clear them. The sky was a dull grey, and with the jackdaws circling and squawking at us from their roosts above, it did not make for a very pleasant walk.

Worst of all, as I was walking behind the pair, I noticed that Mr Hart was taking the opportunity to be intimate with Lucinda. Of course, he would now prove me wrong and not act the respectful host just when I had written to Max saying he was!

He would point out something trifling to distract me, and when he thought I was not looking, he would hold her hand in his! However, I cottoned on soon enough and cleared my throat loudly to indicate I had seen through his ruse, and he quickly stopped that nonsense. Lucinda did not seem to mind his impropriety and looked over her shoulder at me and shrugged slightly (and almost resentfully, I thought), as if to say, 'Does it matter? He likes me.'

Aunt had been right when she had warned me in

Steventon to stay vigilant. I was going to need eyes in the back of my head where Mr Hart was concerned.

I had been giving him the benefit of the doubt about the exterior of the castle and hoping that the front was in a better state of repair. But when we came to stand upon an unraked gravel drive with weeds poking through, I was dismayed to see the front had as much crumbling and gaping stonework as round the back. Jane and Mr Smith-Withers wandered off to a slimy green pond to see if it contained any fish, leaving me alone with Lucinda and Mr Hart.

'So what do you think, ladies?' said Mr Hart, smiling pleasantly. 'Does Hartmoor meet with your approval?'

I noticed Lucinda kept peeking at the portico as it had another of those gargoyles crouched on top of it. The grinning creature was certainly unnerving. She nodded briefly at Mr Hart but did not say anything nor look too enthused. I had no such qualms, however, and could hold my tongue no longer.

'Your castle looks quite different to the sketch you drew us in Bath,' I remarked. 'Pray, why did you not draw its true likeness?'

A flash of annoyance crossed Mr Hart's face as he turned to me, but his agreeable features quickly smoothed. 'I do not know why you think it is so different,' he said. 'Everything in the sketch is as you see it now.' He gestured at the turrets. 'What do you think, Lucy? Do you not think it a good likeness?' he asked, turning his attention to Lucinda.

'Oh yes, Dory, I believe so,' she said, tearing her eyes away from the gargoyle and looking up at him. He smirked at her in a self-satisfied kind of way.

I did not know what rattled me more: them calling each other Dory and Lucy or the fact he was trying to pull the wool over my eyes.

Drawing myself up to my full height, I gave him a stern glare.

'Mr Hart', I said firmly, 'may I remind you it is proper to address my niece as Miss Fitzroy. And forgive me for saying so, but your castle is in a shocking state of disrepair. It needs extensive masonry work—'

'It has a few missing stones.'

'It has more than a few. And there is a gargoyle, for goodness' sake!' I exclaimed, pointing at the stone creature with a shudder. 'You did not draw that!'

'It is difficult to draw,' retorted Mr Hart stiffly.

I gave a cold little laugh. 'Surely not for a superior artist such as yourself.'

'I had only a short amount of time to sketch. If I had had an hour or two, then I believe even I could have met your high standards of realism,' he said, his voice dripping with sarcasm. 'Forgive me, but criticising my abode when I have been kind enough to invite you to stay is not good manners.'

'And it is not *good manners* to deceive us about said abode in the first place!'

'There is no deception, woman—only your determination to be bloody pedantic!' Mr Hart spat, his jaw tight and eyes dark and narrowed.

Gracious, this was escalating quickly. But it was satisfying to crack his smooth veneer and catch a glimpse of who he really was. My heart was bouncing in my chest as he took a step towards me, his eyes boring into mine. But strangely, at that moment, I was quite unafraid and riled enough to batter him if need be. I curled my hands into fists against my sides in preparation (though I doubted I would be able to do much damage—he was not broad, but he was tall and had strong wiry arm muscles. I had witnessed them when he had rolled up his shirtsleeves on the journey here).

Lucinda, who had been swinging her head backwards and forwards between us like a pendulum, spoke up nervously. 'Ah, I believe Jane and Mr Smith-Withers are ready to continue the tour ... I will go and tell them we are coming now.'

With a fearful glance at Mr Hart, she scurried off to the others, who were looking over curiously.

Realising he had scared her, Mr Hart stepped back and

hooked a finger into his cravat to loosen it, as if to cool down. Indeed, he was breathing heavily and had high colour in his cheeks. He chewed his lower lip and glanced at me, and I could see he was trying to figure out how to best manage the situation. But I did not want to be managed. All my earlier worries about confronting him had disappeared. It felt good to speak up and air my feelings, and I was itching to push him further and ask him a few choice questions about his father to see how he reacted. However, Mr Hart had other ideas.

'Come now, Felicity,' he said placatingly. He tilted his head at me and smiled like his usual smarmy self. 'We are having a pleasant tour. You do not want to spoil it for everyone, do you? Let us shake hands and be friends.' He held out his hand to me, but I did not want to touch his bare skin with my own. It was much too dangerous when I was in this fizzing kind of mood. So I refused to take it.

'It is *Mrs Fitzroy*,' I said sharply. 'And I don't want to be friends with you.' I stalked off towards the others, ignoring the pained expression on his face because I did not believe he felt any hurt whatsoever. It was all part of his ploy to trick us. For what reason, I did not know yet, but I was determined to find out!

'Whatever was that about, Flissy?' asked Jane as I reached them. 'Why were you and Mr Hart quarrelling?'

I glanced back and saw that the gentleman in question was kicking at a stone ledge of an old dried-up fountain with the toe of his boot, causing chips to fly off. With his shoulders up around his ears, he looked like a sulky child that had been given a telling-off.

'I simply pointed out that the castle he sketched for us was nothing like it is in reality,' I said, surprised that he was behaving in such a manner when I had moved on from our spat already.

Mr Smith-Withers clicked his tongue in an exasperated fashion. 'You should not have done so, Mrs Fitzroy. Dory is a sensitive *artist* and suffers greatly when people find fault with his work,' he said, giving me a contemptuous look. 'I will see how he fares. He may wish to rest and take tea indoors.'

I rolled my eyes at his departing back.

'I might go and see if Mr Hart is all right too,' said Lucinda anxiously. 'I very much wish to see the library, so I hope he can continue with the tour.'

I was pleased that she was back to addressing him formally. Her calling him Dory had brought to mind Cecilia Spencer. She must have heard Mr Smith-Withers addressing him so.

'Yes, all right,' I told her. 'We will do a turn about the drive in the meanwhile.'

Lucinda ran off, and I linked arms with Jane.

'I am sure Mr Hart will recover in due course,' she whispered to me as we strolled around the drive, and I fought the urge to laugh.

'If he is *that* sensitive about his art, then perhaps he should give it up and find a more useful occupation,' I replied.

'Like what?' queried Jane.

'I don't know—a butcher, a baker ...'

'A candlestick maker,' she finished with a giggle.

I shushed her quickly. For if *delicate* Mr Hart should hear us laughing about him and become reoffended, he might cancel the tour altogether. Then Lucinda would be upset at not seeing the library. I supposed I should try to be civil to him to keep the peace. Otherwise, the remainder of our stay would be extremely awkward. I also did not want him cutting it short before I learned anything important.

* * *

Fortunately, Mr Hart did recover enough to continue and gave us a tour of the grounds near the castle. These consisted of a rabbit-infested meadow and an orchard with around two dozen apple trees that needed a good prune. There was also a vegetable garden near the kitchen, which was in a much healthier state with neatly planted rows of carrots, turnips, cucumbers, and cabbages. I suspected Maurice tended that.

'Now for the pièce de résistance, the library,' declared Mr Hart.

'Ooh, goodie,' said Lucinda, clapping her hands, and he smiled at her.

'Yes, I have not forgotten, although I did consider leaving it for another day as I did not feel up to it.' He looked at me with a wounded expression. However, I averted my eyes and stared pointedly at a cabbage. Obviously, I was still not forgiven, and Lord, was he milking it!

The library was accessed through the smaller south turret, and we had to ascend a spiral staircase to reach it. Mr Hart led us up, and we followed him in single file, clutching at a rope railing. 'Watch your heads at the top,' he cautioned. 'The doorway is low and has an overhanging stone. I have banged my head on it several times.'

Pity he does not bang his head on it now, I thought. *It might knock some sense into him.*

Up until now, I had not been particularly impressed with anything on the tour (including Mr Hart's attitude!), but this changed when I ducked through the doorway and beheld the splendid library. Curved wooden shelves rose six high and were filled with hundreds of leather-bound volumes. Round porthole-style windows, set at intervals throughout the turret walls, ensured that there was enough light to see by; and if not, there were plenty of candles and lanterns waiting to be lit. Woven rugs had been placed on the flagstones to make it cosy, and there were several comfortable chairs with folded blankets in the middle of the space. I imagined you could curl up here and read to your heart's content or at least until you got too hungry to concentrate.

'Oh, it is wonderful!' cried Lucinda, running over to a shelf and immediately starting to browse the titles.

'I think you have lost Lucy for the rest of the stay,' Jane commented to Mr Hart.

He chuckled, looking pleased. 'And do you like it too, Miss Austen?' he asked her.

'I do, very much so,' she said, looking around with a small smile. 'As libraries go, this is one of the most unusual I have ever been in. But I have a test to ascertain its true excellence—does it contain any romance novels?'

Mr Hart bowed. 'Of course, there is a whole section dedicated to the latest ones. Please follow me.'

Now we have lost Jane too, I thought, amused.

They went off, and I was left with Mr Smith-Withers, who had plucked an encyclopaedia-sized book from a bottom shelf and was seated in an armchair. It seemed to contain nothing but maps, but if that interested him, who was I to judge?

Idly, I wandered along the nearest shelf, peering at the titles. It was a whole row of Shakespeare's plays and sonnets bound in rich red leather with gilt-tooled spines. I was interested in the Bard's works per se, but not enough to sit down and read any at present. Yet it appeared we were to be here until luncheon the way everyone was settling in. *Perhaps I should go and peruse the romance novel section too?* I was just about to when I spied, on the next shelf over, *The Monk: Volume One;* and nestled next to it were volumes two and three. Oh, Jane would be thrilled. She could read the next instalment here and need not wait for it to become available in Bath. I looked around to call her over, but she was animatedly discussing something with Mr Hart. No matter, I would tell her later.

My fingers brushed the spines of the books next to *The Monk* and landed on another familiar title: *Fanny Hill*. I jerked my hand back, as if it were burned, and looked around. But no one had noticed anything. Harriet had returned her banned copy of *Fanny Hill* to cousin Erica as soon as she got engaged to Evan, but I could still recall us giggling over some of the more lurid scenes. It was definitely educational, but not the kind of book young ladies should be reading. I would not, therefore, be recommending it to Lucinda. Seraphina would kill me if I did. But how funny to discover a copy here!

There were a number of books in plain black leather covers sitting next to it. Curiously, I pulled one out and turned to the title page: *Teaching Molly* by Anonymous.

It seemed to fall naturally open at a certain page, so I skim-read a couple of paragraphs. As I did, my eyes widened. A gentleman was visiting a housemaid called Molly in her chamber and was not being shy about his intentions.

> *He requested politely that Molly remove her chemise, but she refused, calling him a beast for asking. Yet to his frustration, she began teasing him by untying it and showing him a bare silky shoulder, then a glimpse of her white voluptuous bosom. This whipped him into a impolite and uncontrollable passion. He started chasing her round the room, whereupon there was much giggling (from her) and grunting (from him). She made a bid for escape out the door and almost achieved it, but he caught hold of her chemise at the last minute and unceremoniously ripped it from her. Molly, naked and laughing, was thrown onto*

the bed, where he proceeded to unleash his fervent
desire and teach her an enjoyable lesson ...

Blushing furiously, I slapped the book shut and shoved it back into its rightful place on the shelf. Good Lord, now I knew why the book's cover was so discreet. I seemed to have stumbled upon the library's smut section. No wonder Mr Hart had spent practically every waking moment of his teenage years in here when he was not at Eton!

'Find anything you like, Mrs Fitzroy?' a low voice said from behind me, and I spun around guiltily to find Mr Hart leaning casually against the bookshelf. He took one look at my pink cheeks and chuckled. I groaned inwardly. Trust him to come across me riffling through erotica. How utterly embarrassing! But maybe I could brazen my way through it.

'No, not on this particular shelf, Mr Hart,' I said, shaking my head at him reproachfully. 'You would do well to keep these books under lock and key in case any innocent young ladies happen upon them by accident.' I looked pointedly at Lucinda, who was curled up in an armchair, her nose in a book.

'So you do not put yourself in the category of "innocent young lady" then?' he drawled. I glanced back at him, and he was staring at me so intently that I gulped.

'Well, no, of course not. I am married and well versed in

what occurs in the bedroom,' I said decorously. I meant to give the impression that I was a mature woman and had no need of such silly books, but I realised that saying I was well versed in the bedroom was not a good thing to tell a rake.

'Indeed,' he replied huskily.

Oh no, this was dangerous. I needed to get off the subject of 'the bedroom' immediately. 'Er, so shall we be having luncheon soon?'

'Yes, in a little while. Hmm, I wonder what was it about this book in particular that you were so absorbed in,' he said thoughtfully.

To my horror, he reached across and plucked out *Teaching Molly* and unabashedly flipped to the page I had been reading! It was either to get back at me for my earlier admonishment or to make me feel even more excruciatingly uncomfortable than I already did. Whichever it was, it worked. My ears burned in shame as he scrutinised the passage with a smirk on his face, obviously enjoying my discomfort.

'Well well well,' he said, closing the book. He placed it back on the shelf, accidentally on purpose brushing my shoulder as he did so. 'How interesting that out of all the books in the library, you should gravitate to this one.'

'I did not "gravitate" to it!' I hissed. 'I was simply browsing and *happened* upon it.'

'Thousands would believe you. I do not,' he said. 'But have no fear, Mrs Fitzroy. Your secret penchant for erotic literature is safe with me.' He tapped his nose.

My mouth dropped open, incensed at this.

'But ... but ...' I stammered.

'Uh-uh, the lady doth protest too much, methinks,' he said, wagging a finger. His laughing eyes lingered on mine and then lowered, most audaciously, to my décolletage! I was shocked into silence as he scoured my cleavage, then slowly raised his gaze back up to mine with a knowing smile. I stared at him helplessly, feeling like he had trapped me into a corner. Oh, he looked like an angel, but he was the devil incarnate and the worst man I had ever encountered!

'Mr Hart?' Lucinda's dulcet tones broke the spell he was weaving over me, and both of us whipped our heads round simultaneously to look at her.

'Who is Harrington Hart?'

Mr Hart blinked. 'Pardon?'

'Harrington. He has written his name all over this book. Look there, on the front page.' She pointed to it. 'And also here, in the margin.' She jabbed a finger. 'But here, he shortens it to Harry.' Lucinda sniffed. 'Whoever Harry is, he does not seem to appreciate that other readers do not want to see his graffiti.'

Mr Hart walked over to Lucinda and took the book from her outstretched hand. He looked at the pages with the offending signature but did not say anything.

'Who is Harry, Mr Hart?' I prompted, glad that he had been distracted from torturing me by the bookcase.

'My elder brother,' Mr Hart said flatly after a pause.

Lucinda and I looked at each other. 'Your brother! But I thought you were an only child?' I said, confused.

'No, I never said so.'

'Well, you never mentioned you had a brother.'

Mr Hart handed the book back to Lucinda and perched on the edge of an armchair. Jane was trying hard to look as if she were fixated on her book, but I did not blame her if she was listening in. He had a brother!

'We had a falling-out. We try not to be at the castle at the same time.'

Oh no, I thought. *Not two Mr Harts in existence.* 'Is he ... like you?'

'Not much in personality, though we do look rather similar. My father mixes us up quite frequently.'

'It's the Hart bloodline,' piped up Mr Smith-Withers from his map reading. 'You all look the same.'

'The painting in my room ... *He* is definitely one of your relations,' I said, rubbing my arms. My shawl was still obscuring the painting as I had not been able to bring myself to take it down, so I was half-chilled.

Mr Hart glanced at me. 'Yes, that's Royden Hart, my uncle. He was a bit of a dab hand with the sword.'

Mr Smith-Withers guffawed. 'And with the ladies! He got into a spot of trouble with a friend's wife and came to an untimely end. He was only thirty!'

'He was murdered?' exclaimed Lucinda, sounding shocked, and even Jane looked up from her book at that.

'Yes, he was run through with his own sword,' confirmed Mr Hart. He pressed his lips together tightly and did not seem pleased that Mr Smith-Withers was doling out family history without his consent. But now I knew about Royden Hart's demise, those eyes made more sense. *No wonder he looks so annoyed—he was cut down in his rakish prime.*

'He's still giving us trouble too,' continued Mr Hart. 'One of our previous maids refused to clean your room, Mrs Fitzroy. She said it felt like Royden was looking at her from the painting and that it gave her the creeps. You are much too sensible to believe such a notion surely?'

I shuddered. 'Actually, I happen to agree with her. I can't say I like that painting much myself.'

'There is no need to worry. You will be quite safe in that room,' he said quietly. And I felt slightly comforted by him saying it, as much as one could be comforted by a rogue.

'Yes, you will be quite safe in there!' crowed Mr Smith-Withers. 'His ghost tends to frequent the orchard, the dining hall, and ... the pink bedroom.'

'Oh no, please noooo,' whimpered Lucinda. Her eyelids fluttered, and to my horror, she looked ready to faint.

Chapter 15

Mr Smith-Withers hurriedly told Lucinda that Royden's ghost was something he had never seen himself, and it was only the product of servants' vivid imaginations.

But it was too late—the damage was done. She was almost catatonic with fear at what he had said, no matter how much I chafed her hands and spoke sense to rouse her. Mr Smith-Withers stood by unrepentant, saying, 'How was I to know she would react like that?'

I could have cheerfully strangled him. Whether the story was true or not, Lucinda was highly strung and possessed a vivid imagination herself due to all the reading she did, so I was not looking forward to having to reassure her that Royden's ghost would not appear in her bedroom tonight. However, Mr Hart—most impressively, I had to admit—took control of the situation and single-handedly soothed her without the need of smelling salts.

He suggested calmly that it was time for luncheon and asked if she would allow him to escort her back. She nodded and took his arm, and he supported her down the stairwell. And as we walked to the main entrance, she leaned on him;

and he spoke to her softly, saying something I could not hear. But his words seemed to have a miraculous effect as she stopped quivering, and her colour returned.

Not knowing exactly what he was saying bothered me a little, but I did not like to interfere since the girl had been severely afraid, and he was doing an admirable job of handling the situation.

My own recent encounters with Mr Hart and what I thought of them could wait. Lucinda's well-being was my primary concern.

'Are you all right now, Lucy? I am sorry that man's thoughtless remark frightened you so,' I said gently when she had composed herself and we were in the dining hall.

'I am well. Thank you, Aunty Fliss. Mr Hart has promised me that it is only a story and I need not worry. He was very kind, and I feel a bit silly for acting as I did.'

'I can stay with you tonight if you need me to—'

'There is no need,' she said quickly. 'I mean, thank you for offering. But I would like to prove to Mr Hart that I can be brave and am not a child.' She gave a hollow laugh.

I pursed my lips and said nothing further.

The simple meal of potato soup and lightly salted cucumber sandwiches, as well as fruit, biscuits, and cups of refreshing tea, helped restore a semblance of normalcy to our party; and no further mention was made of ghosts. But there was still an absence at the table that had not been explained.

'Mr Hart, will your father be joining us for luncheon?' I asked.

He was in the middle of eating a cheese sandwich Maurice had made specially for him as, apparently, 'Master Dorian does not like cucumbers' (a pity as the garden was full of them).

Pausing to wipe his mouth with a napkin, he said, 'Unfortunately, he is not up to socialising today, Mrs Fitzroy.'

'Oh, is he ill?' Jane enquired, and I was glad she had asked the question. Indeed, this was the first time we had heard that Mr Hart Sr was in some way incapacitated. I had assumed he was reclusive.

'He does not have a strong constitution' was Mr Hart's reply, and he resumed eating his cheese sandwich as if the subject were closed.

But I wanted to keep it open.

'I am sorry to hear that as we were looking forward to meeting him. When do you think we shall?'

Mr Hart looked at me with an unreadable expression. 'I cannot say exactly. But he knows you are all here and sends his greetings.'

'I see. Well, I hope he will feel up to meeting us soon.'

'Thank you. I hope so too,' he said and took a large bite of his sandwich to make it clear that the subject was now well and truly closed.

I nodded and continued with my meal, but a knot of unease lodged in my ribcage. What was wrong with Mr Hart Sr that he could not even have luncheon with us?

After we had finished, Mr Hart suggested a quiet afternoon in the parlour with tea served at three o'clock, to which everyone readily agreed. I said that I would join them shortly, but that I wished to write to my husband (really, I wanted to speak to Maurice in the kitchen).

'*Another* letter, Mrs Fitzroy?' said Mr Hart. 'Have you not just written to him?'

'That was a brief note. I wish to write a longer letter describing your atmospheric castle.'

I thought the compliment might make him relinquish me, but he was intent on keeping our group together.

'You can do that easily in the parlour,' he said with a frown. 'There is a writing table, along with ample paper, ink, and quills—for you as well as Miss Austen.'

'Ah, Miss Austen may like to use the table herself.'

I crossed my fingers and hoped that Jane would take the bait.

She nodded. 'Thank you, Flissy. It is true. I am itching to write after our tour.'

'You see, Mr Hart, I must use the table in my room. But I am a fast writer, and I shall join you in half an hour. You shall hardly know I was away.'

I smiled as innocently as I could, and he inclined his head, but he did not look pleased.

With the notion that Mr Hart might come and fetch me if I was a minute later than half an hour, I knew I had little time in which to act. As soon as everyone had disappeared into the parlour, I did an about-turn and flew silently down the stairs and along the hallway to the kitchen.

Maurice was startled, but not overly surprised to see me, thanks to my forewarning of offering him assistance. He was in the middle of preparing a tray of food.

'Is that for Mr Hart Sr's luncheon?' I enquired.

'It is indeed.' *Oh, so he does exist*, I thought, a pulse of excitement running through me.

'Might I take that up for you? You must be busy down here.'

'If you do not mind, that would be helpful. Thank you.' He wiped his forehead with his sleeve, looking harassed. 'The assistant cook is due to arrive shortly, and I need to be here to show them what to do.'

'It is no trouble! If you would kindly give me directions to his apartment,' I said, lifting the wooden tray up and down experimentally to see how heavy it was. It held a plate with a cheese sandwich, an unpeeled boiled egg, an apple, and some biscuits. So it was not overly laden. I noted that Mr Hart Sr also did not like cucumbers.

'Yes, of course. If you go down the hallway that leads to the back entrance, there is an oak doorway about halfway along. Through it is a stairwell that leads up to the main turret. It is a bit dim, but there are arrow slits in the walls that provide some light. Mr Hart's room is the first door on the left. He does not like to be disturbed ... So leave the tray outside the door, knock twice, and he will collect it when he is ready.'

I gulped. It all sounded strange and spooky indeed, especially after Mr Smith-Withers telling us about Royden Hart's ghost flitting about the place. Maurice obviously had nerves of steel to live here, and I wondered if I should offer to stay in the kitchen and greet the cook while he took the tray. But this could be the only chance I had to solve the mystery of Mr Hart's father (and of course, I was going to have to disobey instructions and go into his room to do so).

With a resolute breath, I hefted the tray and went off down the hallway to find the oak door.

The castle was not built for traversing a tray of food up a stairwell. Lord knew how Maurice did this. I was having a lot of trouble both keeping my balance and stopping the food from sliding off, especially the apple and the egg—they kept rolling around on the tray alarmingly. A blast of wind whistled through an arrow slit and wrapped around my neck like icy fingers. I almost flung the lunch into the air and made a run for it.

Emerging out of the stairwell at last, I peered tentatively down a gloomy stone-walled hallway with ancient threadbare carpet. *Do not think of Royden Hart!* I told myself firmly. But if ever there was a time for his ghost to appear, this was it! Fear was causing my limbs to seize up, but time was also ticking by, so I gave myself a set of stern instructions to force my feet to move.

It is the first door on the left. You will knock and open the door and greet his father. Do not be afraid.

This seemed to work, and upon following these dutifully, I found myself in a sparsely furnished room. A man with unkempt grey hair and a patchy beard was sitting by the window, reading a book. His grizzled appearance made him look old, but in truth, he could not have been more than fifty. He was dressed in simple trousers, a grubby white shirt, and a leather jerkin.

'Good day,' I said to him, nervously clutching the tray.

'Good day,' he replied gruffly, then looked closer at me with suspicious eyes. 'Who in heaven's name are you? Where is Maurice?'

'I am one of your guests, Mr Hart. My name is Mrs

Felicity Fitzroy, and I am assisting Maurice by bringing your luncheon,' I said, indicating the tray with my chin.

'One of my guests?' he repeated, sounding amazed.

'Yes, my niece and my friend are here with your son and his friend Mr Smith-Withers.'

'Humph, the lawyer,' said Mr Hart and beckoned me to bring the tray to his table, which I did. He immediately took a bite out of the sandwich and began peeling the boiled egg. 'Yes, I knew *he* was here. I did not know Harry was too— he neglected to mention that,' he mumbled through his mouthful.

'Harry? Oh no, we are here with your *youngest* son, Dorian,' I corrected.

'Dorian?' he echoed. 'No, no, he is my eldest.'

I took a step backwards, wondering why he was saying that. How strange.

'Has he not come to see you?' I ventured. 'We arrived yesterday in the early evening.'

He stared at his plate and shook his head once sharply.

'How very bad of him,' I said, quite forgetting myself.

Mr Hart's expression turned stony, and he lifted his eyes to gaze at me, then looked at the half-peeled egg in his hand. 'Yes, very bad,' he said slowly and tightened his hand until I heard the shell crack. 'Bad egg,' he mumbled, and much to my dismay, he kept repeating it over and over. 'Bad egg, bad egg, bad egg …'

'Mr Hart, please stop. I am sorry,' I said, feeling awful that I had triggered some kind of nervous complaint in him.

'Very *bad egg*!' he shouted and then, without warning, threw the egg violently at the stone wall in front of him, where it exploded into a mess of white, yellow, and pieces of shell. I stood there, gaping.

Shocked and frightened by his behaviour, I ran out of the room, along the corridor and down the stairwell—my feet having no trouble moving quickly now!

Arriving back in the kitchen, confused and shaken, I did not know what had just happened. Was it Mr Hart that his father was referring to as 'bad'? Or was it indeed the boiled egg? Whichever it was, there was no doubt that he was suffering from some kind of mental condition.

I had no time to ask Maurice about it as I needed to go to the parlour forthwith and act calmly as if I had been writing a letter to Max. I did so and pulled it off admirably as no one suspected a thing.

The rest of the afternoon passed quietly with reading and light conversation. But the encounter with Mr Hart Sr stayed uppermost in my mind, and I mulled over it constantly, wondering if I should attempt to talk to Maurice again to discover more.

After supper, a game of cards was suggested. But Lucinda said she was tired and wished to go to bed, and that immediately set Jane and me off with yawning. We bid good night to the gentlemen, who were staying up to have a glass of port.

But at the bottom of the stairs, I hesitated, looking towards the kitchen.

'Are you not coming up, Aunty Fliss?' asked Lucinda.

'In a moment ... I might fetch a cup of milk to help me sleep. My head is a bit frazzled. But do you need me to come with you to your room first?'

She put her shoulders back and lifted her chin. 'No, I will be perfectly fine.'

'All right, brave girl. Pleasant dreams, and see you in the morning.'

She blew me a kiss and ran up the stairs after Jane, who called out, 'Good night, Flissy!' from the landing.

Excellent, I thought. *Now I can talk to Maurice.*

But when I reached the kitchen, it was cold and empty, and Maurice was not there. Sighing, I poured myself a cup of milk anyway from the earthenware jug in the larder and stood by the window, sipping it while looking out at the vegetable garden. The moon was rising, lighting up the cucumbers growing there, which made me think of cheese sandwiches, Mr Hart, his father, and exploding boiled eggs.

Hopefully, I would be able to sleep with all that whirling around in my head!

Placing my empty cup in the sink, I turned and saw the outline of a wooden door—it was the one that led to the parlour, the one I had gone through with Maurice on the first night. One thought joined to another in rapid succession and led me to an obvious conclusion: Mr Hart and Mr Smith-Withers were conversing in the parlour ... And if I listened in, I might discover some truths!

The candles in there were still burning, but barely, and it was nerve-racking to walk down the ill-lit passage alone. But I steeled myself to do so, keeping one hand on the rough stone for guidance and feeling the way in front with one outstretched foot after another.

Eventually, I reached the parlour door, which had a strip of glowing light underneath, and heard the low rumble of male voices. I placed my ear against the wood, but it was solid and too thick to hear properly.

With a thudding heart, I inched the door open a crack, and their muffled conversation came through loud and clear.

'And she *is* uncommonly pretty,' said Mr Smith-Withers. 'Plus her dowry makes it an advantageous match. Well done, you. All those mornings you dragged me around the pump room were worth it.'

Mr Hart chuckled, and I heard the sound of glasses clinking.

'Now if Father would only sign his updated will ... It is taking forever.' He let out a frustrated sigh. 'How was he this morning?'

'His confusion is growing, especially with my encouragement. This morning, he firmly believed that you are the eldest and Harry the younger. But then he slipped back into lucidity and yelled at me to leave.'

'Hmm.'

'I will keep working on him,' said Mr Smith-Withers.

'Good, good, and I too with Lucy. She is enamoured enough by now, I think, to accept a proposal soon.'

'You should watch out for the aunt. She could be a hindrance to it.'

'Leave her to me,' Mr Hart said.

'Oho, what are you going to do with her?'

'I'm not sure. But she is not unaffected by me, I think. Perhaps I can charm her into submission.'

Mr Smith-Withers chortled. 'It is not working so far.'

He said something in a low voice to his friend and laughed. My cheeks burned, imagining he had said something indecorous about me. *Oh, I was right in calling that man a weasel!*

'No, not that,' replied Mr Hart. 'Even if I have been

thinking it. I have to keep my eye on the prize. I will propose to Lucy soon and consummate our engagement. She is practically begging for it anyway, and I do not want to wait for the wedding.'

Mr Smith-Withers guffawed drunkenly at that. 'Indeed!'

'Then with the will signed, I will be heir, and Harry shall have his loose change. When Father eventually carks it, the castle shall be mine. And with Lucinda's generous dowry, I shall have a stipend to fund my lifestyle plus capital to restore it to its former glory. And you shall have your cut, of course, Smithy, and visit whenever and with whomever you like.'

There was another clinking of glasses.

'And what will you do with your wife in the meanwhile?'

'She can live here, while you and I partake in the pleasures of the Season in Bath and London. I'll tell Maurice to relinquish his nursemaid duties of father to her and *she* can empty the old man's piss-pot.'

The two of them laughed uproariously, fuelled by port.

I could not believe my ears. So this was Mr Hart's devious plan: to marry Lucinda for her money and cast her aside without a care so he could continue his reprobate ways when she doted upon him—even loved him. It was clear that he did not love her one jot and was involved in a terrible deception—of his own father no less! A fury rose in me so great that I nearly burst through the door and clawed his eyes out.

However, before I could move a muscle, something ran over my foot and started scrabbling at the crack in the door. A small brown field mouse shut up in the passageway had seen its chance for escape and life and decided now was the ideal time to make a run for it. Luckily, I did not mind mice and did not think to scream, but that did not matter because it started squeaking—very loudly—and roused attention anyway.

'What the devil is that noise?' asked Mr Smith-Withers from within.

'It sounds like a *mouse*,' replied Mr Hart, sounding equally perplexed. 'It seems to be coming from the ...'

I shrank back from the door and fled as quietly as I could down the passageway, with the mouse hot on my heels.

Chapter 16

The next morning, I was awake at dawn, having slept fitfully. Staying in bed was tempting. But I had locked all our bedroom doors, even Jane's, and pocketed the individual keys. After what I had heard last night, I wasn't taking any chances with Mr Hart or Mr Smith-Withers either, especially as they had been on the port.

But now I had to unlock the doors before Lucinda and Jane awoke and wondered why they were locked in. Thankfully, both were still dead to the world as I undertook my task and then padded shawl-less and shivering back to my room.

Lying in bed, the covers pulled up to my chin, I wondered what on earth to do now. One thing was very clear: I could not let Lucinda marry Mr Hart. Unfortunately, he was right—his plan to beguile her had worked, and she was now besotted. If he proposed to her, she would definitely accept him.

There were only two ways I could think of to prevent the union, and neither of them was guaranteed to succeed. The first way was thus: Before Mr Hart proposed, I could prepare Lucinda and tell her that I had an inkling that he might. She would no doubt be excited to hear it, but then I would say, 'But, dear, it would be best to tell him you would like to wait until your father has given his blessing. It is the proper thing to do, and you do not want to upset him, do you?'

Lucinda was very close to Tobias, so the fear of angering her father might hold some sway over her. If I could get her away from the castle and back to Bath, Mr Hart would not have as much power. And I could gently sow the seeds of doubt about his character with Jane's help (of course, I would have to tell my friend the truth about him beforehand). Hopefully, by the time Lucinda went home to York, she would have come to see Mr Hart as the rogue he was and refuse him.

However, one big problem with this was that Mr Hart might start his own campaign in retaliation and persuade Lucinda, by letters and visits to Queen Square, that everything I said was a lie because I was jealous or bitter or some such nonsense. He might pursue her to York and charm his way into the hearts and minds of her family, and the marriage could still take place.

The second way was to rip the bandage off and tell her in no uncertain terms what I had overheard in the parlour last night. But this, I knew, would upset her tremendously—to the point that she may not want to believe it and turn against me and run straight into Mr Hart's tangled web like a little fly. If I tried to pry her away from him, then I might have an elopement on my hands.

What a blasted mess! I wished I had been strong enough to withstand the pressure from everyone to come to the damned castle in the first place. If I had also told Elizabeth and Jane of Ceci and Dory being caught in bed together immediately after I had learned it, then I might have prevented this distressing scenario. It was my own fault. I had not wanted to be the 'dull, boring aunt' and spoil everyone's good time.

Even Max had sensed something untoward and written instantly to express his concern, but I had been too proud to tell him the truth and ask for his help. In fact, I had blatantly fibbed to give the impression everything was under control so he thought I was capable and mature. Oh, if only I had written saying I needed him and to please come and take us back to Bath immediately! He would have leapt into his carriage and shown up at the castle before Mr Hart could enact his wicked plan. I blinked away bittersweet tears.

But if he knew the truth of the situation, Max would be loath to let me go away again, and he would certainly lose any faith in my ability as a chaperone. I had to sort out this matter on my own. As I lay there pondering, I realised I was overlooking the most obvious solution and another way I could save Lucinda—it was time to confront Mr Hart.

I chose my moment after breakfast and asked discreetly, out of hearing of the others, for a private meeting. Mr Hart looked at me curiously but did not reject my request. With a shrug, he said, 'By all means. We can talk in my study.'

His study was located on the other side of the parlour. But unlike the parlour, which was sizeable even though it had a low ceiling, the study was a compact room. It had space for a flat-top mahogany desk featuring several brass-knobbed drawers, as well as a small settee, but no other furniture. The castle was odd in that respect. Some rooms, like the dining hall, were absurdly large, as Jane had pointed out. Others, like Mr Hart's study, were miniscule. The architecture had no sense of logical proportion. It was as if the inhabitants' comfort was a low priority on the scale of things.

Indeed, when it came to comfort, I would rather have been in a larger room for this meeting as the size of it placed Mr Hart and me in rather closer proximity than I would have liked.

He indicated that I should take a seat on the settee while

he perched on the edge of the desk.

I glanced around at the framed pencil sketches on the panelled walls, mainly of birds and country landscapes. 'Did you do these?' I asked, recognising his style of sketching.

He nodded. 'Yes, when I was at Eton. I found it a pleasant respite to take off into the grounds with my sketch pad rather than listen to law lectures. Such a pastime did not help my grades, though.'

'I did not know you had a background in law,' I said, interested despite myself.

'Yes, that is how I met Smithy, er, Mr Smith-Withers. We were in the same year.'

'I see,' I said, my countenance hardening at the mention of that gentleman.

'But I gather you did not ask for a private meeting to discuss my sketches, no matter how unrealistic you deem them to be,' he said in a teasing tone. He swung his leg, which was encased in a black riding boot and well-fitted fawn breeches, and I was struck again by how long and lithe his limbs were. His manner of walking was always rather graceful too, but purposeful, like a confident whippet.

I collected myself to deal with the matter at hand. Staring at Mr Hart's legs was not at all what I was here for!

I sat up straight on the settee and clasped my hands in

my lap. 'No, I did not,' I said. 'I wish to discuss a much more serious matter.'

'Goodness,' said Mr Hart in the same light teasing tone. 'I am all ears.'

I took a breath and steeled myself. What I was about to say would no doubt wipe the smile off his face.

'Certain information has come to light about your intentions towards my niece, Mr Hart,' I began, trying not to let my voice betray my nervousness. 'I have come to ask you, well ... to beg you, really, to leave her alone.'

There was a silence, and Mr Hart stopped swinging his leg.

I did not want to, but I forced myself to look at him. 'Please,' I added, thinking I should be polite about it.

'I am not sure what you are talking about,' he said slowly.

'I am talking about the plan you have concocted with Mr Smith-Withers: to marry Lucy, take her dowry, and cast her aside while you continue to live a life of debauchery—as well as deceive your father into becoming heir of Hartmoor.'

Mr Hart's left eye twitched, and I could tell I had caught him unawares.

'Well, well. Someone's been sneaking around and listening at doors,' he said, his teasing tone gone.

'I am not here to accuse you or judge you or anything like that. My concern is purely for Lucy. All I ask is that you do not go through with your intention to propose and leave her be,' I said, hardly believing I was daring to speak to him so plainly.

'And if I will not?'

Glad that he was speaking plainly too and not bothering to deny he was a scoundrel any longer, I pressed on.

'Then I will have no choice but to out your plan to everyone I know, and then the word will spread. By the time next Season comes around, you will never again be able to hold your head high in good society, in Bath and even perhaps London.'

'But who would believe you?' he said, sounding faintly mocking.

'I have testimony from another to back up my story.'

'Who, pray tell?' To my chagrin, he did not sound as worried as he should be.

'Cecilia Spencer, of course,' I said triumphantly. 'She has told me all about your sordid affair.'

Mr Hart rolled his eyes. 'Ceci! She was infatuated with me. Everyone knew it. It is why her mother separated us. She couldn't keep her hands off me in public. I doubt anyone will take Ceci's word over mine.'

Blast, he might be right about that, I thought, remembering Cecilia had also been quick to defend him when I had dared to criticise her *Dory*.

'Then ... then I will pay you five hundred pounds to leave Lucy alone,' I said, pulling out another ace out of my sleeve since the first one had failed.

'Oho, so now you are bribing me? Wonders will never cease!' Mr Hart said, sounding amused.

I gazed at him steadily. 'Call it what you want. My offer stands. What is your answer?'

'Five hundred would not inspire me to get out of bed in the morning and take a piss,' he said, folding his arms.

I wrinkled my nose. 'There is no need to be coarse, Mr Hart.'

'My apologies. In plainer and *less coarse* language, no, I will not accept five hundred pounds.'

'A thousand pounds then.'

'You are getting slightly warmer. But I think you can do better than that, Felicity,' he replied.

'One thousand five hundred pounds,' I said.

He shook his head.

'One thousand eight hundred pounds.'

Mr Hart's eyebrows raised. 'Ooh, that might inspire me to get out of bed,' he said with a laugh, shifting on the desk. I kept my eyes firmly on his face, away from his breeches.

'But it's still not quite enough.'

'Three thousand pounds,' I said, growing desperate. 'And that is my best offer.'

Mr Hart whistled. 'You would pay me that much?'

I lifted my chin. 'Yes, for the sake of my niece's reputation and future happiness, I would.'

In truth, I felt a little faint as I had not meant to go that high. But my personal allowance was mine to do with what I liked, and it was in a separate account, so I could easily access it without Max knowing. I was quite prepared to go without new gowns, accessories, and any other trifles if it would deter Mr Hart from his pursuit of Lucinda.

However, the man was so ill-bred he did not even have the manners to accept the money immediately and say he would agree to my terms. Instead, he looked thoughtful, as if he was turning my offer over in his mind and looking at it from all angles.

'It is very generous of you. But after careful consideration, I will have to refuse it,' he said at last.

Oh no, I thought, my mouth going dry.

'W-why must you refuse it?'

'Because if I took your bribe, it would sully our acquaintance.'

He grinned and started swinging his leg again.

'*Sully our acquaintance*'? *The nerve of him! Our acquaintance was already well and truly sullied.*

'Is there anything I can give you to make you stay away from her?' I asked shakily.

'Hmm, I wonder ... What can you give me?' He tapped his chin thoughtfully.

My eyes closed briefly, knowing exactly where he was going with that line of thinking—he was a rake after all.

'That is impossible,' I said flatly.

'Oh, so you know what I'm considering. I thought you might, considering your penchant for erotica.' He smirked, and I swallowed hard.

'It will not get you your money, if that is what you are after.'

'No, perhaps not. But enjoying myself with you will go some way to easing the pain of losing Lucy ... if that is what is to happen.'

'Pain?' I said scornfully. 'You will not feel pain—more like the pain of losing her dowry. But there will be other women you can pursue. Leave my niece out of your schemes.'

There was a long silence, as if he was considering my words.

Then he spoke. 'Very well,' he said simply.
I blinked at him.

'So you will not pursue her?'

'No, I won't. You have my word.'

I heaved a sigh of relief. Thank goodness, Mr Hart had decided to choose wisely for once in his life.

On the face of it, it seemed too easy. But short of getting it in writing, what else was I to do? I had to take his word for it.

Perhaps it would be all right. At least he now knew I had the measure of him and would desist or face the consequences.

'Very good. Now please make arrangements for our immediate departure back to Bath,' I said, giving him my best haughty face to show that I meant business.

'I'm afraid I cannot do that,' he replied smoothly.

My haughty face faltered slightly. 'You must. I demand it!'

'The carriage is being repaired and will be ready only on Saturday.'

'A likely story!' I scoffed.

''Tis true ...'

I stood and made to leave, having had enough of his lies. But quick as a flash, Mr Hart was off the desk and in front of me, blocking my way.

'Felicity, wait!'

Before I knew what was happening, he was clasping me against his chest, and the nearness and masculine heat of his lower body made me shudder.

'What if I want you to stay?' he murmured in my ear. He had not shaved, and I felt the rasp of his beard on my temple and smelt the remnants of port fumes emanating from his skin.

Was this his way of 'charming me into submission'? If so, I did not like it or want it.

'Let me go!' I tried to wriggle out of his grasp, but his arms were strong and held me firmly.

'Just one kiss.'

'No!'

'I think I deserve it as payment for being so accommodating.'

He moved his mouth to mine, but I ducked my head at the last minute, and it landed somewhere in my hair. Then I stomped hard on his boot with my heel.

'Ow! Dammit!' he swore and released me to attend to his foot. I scuttled around him to the door and leaned on the knob for support, shocked that he had tried to kiss me.

If I'd had a riding crop, I would have whipped him for attempting such a thing with a married woman!

A smile curled on his lips as he took in my flushed cheeks and heaving bosom. 'You enjoyed that,' he said with a smirk.

'You mistake my disgust for enjoyment, Mr Hart,' I said breathlessly. 'If you ever try that with me again, you will have injuries more serious to contend with than a sore foot!'

But I knew my words would have little effect on a man like him. Before he could try anything else or detain me further, I flung open the door and beat a hasty retreat from his study.

***

The encounter with Mr Hart left me severely shaken, and I clung to the stair banister for support while making my way up. Everyone was in the parlour, so I thought I would be able to recover my battered senses in private before I was missed.

However, at the top of the stairs, I ran into Jane, twirling her bonnet. 'There you are, Flissy! We are planning on going for a walk. Mr Hart said there was a lovely stream.'

The mention of his name was too painful to bear, and my legs threatened to collapse. It was most alarming, but I managed to keep my grip on the banister. Otherwise, I would have toppled down the stairs!

Jane let out an exclamation and spun into action.

She hauled me up along the landing and into her room. I

fell onto her bed, gasping with emotion, and buried my face in the eiderdown. It was a pretty light blue, but it was soon covered with dark blotches as it became a large silk handkerchief to soak up my tears.

'Flissy, oh my goodness!' Jane said, sounding startled. But I was too racked with sobs to reply, so she sat beside me and patted my arm and talked soothingly until I had gained some composure. I sat up, wiping my eyes, and let her hug me.

'Hush now. Are you missing Max? Is that it?' she asked, hooking her chin over my shoulder and rubbing my back. 'It is perfectly understandable, and I am sure he feels exactly the same.'

I swallowed. Jane hugging me had brought to mind a clear image of Mr Hart's arms around me in a vice-like grip. Hot guilt washed over me. It had not been a quarter of an hour since he had done so, and I could still feel his breath in my ear and his stubble rasping along my cheek. I scrubbed at my face ineffectually, but I knew only a good wash would help.

I let out a sob. 'Oh, Jane ...'

'It is all right. You can tell me all about it. I promise not to add our conversation to my book.' She huffed a friendly laugh, but her saying that did not cheer me up.

I took a deep snivelling breath. What I had to say might

be too good for her to resist writing about!

'It is n-not about Max. It is Mr Hart. I w-was w-with him just now in his study.'

Jane drew back, looking at me. 'But why?'

I bit my lip, wondering how to put it delicately. But there was no delicacy to what was occurring—it was raw and real.

'I bribed him—to stay away from Lucy.'

'You what?!'

'Shhhh, keep your voice down.' Quickly, I told her everything, starting with my conversation with Cecilia at the baths and finishing with Mr Hart trying to coerce me into an intimate liaison. 'It was shocking to me that he even suggested it. He did not seem to care one jot that he would be breaking Lucy's heart, let alone ruining the reputation of a respectable married woman,' I said in a low voice. 'He is truly as corrupt a man that ever lived.'

By this point, Jane's face had drained of all colour; and she placed a hand on her forehead, as if my words were causing her great pain. 'I do not want to believe it,' she whispered. 'But I know you would not lie.'

I felt awful causing her such distress. The shock was doubly great for her because she had been completely taken in by Mr Hart, and up until now, she had believed him to be a paragon of virtue. And she may have even been thinking of weaselly Mr Smith-Withers as a potential suitor!

'Believe me, I wish it was a lie, but it is more like a nightmare I wish I could wake up from!'

'But you have sat on this information about Cecilia Spencer since the baths, and I queried your trust in Mr Hart on the first night we arrived. I distinctly remember doing so. Why did you not tell me what had occurred between him and Cecilia then?' she said accusingly.

'Because at that stage, I was still giving him the benefit of the doubt and holding on to the hope that he had changed his ways for Lucy's sake,' I said defensively. 'But the more information I uncovered about him, the worse it got ... And now he has displayed his true colours, in all respects.'

Jane rubbed her hand over her chin distractedly. 'Lucy ... Oh no, she is going to be devastated when we tell her. She thinks so highly of him.'

'I know.'

'Oh, this is too bad of him. I thought he was a gentleman of good breeding, but he is nothing but a sly dog! How could he artfully deceive us like this?'

'Money,' I said flatly.

'But then why did he not accept your offer? It is more than generous.'

That was a good question indeed.

It appeared I had won. He had agreed to leave Lucinda alone, which was a huge relief, but we were still trapped here until his carriage was 'repaired'. So I did not trust him fully to keep his word and stay away from her. He was a man without morals, so really, I would be a fool to believe him.

Chapter 17

'I must have convinced him to change his mind. But who knows what is in his head? It is a dark and dishonourable place. We cannot trust him an inch.'

I was reluctant to tell Jane about Mr Hart's attempt to kiss me. But if things turned ugly, he might try to twist things and say I had thrown myself at him or some such nonsense. So it was best that she knew everything.

'Ah, there is one further thing that I need to tell you.' I steeled myself. 'Please know that I did nothing to encourage this.'

'What is it?' Jane sounded wary, as if she did not want to hear any more bad news. But I had to confess it.

'Mr Hart tried to kiss me in his study. It was after I turned down his reprehensible suggestion that he become ... intimate with me. I made to leave, and he grabbed me and attempted it. Of course, I struggled to get away and did not submit to his advances.'

Jane took my hand and squeezed it. 'How awful for you,' she murmured.

'It was,' I agreed, my mind conjuring up the scene with Mr Hart again. I fancied I could still feel his strong arms around me and the heat of his body. 'Awful a-and mortifying.'

'What did you do?'

'I stomped on his foot, and he let me go. That's why I was so overcome on the stairwell when you found me.'

Jane shook her head, and her lips curled in disgust. 'He is abhorrent. My opinion of him has been lowered even further, if that is possible. We need to leave immediately.'

'I agree. We just need to find a working carriage.' Jane looked at me enquiringly. 'He said his one is being repaired,' I explained.

She rolled her eyes. 'I do not believe that for a second. There must be another way, even if we have to walk to that nearby inn he mentioned ... though I do not know where it is. But we could ask someone.'

'Maurice said there is a mail coach that passes by the castle to collect the mail in the morning and afternoon, and it then travels onto the inn,' I said slowly. 'We could catch it and stay at the inn until we make arrangements to travel to Bath.'

'Perfect! We'll leave tomorrow morning then.'

'Can we not leave today?' I asked, eager to be on the

move now that we had the inklings of a plan.

'We need time to break the news gently to Lucinda about Mr Hart. I fear once she finds out, she is not going to be in any fit state to think rationally. She may try to attack him.'

Gracious! I thought. *That might be quite fun to witness!*

'Or she might be a limp inconsolable wreck,' continued Jane blithely. 'We need to choose our moment carefully. I think, in the meanwhile, we should start packing but keep our eyes and ears open for information that may aid our escape. We should act as normal with Mr Hart and Mr Smith-Withers and go on this walk to the stream so they do not suspect anything.'

'Excellent,' I said. 'I will find out from Maurice exactly when the mail coach arrives. And we will reconvene here before dinner for an update on our progress.'

We saluted each other like military generals, grinning as we did so. But there was a lot that could go wrong before we were free of Hartmoor and safely back in Bath. It was imperative that we did not underestimate Mr Hart. He might live in a castle, but he was decidedly the opposite of an chivalrous prince!

By the time we readied ourselves for the walk, however, it was too late. The other three had given up waiting for us and were already gone. I was unnerved at the thought of

Lucinda alone with the two men (I refused to call them 'gentlemen'!). But Jane said it was the perfect chance for me to talk to Maurice about the mail coach without raising suspicion.

Pushing my worry aside, I headed along to the kitchen and discovered a tall middle-aged woman in a grey dress, white apron, and cap dismantling a cold roast chicken at a startling pace. The legs and wings had been removed, and she was slicing into the breast meat with swift strokes of her sharp knife. She was, I assumed, the assistant cook.

Maurice appeared out of the larder, carrying a new loaf of bread.

'Ah, Mrs Fitzroy! This is Mrs Webber,' he said, introducing her with a tilt of his head. 'She will be assisting me in the kitchen until the end of your stay.'

Which will be much sooner than expected, I thought. I greeted her politely, and she stopped slicing and bobbed a curtsy. When she returned to the chicken, I beckoned Maurice aside, and he shuffled over.

'Was there not supposed to be a maid as well?'

'There was, but no one replied to the advertisement,' said Maurice in a low voice. 'But it is not surprising. The local girls are afraid of the castle and believe it is haunted.'

'By Royden Hart?'

'Well, yes. But it is just gossip. I have never seen anything resembling a ghost, and I have worked here for twenty years.'

Hmm, I was beginning to think Royden's nephew was the real reason that the maids did not want to work here. If Mr Hart was apt to take liberties with me, he would not think twice about accosting a pretty maid—all the more reason to leave as soon as we could and sever our acquaintance with him.

'Maurice, you mentioned the mail coach stopped by here in the morning and afternoon. Is it usually punctual?'

'Yes, madam. It arrives promptly at eleven o'clock and three o'clock. I can set my watch by it.'

I told him that I wished to know as I was writing another letter, which was true—I was going to write to Max to tell him that we were going back to Bath early. Maurice did not need to know that I myself would be on the coach clutching said letter! Although I had a good feeling about Maurice, he was still the family's butler and no doubt had an ingrained loyalty to Mr Hart, being the son of his employer. That being said, I did not want to involve him any more than necessary. But I planned to leave him a note excusing our abrupt departure and thanking him for his hospitality.

There was nothing else to do but return to the parlour and wait anxiously for the others to return for luncheon. I was trying to act outwardly composed, but my imagination was running wild now that I knew what Mr Hart was capable of. I paced, I bit my fingernails, and I looked out the window so many times that Jane said I needed to calm down as I was making her extremely nervous. When I finally heard footsteps in the foyer and Lucinda's girlish tones exclaiming about something, my relief was palpable.

Mr Hart poked his head around the door, and I stopped midpace and stared at him.

'Ah, ladies, there you are! Apologies for abandoning you. But please do feel free to take a stroll after luncheon to the stream if you wish. It is not far and a delightful scene at present with numerous wildflowers in bloom.'

But there was no way on earth that I was going to leave Lucinda alone with him and his friend again.

'That is quite all right. Lucinda mentioned she wanted to go to the library this afternoon, so Jane and I will accompany her.' *And tell her all about you.* 'There is no need to join us. I am sure you wish to spend time with Mr Smith-Withers without female company for once.'

I glanced surreptitiously at Jane, and she looked approving at my sharp-wittedness.

Mr Hart nodded. 'As you wish. Luncheon will be served shortly.' His gaze snagged on mine, and he smiled.

'May I say how becoming you look today, Mrs Fitzroy! Have you done something different with your hair? Or perhaps you are wearing a new dress?' His impertinent eyes raked me from top to toe, and I was again reminded of the encounter in his study—of my body pressed against his.

'My hair is as it usually is, and my dress is not new. But I thank you for the compliment,' I returned stiffly. But my heart rate increased from the way he continued to gaze approvingly at me, and my nerve endings tingled. Smirking at the colour creeping into my cheeks, he withdrew.

Jane giggled when he had gone. 'I can see what you mean. His attempt at seduction is laughable. How false he is!'

'Quite,' I said weakly. 'Very false indeed.'

I was not looking forward to having luncheon with Mr Hart in attendance, but my stomach had other ideas. Roast chicken, salad, and freshly baked bread were on the menu. So it was rumbling in anticipation. Mr Smith-Withers and Mr Hart were already seated in the dining room, with Lucinda in the middle, when Jane and I came in. We took our usual seats opposite them.

'Hello, Lucy. Did you have a nice walk to the ...' I began as I sat down. But as I did so, there was a slight rustling sound, and I realised something was on my chair. Reaching beneath my dress, I drew out a vibrant posy of pink and purple wildflowers tied with a white ribbon.

'Gracious, this is lovely. Thank you, Lucy,' I said, twirling the posy so I could view it from all angles. 'But you should have handed them to me as I was about to squash them flat!' I laughed and placed the flowers beside my plate and shook out my napkin.

Lucinda looked at the posy, then at me. 'I did not give you the flowers, Aunty Fliss,' she said.

'They are from me, Mrs Fitzroy,' said Mr Hart after a pause. 'You did not accompany us to the stream, so I picked them for you.'

'Oh, er, thank you.' I assumed he had also created a posy for Jane, but when I glanced at her place setting, she did not have one. How awkward!

The food came out then, with both Maurice and Mrs Webber serving, and I concentrated on filling my plate. But I could see Lucinda was staring at the flowers with a tight expression, and my face grew hot with embarrassment. She had obviously not received a posy from Mr Hart either and was upset about it. I almost thrust it at her and said, 'Please have it! I do not want it!' But the posy was not the problem. It was the fact that he had picked the flowers especially for me and had slighted Lucinda deliberately in front of everyone. Oh, I knew what he was doing—he was playing the martyr and showing that he was following my order to leave Lucinda alone. Yet did he have to do it in such a hurtful fashion? I supposed I should not have expected kindness from him!

Indeed, Mr Hart was sucking on chicken bones, stripping them clean, and tossing them onto his plate without a care—no doubt enjoying the emotional havoc he was wreaking at the table. Mr Smith-Withers was just as bad—he rubbed salt in her wound by making a pointed comment on how lucky I was as he had *never* seen Dory give flowers to anyone.

Lucinda picked at her meal with a disgruntled expression and hardly ate anything. I watched her with concern. This was not good. However, I consoled myself with the fact that we were about to tell her everything in the library, which would explain his behaviour. The information about his true character would cause her even more pain, but at least her anger would not be directed at me!

But the flowers had done more damage than I had perceived. When I asked her at the bottom of the stairs about going to the library, she said she would rather read in her room and ran up before I could say anything. Soon, a door closed along the corridor with a muffled, but resounding bang. I could have cried with frustration.

Jane grasped my arm and said softly, 'Perhaps leave her to calm down and let us speak in my room.'

There was nothing else for it. Having Jane on my side was such a relief at least. I was glad I had met her on the stairs when I did and told her what was happening. If she had gone off with the others, Mr Hart may have said something to cause her to be hostile with me as well.

I tossed the offending posy on the bed and flopped down next to it with an exclamation of annoyance. Jane took some folded petticoats out of the dresser drawer.

'Do not let him get under your skin, Flissy,' she said. 'He is playing games to get a reaction.'

'Well, it is working,' I said through gritted teeth. 'Oh, I could strangle him for giving me these damned flowers! Did you see Lucy's face? She was crushed.'

'Yes, she is very sensitive when it comes to him. We will need to tread carefully,' said Jane sagely, packing the petticoats neatly into her carpet bag. 'But we shouldn't leave it too late either.'

'No, we should not,' I said soberly. 'As he could stir her into a jealous rage, and she might try to attack me!'

Unable to bear looking at the flowers a moment longer, I got up, cracked the mullioned window open, and threw the posy out. I felt no guilt about it. No matter how pretty they were, they were not worth holding on to if they caused a rift between Lucinda and myself. Watching the flash of pink and purple tumble into the bushes below, I instantly felt better, as if I was proving to myself that I would not be swayed by him.

I slammed the window shut with a victorious 'Take that!'

'Well done!' Jane crowed. 'We will fortify our battlements, and he shall not breach our defences!'

I spent the rest of the afternoon in Jane's room, writing my letter to Max and the note to Maurice, while she worked on her novel. By the way she was writing furiously, I gathered that at least our circumstances were proving favourable for her creative energy!

When we eventually descended for supper, Jane warned me to be on guard against Mr Hart's emotional tricks and not to let him traverse my moat. She seemed intent on using castle metaphors as if we were in a battle. But I supposed we were, and I should don my armour if I wanted to come out of this unscathed.

Almost at once, I was in the thick of the fray. Mr Hart flirted brazenly during supper in the dining hall, giving me amorous looks and bestowing outrageous compliments that would have made me laugh if Lucinda had not been glowering into her soup. As it was, I had to deflect and ignore his comments until I was exhausted.

Moving to the parlour, I hoped he would leave off, but he had worse stratagems up his sleeve.

'I thought I might read a passage aloud from a book I am enjoying,' he announced, standing by the fireplace.

'Oh yes, do. If it is what I think it is, then it will be very pleasing,' said Mr Smith-Withers, rubbing his hands together.

I assumed that he was going to read something spooky to scare Lucinda witless, but he remarked, 'You should also find it very pleasing, Mrs Fitzroy, since I saw you perusing the volume enthusiastically in the library.' This made me extremely wary. My suspicions were confirmed when he whipped out a book with a black leather cover out of his pocket, and I knew it all too well: *Teaching Molly*.

Blood throbbed in my temple as he flipped slowly through it, looking for a specific passage, humming and harring to make me squirm. *Oh no, please do not let him read the chase scene in Molly's chamber!* I thought, panicking. *Anything but that!*

Finding the place he wanted, Mr Hart cleared his throat theatrically and read, 'After several weeks, he became accustomed to Molly's coy glances when she served him supper. Though no one else at the table noticed anything amiss, it was like a secret game between them. He began to learn too that she gave signals meant only for him. Placing a bread roll on a plate to his left meant that she would be amenable to a visit; to the right meant she was not. As it had been three nights since he had last visited her, he was hoping the bread would be on the left. "Left, left, left," he prayed as she approached. And under the table, he felt himself growing—'

I leapt up from the sofa and ripped the book out of Mr Hart's hands. 'That will be quite enough of that, thank you very much!'

Mr Smith-Withers guffawed, and Mr Hart smirked at me. 'Oh, come now, Mrs Fitzroy. I was just getting to the good part.' He stretched out a hand and wiggled his long fingers. 'Give it back and let me read some more. It is most entertaining.'

'No, I will not,' I replied, hiding the book behind me.

'Why will you not give Mr Hart the book, Aunty Fliss?' asked Lucinda plaintively from the sofa. 'I want to hear what happens next ...'

'It is rather boorish, dearest. Mr Hart has not given any thought to its suitability for his present audience.'

I gave him a chilly smile, and he bowed, his eyes glinting.

'Oh, well. Then maybe Aunt Jane can read to us from her new novel? Since she has it right there in front of her,' said Lucy.

'Miss Austen, writing a novel?' said Mr Smith-Withers. 'Well, I never!'

Lucy clapped her hands. 'Oh yes, she is such a good writer! Mr Smith-Withers, you will find it even more pleasing than Mr Hart's book.'

'I very much doubt that,' I heard him say under his breath, and Mr Hart grinned.

Jane, who had been writing steadily at the table over by the window throughout this exchange, now lifted her head. 'Pardon?'

Chapter 18

With much prompting and coercing from Lucy and me, Jane finally agreed to do a reading. 'The story is by no means complete,' she said, standing by the fire, clutching her pages. 'And this part has been roughly written so it needs severe editing—'

'Yes, yes, we understand. Afterwards, perhaps we can return to *my* book,' interrupted Mr Hart.

He looked across at me, sitting in the armchair. But *Teaching Molly* was well out of sight beneath my derriere and would be following the flowers out the window later on.

Jane cleared her throat and, looking slightly worried, proceeded to read out a scene in which her impressionable main character meets an obnoxious young man. It was subtly disguised hyperbole, but she had obviously borrowed from Mr Hart's propensity for empty flattery and Mr Smith-Withers's tendency to talk himself up. It was brilliantly funny, and I had to bite my lip to stop myself from laughing.

'Well, well,' said Mr Hart, looking surprised and a little disconcerted when she had finished. 'That sounds like it will be a very ... interesting ... novel.'

'Thank you,' said Jane with a nod. 'It is actually a cautionary tale, so young women can avoid forming attachments with unsuitable men.'

Mr Hart exchanged a glance with Mr Smith-Withers, and the two of them said nothing.

Oh, Jane, I thought worriedly. *Why did you have to go and say that? Now they know that you know too!*

I made a show of yawning. 'I think it is time for bed.'

'But it is still early,' Lucinda complained.

But I was decided—the less time she spent in the company of these two unsuitable men, the better. 'Yes, Lucy, please.'

'All right,' she grumbled.

'If the day is fine tomorrow, then we can go raspberry picking,' Mr Hart said to her, and she seemed cheered by that.

We ladies bid the men good night and left them to their port and sordid conversations.

I nudged Jane as we went upstairs.

'Shall we tell her now?' I whispered.

'Maybe it is best to let her get a good night's sleep,' she whispered back.

I nodded mutely in agreement. Keeping silent was preferable than being up all night with Lucinda sobbing her heart out. But how on earth were we going to get her onto the mail coach tomorrow? It was worrying me a lot, especially now that Mr Hart had promised to take her raspberry picking.

I waited until I thought Lucy and Jane were asleep and crept along to their doors and safely locked them in again. But my anxiety about the next day meant sleep eluded me entirely. Not only did I have the godawful painting of Royden Hart in the room, but also *Teaching Molly*. So the room was roiling with bad energy. I wanted to throw the volume out the window, but when it came to it, I could not bring myself. It was a book, after all—even if it was an unsavoury one. However, if I could not rid myself of the book, at least I could do something about the painting—and get my shawl back.

Avoiding looking at Royden Hart, I unhooked it from the wall, fumbling a little as the gilded wooden frame was heavy. With some difficulty, I dragged it over to the door and nudged it out into the passageway. I then shut and locked the door. Instantly, I felt lighter and more at ease from not having him in the room.

Wrapping my shawl around me, I held the candle up to the panel where the painting had hung to make sure I hadn't damaged it. Outlined in the flickering yellow light was a small square measuring about as broad as a hand's width. Intrigued, I inspected it more closely. Was it a repair? If so, it was badly done as there was a small gap around three of the sides. I inserted a fingernail and tugged at it lightly, and it swung open like a flap of skin. Inside the panel was a small knob-like brass lever. Tentatively, I grasped it, but the knob did not yield no matter which direction I yanked it. In frustration, I pushed at it with the heel of my palm forcefully and got a fright when it suddenly sunk in. A light cracking noise around the panel accompanied it; and I discovered, with some experimental tugging, the panel could be opened like a door!

I could not believe my eyes. So this was what Royden Hart had been guarding—a secret passage. Did Mr Hart know about it? Presumably, he did. Thrusting my candle into the space, I saw the passage was dark, but quite dry with a slight downward slope. If I angled my head to accommodate the ceiling, I could probably walk along it quite well. But where on earth did it lead?

Fear and curiosity battled for supremacy, but curiosity won, as it always did with me. We were leaving tomorrow, so I would not get another chance to explore, and I was too inherently nosey to let the opportunity pass. I might discover some kind of evidence I could use against Mr Hart in court, if it ever came to that. Decision made, all I had to do was take the first step ...

I was half expecting the passage to lead nowhere more interesting than the dungeon. But after a short cramped walk, I came upon a wooden door. Turning the handle, I found it wasn't locked and that it opened into a small chamber.

A desk and chair were the only furniture in the room, but it had a lived-in feel. An opulent oriental rug covered the floor, and the chair was wide and slouchy with a footstool. But as the walls were papered with sketches (half-drawn birds in flight, autumn leaves, and bucolic landscapes, in the same style as those in Mr Hart's study), it convinced me without a doubt that I was in his art studio. If I was going to find anything to use as evidence, it would be here in this room.

Eagerly, I set my candle on the desk and started pulling out the desk drawers. But sifting through the papers contained in them turned up nothing but receipts for art materials sent from London. I was busily leafing through a sketch pad when a voice said softly behind my left shoulder, 'Can't sleep, little mouse?'

Swivelling, I saw another doorway had opened without

my noticing, and a shadowy figure was standing in front of it. I almost screamed bloody murder, but then the figure came forward into my circle of candlelight. It was Mr Hart, sans cravat, wearing loose linen trousers and a black silk dressing gown. He did not appear to be wearing a shirt underneath.

'W-where did you c-come from?' I stuttered, my heart thumping in my throat.

He shrugged. 'The library. The door is behind one of the bookshelves. But it seems you are cleverer than most guests, little mouse, as no one has ever discovered the other entrance behind the painting.'

'D-do not call me t-that,' I stuttered, still trying to catch my breath in lieu of the fright he had given me.

'I can call you what I like since I have caught you red-handed going through my private affairs.'

Mr Hart sauntered over, and I slapped the sketchbook shut guiltily. There had been nothing in it but similar drawings to those on the wall anyway. He flopped into the chair beside the desk and propped his legs on the footstool, crossing them at the ankles. The edges of his dressing gown parted, baring a smooth chest ridged with muscle; and I gulped, averting my eyes, and pulled my shawl tighter around me. Thank goodness I had not changed into my nightgown and was still wearing my day dress. Being alone with him like this was improper, but my situation was even more precarious since he was an unscrupulous rake.

'If you want to peruse my drawings, these might be of more interest.' He reached down the side of the chair and tossed a sketch pad on the desk. It landed with a smack, making me jerk backwards. I hesitated, staring at the soft brown vellum cover. The way he was looking at me with a lazy smirk made me reluctant to open it.

'Well, go on, since you're so curious,' he urged. 'I must say, it is quite flattering to have someone take such an interest in my artwork.'

I flipped through the first few pages, which were pencil sketches of Cecilia Spencer sipping tea (she was easily recognisable as he was a good artist—I would give him that much!). Then came one with Cecilia looking over one bare shoulder with a faint smile.

I puffed out my cheeks. The next was drawn from the shoulders up, with her hair loose and fanned out around her head on a pillow. But the expanse of skin made it obvious she was not wearing much. I gulped. Mr Hart was watching me closely as I turned the pages, no doubt wanting me to gasp in prudish horror so he could laugh. I was not going to give him the satisfaction.

He shifted his hips in the chair, causing his dressing

gown to fall open wider and reveal more of his chest. He did not bother to cover himself when he saw me looking.

'What do you think of them?' he asked (as if *my* opinion mattered to him!).

'They are well drawn,' I said slowly. 'Did Miss Spencer agree to model for you?'

He nodded. 'I think she thought I was Vermeer or something, and she'd end up in the National Gallery. Dear Ceci.'

His lips twisted ruefully, and he gestured at the sketch pad. 'Keep going.'

I turned to the next page and nearly gasped aloud. Cecilia was completely naked and lying full length on a settee. The sketch left nothing to the imagination. Her body was drawn in detail, though her expression in this one was unsmiling ... Oh good Lord, I did not want to see any more! Indeed, I wished to now unsee it!

I closed the sketch pad, struggling to keep my composure. 'It seems that you have compromised Miss Spencer's reputation in more ways than one, Mr Hart,' I said evenly. 'Did she ask for these drawings back after you were banned from seeing her?'

'Of course, but I see no harm in keeping them if they are for my eyes only, though they *are* part of my portfolio,' he mused. 'I am thinking of applying for art school, you see. Who knows, she may end up on the wall of the National Gallery for everyone to gawp at after all.' He laughed, a touch cruelly, I thought.

'I should go. It is late,' I muttered, pushing the sketch pad aside and standing up. But Mr Hart shot out of his chair at lightning speed and stood in front of me.

'Not so fast,' he said, and I was forced to step back so that I was pressed against the edge of the desk.

My legs trembled as he inched closer, and fear must have shown in my face as he murmured, 'I will not hurt you— only encourage you to give in to your desire.'

'That will never happen as I do not desire you.' To my dismay, heat crept into my cheeks, belying my words.

He laughed softly. 'Then why are you blushing, Mrs Fitzroy?'

With a finger, he softly traced my cheekbone, and the blood in my veins fizzed. But I could not move as his position prevented me from accessing the door back to my bedroom. Gently lifting my chin, he tilted my face to the candlelight. 'Your bone structure is quite exquisite. Would you like me to paint you? I have been experimenting with oils.'

I shook my head abruptly, making him chuckle.

'We could do a *Girl with a Pearl Earring*-type pose. It

would be fully clothed and so seemly that even your husband would approve. You could hang it in the dining room, and he could look upon my fine work every morning at breakfast.'

They shouldn't have, but his words struck a nerve as I was reminded of my dead mother's portrait.

Tears pricked my eyes, and I turned away, not wanting him to see that he had affected me. But he grasped my jaw and turned my head back towards him so he could look into my watery eyes. I was like a wooden puppet in his hands.

'What is it? What did I say?' he asked, sounding concerned, but I knew it must be a feigned consternation. Why would it be anything else?

'My mother died whilst giving birth to me. Until recently, her portrait hung in the dining room of my family home. My father has since moved it to the parlour. I ... I think he must be trying to forget her.'

Mr Hart's gaze softened. 'If I had known that about your mother, I would not have said it.'

He wiped a brimming tear from the corner of my eye with his thumb. It was a strangely intimate gesture, but I allowed it. If I was pliant, he might relax his attention, and I could scuttle past him to the door.

'How could you have known? You do not know the first

thing about me,' I replied flatly.

'I know that there is an attraction between us that burns as bright as a flame—no, no, do not do that, Felicity,' he said, frowning as I rolled my eyes at his flowery falsehood.

'You would be attracted to a stump of wood if it was wearing a muslin dress,' I said with a sniff.

'That is not true. I actually have very particular tastes ...'

'What? Married women?'

His lips twisted in amusement. 'No, beautiful, smart, funny women.' His warm fingers trailed down my neck, brushing over my pulse point, which was fluttering erratically. He shifted closer, pressing a leg in between mine, and the way he was looking at me was causing goosebumps to stud along my flesh. Though my body was responding to him on one level, I was not stupid. He was relaxing me on purpose, melting my resolve, so he could seduce me.

'Ah, what about your own mother?' I asked to get him off the subject of our mutual attraction (which I was going to deny until my last breath). 'I have never heard you speak of her. Is she locked up somewhere in the castle too? Like your poor father.'

Mr Hart's expression hardened. 'My father is neither poor nor locked up. What do you know of him?'

'I know he is ill and confused, and you have not once been to visit him since we arrived. And I know you are trying to make him sign the castle over to you—not exactly the behaviour of a loving son.'

Mr Hart smiled grimly. 'I see. So you feel sorry for him, do you? Well, I do not. He caused my mother's death, so I can never feel love nor pity for him. I can only despise him.'

I was a bit shocked at that. 'H-he killed your mother?'

'In a way. He never loved her the way she loved him. Oh, he may have held some affection for her at the start, but it didn't stop his womanising ways. He was usually discreet about his affairs, but one night, he foolishly arrived from London with his latest mistress in tow. It was too much for my mother, and she rode off on her horse in despair. A search party was sent out. But it was a wild, stormy night, which made conditions difficult for searching. They eventually found her horse, but not her. She was discovered two days later with a broken neck.'

He said it dispassionately, but I could tell from his eyes there was great pain there. 'Oh, how terrible. How old were you?'

'I was eleven. And my brother, Harrington—or Harry, as he prefers—was thirteen. After that, my father packed us both off to Eton so we weren't around to interfere with his "lifestyle". With a father like that, there was no hope for me. I was destined to follow in his footsteps ... until I met you.'

He leaned in, his lips moist and parted, and I realised he was about to kiss me. If that happened, I knew Max would be lost to me forever.

'No!' I gasped. 'Do not attempt it! I love my husband. I want only him.'

In desperation, I twisted my head at the last minute so his lips bounced harmlessly off my cheek instead.

'Such a doting wife,' Mr Hart murmured, his nose in my hair. 'And such a little liar. You want me too—I know you do.'

He grasped my dress and slowly pushed it up around my thighs. 'If my fingers searched between your legs, I know what they'd find: an ocean of longing.'

'I think not,' I replied tartly, yanking my dress down. 'You would find a dry, sandy beach that was perfectly content.'

Mr Hart laughed. 'That does not sound conducive to having children.'

'I do not want children, and neither does Max.'

He lifted an eyebrow in disbelief, staring at me. 'Is this a religious thing? Are you a married nun?'

I huffed a laugh. 'No! I do not have to explain our relationship to you. Stop it, Mr Hart!' This last was exclaimed as he again tried to pull up my dress, and there was a brief struggle that nearly caused the fabric to rip. Fearing that he would throw me onto the desk and 'teach me' like Molly, there was nothing else I could do but slap him *hard* across the face.

It seemed to bring him out from his lust-driven urge, and he sprang back, clasping his cheek and cursing me. 'Why the devil did you do that?'

'Because you did not stop when I asked you to! Please desist from trying to maul me and give me leave,' I said, adjusting my dress and smoothing my hair, which was in such disarray it was like I had been wrestling in a bush.

Silently, Mr Hart stood to one side, looking sour. But to my relief, he let me collect my candle and pass.

As I did so, I saw the imprint of red fingermarks like warpaint on his left cheek. He had deserved it, but I had never struck anyone in my life before, and I felt ashamed. 'Mr Hart ... Dorian ... I ...'

'Just go, Felicity,' he mumbled.

Not knowing what else to say and feeling tired and drained, I slipped through the door and crept along the passageway back to my bedroom. My smarting hand was a stark reminder of our seedy encounter. The sooner we were all in the mail coach heading to the inn, the better.

***

It seemed but a minute that I was asleep when I was woken by a short sharp cry. I sat up, peering into the darkness, and Jane stirred next to me.

'What was that?' she asked groggily.

I had decided to spend the night locked in her room after the encounter with Mr Hart as I now knew he had access to my room through Royden's panel. After I had turned into Madam Slap, I doubted he would try anything else, but I did not want to take any chances.

'It sounded like Lucinda. Stay there. I will go to her. She probably had a bad dream.'

It took me a few minutes to fetch my shawl and find the keys. Then I was padding to Lucinda's room. Quietly, I unlocked her door at the same time as I knocked, so she didn't hear me turning the key.

'Lucy? Are you all right?' I called softly.

No reply came except for a stifled whimper.

I moved forward cautiously with my hand outstretched. It was so dark in here, and I did not want to stub my toe on one of the solid oak bedposts.

I felt along the edge of the counterpane until I touched her hand. She jerked it away with a gasp.

'It's me, dearest.'

'Oh,' she said, sounding relieved.

As my eyes adjusted to the darkness, I saw she was lying on her back, the covers in disarray, as if she had kicked them off.

'Did you have a bad dream, dearest?'

'I ... I ... Yes, Aunty Fliss.' She sounded disorientated, as if she was still half-asleep. I smoothed back the hair clinging to her sweaty forehead. Whatever she had been dreaming about must have been frightening to make her cry out like that.

'Hush now,' I said soothingly. 'It is all over now. It was just a dream.'

I pulled the covers up and adjusted them neatly around her and sat there holding her hand. She was trembling like a leaf. I dared not enquire what she had been dreaming about because it might cause me to have a nightmare too!

'Aunty Fliss?' she asked waveringly.

'Yes, dearest?'

'I know we still have several days at the castle, but would you mind if we went back to Bath very soon?'

'Of course not. If you wish to go, we can leave forthwith,' I said, trying not to sound overly excited at hearing this. But in truth, her words were music to my ears. 'How does tomorrow morning sound?'

There was the sound of a breath releasing, and she squeezed my hand emphatically.

'Oh, thank you! *Thank you*. And I am sorry that I have been so out of sorts ... I think I must be homesick.'

'You have nothing to apologise for,' I said quickly. 'This castle could honestly make even the best people turn into trolls.'

She huffed a laugh at that, and I waited until she was comfortable and had drifted off back to sleep before I left her. It was only when I lay back down in Jane's bed that it occurred to me that Lucinda's vehement response thanking me to leave the castle was the mirror image of the one she had given when I had said she could stay.

PART FOUR

A Suitable Gentleman

Chapter 19

'Ah, Mrs Fitzroy, are your companions coming down?' enquired Mr Hart, checking his watch when I entered the dining room the next morning. He and Mr Smith-Withers had not waited and were halfway through their breakfasts.

My hand shook as I helped myself to some toast, two fried eggs, and some bacon from the sideboard. I had practically no appetite, but I had to give the appearance of normality.

'I am afraid my niece is under the weather this morning, and Miss Austen is attending to her,' I replied, sitting down.

'Nothing too serious, I hope?' asked Mr Smith-Withers.

'No, no, just a headache. She slept poorly last night.'

Mr Hart said nothing in commiseration, but he was staring at me with an inscrutable expression, and my skin prickled with unease. A faint redness lingered on his left cheek from where I had slapped him. I averted my eyes from his and concentrated on eating.

'Though it is a pity Lucy is not well enough to go raspberry picking,' I remarked after a short while, as if it were troubling me.

'Yes. Well, that can wait,' said Mr Hart disinterestedly.

I swallowed my mouthful of food and forced myself to say with a smile, 'But there is no need to postpone it. She said she is quite happy for me to go in her place.'

Mr Hart lowered his fork. 'You will accompany me?'

I nodded. 'And Mr Smith-Withers too, of course.'

Mr Hart gave his friend a pointed glance, and Mr Smith-Withers said hastily, 'I have no wish to pick raspberries, but I will gladly partake of them with cream at supper. I shall be in the library if anyone wants me.'

'Excellent,' said Mr Hart, looking pleased. He wiped his mouth with a napkin and settled back in his chair, his eyes upon me.

Excellent indeed, I thought. Everything was going to plan.

* * *

As soon as she had awoken, I had told Jane of Lucinda's request to leave the castle. Jane, like me, thought her change of tune rather queer but agreed with me that at least Lucinda would get into the mail coach without making a fuss.

But the more I thought about it, the chance of us making it onto the mail coach without Mr Hart hindering us in some way seemed slim.

'Jane', I said urgently, 'I think we need to be cleverer about this if we want to escape. Mr Hart ... He may try to stop us from leaving.'

'He cannot,' said Jane staunchly. 'We are grown women, for goodness' sake!'

'But we know about his plan to inherit the castle,' I said soberly. 'He might keep us here to stop us from telling anyone, and he may never let us go. Remember, there is a dungeon with thick walls. He and Mr Mr Smith-Withers could tie us up down there, and no one would hear us screaming. And I did not mention it to Max in my letter so he would not know to look for us down there if he came searching.'

Jane looked horrified. 'I did not think of that. Oh, Flissy, what should we do?'

'I am not sure ...' But as soon as I said that, it became all too clear what had to happen, and my heart sank. I was going to have to sacrifice myself to enable Jane and Lucy to get away ...

***

Mr Hart wanted to go on the raspberry-picking excursion immediately after breakfast, but it was too soon for the mail coach. I managed to delay him for another hour by saying I needed to write a letter to Max. He grumbled at that, but I remained firm, and he acquiesced. No doubt my agreeing to go had softened him up to some extent, and as he probably had some plan up his sleeve to try to compromise me, I knew I was going to have to keep my wits about me. With that in mind, I tucked my letter opener into my dress pocket. Having a weapon of some sort made me feel more confident about being alone with him.

Jane and Lucinda were packed and ready to go with their carpet bags and mine too. While Mr Hart and I were raspberry picking, they would hitch a lift on the mail coach when it arrived promptly at eleven o'clock. Maurice had said this was how Mrs Webber had arrived, so I did not think there would be an issue, and I had given Jane some money to pay the driver handsomely for his trouble.

Lucinda stayed quiet, listening to us talk over our plan, and only nodded occasionally. I was somewhat surprised that she did not question why she and Jane were leaving the castle in secrecy. I thought that she would demand to say goodbye to Mr Hart. But she seemed in very dull spirits indeed, and I assumed she was feeling the effects of homesickness.

The next part of the plan was a little more precarious. I had to make Mr Hart believe that Lucinda was still poorly and that Jane was attending to her, but that she would come down for supper. I would pretend to finish my letter in my room, but really, I would wait in readiness for the afternoon mail coach. Before it arrived, I would slip Maurice the explanatory note I had written for him and say that, as I had a letter, I would take it out to the driver myself. Instead of returning to the castle, I would hop into the coach and request the driver to take me with him to the inn. I would be away before Mr Hart had even noticed I was gone.

'I do not like leaving you here with him,' said Jane worriedly when Lucinda had gone back to her room to wait for Jane's signal.

'It is the only way,' I replied. 'You know how he likes to control things. It is too much of a risk to think he would let all of us waltz out of here freely. We have to be smarter.'

She did not look convinced, and I took her hands in mine. 'Do not worry, Jane. We will be eating supper together at the inn tonight and congratulating ourselves at having escaped the clutches of those two men unscathed.'

'And if they come looking for us?'

'I will tell the innkeeper we are being pursued by a couple of rogues and pay him well if he has some burly friends who can protect us in case they decide to call.'

'All right. But if you do not appear at the inn on the afternoon coach, then I am sending those same burly men to the castle to search for you.'

I swallowed nervously, praying that if she did so, I would be in a fit state to rescue. 'I should go. I cannot keep him waiting any longer. Otherwise, he'll get suspicious, and the mail coach is due shortly.'

'Goodbye. Good luck!' We exchanged cheek kisses, and I left her with a strange mix of nervous excitement bubbling inside of me. For I was eager for our plan to work and to defeat Mr Hart and his friend. In my mind, it had become more than a trio of ladies escaping 'a couple of rogues'—it was now a fight of good versus evil.

I exited the castle with Mr Hart, and we made our way down the path to the orchard. He was clutching a wicker basket and was wearing old breeches and a black linen shirt—his berry-picking outfit, I presumed, so he did not stain his good clothing. Maurice had given me one of his aprons to wear over my dress when we stopped off at the kitchen to collect the basket.

The raspberries were down the back of the orchard, a long hedge full of globules of ripe red fruit. Mr Hart was unusually quiet, but when we had been picking the berries for a few minutes with the basket on the ground between us, he said, 'I am surprised that you agreed to be alone with me after last night, Felicity.'

I shrugged nonchalantly as I detached a raspberry from its stalk and placed it carefully in the basket. I was picking as slowly as possible to give Jane and Lucinda enough time to get away.

'Despite what you might think, I am not affected by you,' I said.

'Is that so?'

I glanced over to find Mr Hart watching my shaking hand with amusement. It was worry that was making my fingers shake and squish the raspberries, not being close to him! Taking a deep breath, I wiped crushed berries and juice onto my apron.

'That one was overripe,' I explained. I had to calm down. He was sharp and observant and liable to suspect something if I did not control myself.

'Mmm, those ones are the best,' said Mr Hart, picking off a couple of fat, juicy raspberries and popping one in his mouth. 'Here.' He offered me the other on his outstretched palm like a peace offering.

'Ah, if we eat them, there will be less to put in the basket,' I said, reluctant to take anything from him.

'There are plenty here. Go on, try one—not that you need sweetening up.' His mouth tilted in a smile.

I sighed. 'Very well.'

I was about to take the large raspberry from his palm, but before I could, he was holding it gently against my lips. The fruit was plump and warmed by the sun, and as I bit into it, some juice dribbled down my chin.

'Whoops,' Mr Hart murmured and wiped it away softly with his thumb, which he then licked slowly, watching me.

My belly tightened, and I turned away, annoyed at myself for reacting to him. He smirked to himself, which made me even more annoyed.

Faintly in the distance, I heard wheels crunching on unraked gravel at the front of the castle, and I knew the mail coach had arrived. I *had* to bear Mr Hart's ridiculous flirtations for a bit longer for the sake of the others. But I did not have to stand so close to him to do so. I moved a few paces away and continued picking, ignoring his presence. But this only seemed to encourage him all the more, and by the by, he was standing next to me again.

'I have to say, I am most impressed by you withstanding my advances, Felicity. Most women would have had their wicked way with me by now.'

'I am not most women,' I said coldly. 'And I am married.'

'That is true for the former, but the latter is not usually an obstacle,' he replied in a confident tone as he continued to rapidly pluck raspberries. 'Well, admittedly, it can be somewhat of a *challenge* to persuade married women to cheat on their husbands, and the endless flirtation can be tiresome. But it is so rewarding when they finally give in to me.'

I shuddered, wondering how many women he had seduced and discarded ... how many marriages he had ruined.

'You, for instance, had me intrigued from the start. From the night we first met at the ball ...'

'Oh?' I said, listening with half an ear for the sound of crunching gravel to resume.

'During our dance, you said you were thinking of me as your husband. And I know it was only in jest, but I started thinking, "What if I was? What if she could persuade me to live a better life?"' He huffed a short laugh. 'But I fear there is no hope for me ... unless you can give me some ...'

I had not really been attending to anything Mr Hart was saying as I was too busy listening out for the reassuring crunch of gravel. There! The sound of wheels moving off down the drive finally came to my ears, and I let out a pent-up sigh of relief. Jane and Lucinda had escaped!

'Felicity ...'

Something about the wistful, but urgent tone in Mr Hart's voice made me glance at him.

'Yes, Mr Hart?' I asked. 'Have you finished picking?'

'You have not been listening to me,' he said querulously.

'Ah, my apologies. What were you saying?'

'I have been trying to convey that I have strong feelings for you ...'

My fingers stilled on the raspberry I was about to pick. A bird warbled in the copse of trees somewhere off to the left, and I could feel the heat of the sun broiling the top of my head through my bonnet.

Incredulously, I turned to face him. *'Pardon?'*

Mr Hart spoke quickly, not meeting my eyes. 'It is a strange thing for me to admit, I know, as everything you think of me I am and probably worse. But last night, you handed me a mirror, and I was forced to face the truth. I do not like what I see, Felicity. I am ashamed of how I acted, and I want to try to be a better man for you.'

He took my limp hand from the raspberry bush and kissed my fingers, then pressed it against his smooth cheek.

'What are you thinking?' he asked with a half smile, gazing at me.

'I am thinking you are ludicrous and c-corrupt,' I stuttered.

'I am. For now. But I want to change my ways. Did you not hear what I said?'

Carefully, I extracted my hand from his, not wanting to

startle him. He was clearly insane. 'Mr Hart, if I am not mistaken, you were telling me about how rewarding it is to seduce married women. In your next breath, you profess to have strong feelings for me ...' I shook my head. 'Forgive me if I am a little confused.'

He smiled at my expression of bewilderment. 'Does not night turn into day? Can not a rake be changed by love?'

I shook my head. 'No, you have no clue about what it means to love someone.'

'You think I am not capable of love?'

'Passion maybe, but not love.'

Mr Hart's face fell, and his expression turned mournful. 'Then who have I been dreaming of at night, and who have I been aching for?'

He stroked my cheek. 'What is love but the joining of two souls? *Our* souls, Felicity.'

'No!' I gasped. 'Please do not say that. I don't believe you.'

Thoughts whirled through my brain. *This cannot be happening. He is trying to trick me. He does not love me. Oh dear, this was not a good plan to use myself as a decoy!*

I attempted to bring some semblance of reason to his assertions, which were starting to sound too serious for my liking.

'Sir, I am flattered by your attention, but the fact remains that I love my husband and am married to him. If we are speaking of souls, then mine is joined to his, and I do not want to be parted from him.'

'I can give you something different—something deeper ... something more thrilling. You know I can ...' He took my hand again and stroked my fingers.

I gave a scornful laugh despite my body lighting up at his touch. What he was saying was completely absurd! 'What you are suggesting would be certain ruin for me, to be connected to a man such as yourself. Have you thought about that?'

He shrugged. 'It is true I am low on funds. But if it is money and your reputation you are worried about, then Smithy is an excellent lawyer. I am sure he could arrange a generous settlement with your husband to keep things quiet.'

I wrenched my hand away from his. 'So this is the truth of it. You want me for my money? What you can get out of a liaison with me?'

'No, it is not about the money. But we will need something to live on and for repairs.' He gestured at the castle. 'Think of it. Once I inherit, you would be the mistress of Hartmoor. We could restore it together.'

'But that is a deception at the expense of your father and your brother.'

'Harry's inheritance is a mere technicality because he is two years older than me. He does not care about Hartmoor like I do. After Mother died, he had no wish to have anything to do with it. As far as he is concerned, it can rot. I do not want that to happen—it is my home.'

He sounded so sincere that I was inclined to believe him. His reaction when I had criticised his sketch of Hartmoor— his vision of how he wanted *his home* to look—had been passionate. Perhaps he had felt that I was saying *he* was flawed when he had wanted me to like him.

I was so confused that I did not know what to believe about Mr Hart. Was he good? Was he bad? All I knew was that I had to make it to the inn—because if I didn't, my life could take a very different turn.

Chapter 20

After the raspberry-picking excursion, I told Mr Hart that I wanted to be alone to think about what he had said. But before going to my room and locking the door, I double-checked Jane's and Lucinda's to ensure they really had gone. All was in order, and they were not in sight. At least that part of the plan had gone smoothly!

Shaken by Mr Hart's revelation, I flopped onto my bed and lay there, going over everything he had said and our conversation as we had walked back to the castle with the brimming basket of raspberries between us. He had wanted me to call him Dorian and not Mr Hart. I had refused.

'You did so last night,' he pouted.

'It was only because I felt sorry for you. I will not make the same mistake again,' I said firmly.

He tried to kiss my hand, but I had pulled mine away. 'Do you ever give up?' I said, half laughing because he was being so insistently ridiculous.

'Not when I find something I want,' he replied, giving me a cocky grin that made my hackles rise.

'You want me only because I'm a challenge,' I retorted.

'I want you because you beat me into submission—and I like that very much,' he added, his voice lowering huskily.

He had an answer for everything and was determined to flirt, so I had thought it was wise to say nothing else to provoke him and come straight to my room. All I had to do now was wait for the afternoon mail coach ... and resist the advances of a devilishly handsome rake ...

A faint click roused me; and I sat up, rubbing my eyes sleepily, then realised with dismay *that I had fallen asleep*! Fortunately, I had dropped off for only a moment as I was so tired after last night's events.

Blast, I thought. *I was supposed to inform Mr Hart that Lucinda was still poorly and that Jane was writing her novel but would be down for supper too.* What was the point of making a plan if I could not remember to action each of the stages?

It was strange that Mr Hart had left me alone and not come pestering me with further flowery declarations of his feelings. I had half been expecting a hastily written love poem shoved under the door à la Mr Humbleton. But unlike my cousin's poor attempts at flattery, a poem from Mr Hart would likely be much more persuasive and possibly even risqué, so I did not want to receive one. Still, there was no harm in checking ...

I got up and wandered over to the door and stooped down to have a look underneath. There was no paper sticking out. Oh well. Thinking I should probably check the time on the grandfather clock on the landing, I grasped the door handle and turned it. However, the door would not open. I pulled harder in case it was stuck, but it would not budge. It took me several tries of uselessly yanking before I had to face facts: Mr Hart had taken the key and locked me in from the other side.

I banged on the door loudly with my fist. 'Mr Hart!' I shouted. 'Are you there? Let me out at once!'

'It is very rude for guests to leave without saying goodbye,' a voice drawled from behind the door.

I fell silent, unsure of what to say to that.

'Especially since I have been an exemplary host, providing accommodation, food and drink, et cetera.'

'Are ... are you angry?' I ventured.

'Fuming,' came the reply.

'Ah ... So you will not let me out?'

There was a pause.

'No, you have vexed me exceedingly. So you can stay in there and think about what you've done.'

There was an undertone of amusement in his voice, so I could not tell if he was joking or not.

Panicking, I yanked on the doorknob fruitlessly.

'Mr Hart, this is not funny!'

'And I am not laughing, Felicity. I am severely insulted, and I am going to need to think of a suitable punishment for you.'

'P-punishment?'

'Yes, I have not decided exactly what yet. But rest assured, whatever it is, you will enjoy it. We will probably be up all night. So if I were you, I would have another nap.'

There was definitely amusement in his tone now. He was enjoying this immensely. I could imagine him grinning away to himself.

'Meanwhile, I am going for a ride to clear my head. Do not bother trying to escape through the secret passage that leads to the library. I've put Smithy on guard. And the ivy outside the window won't hold your weight, so I would not attempt climbing down that if I were you.'

'So much for saying you care for me!' I exclaimed. 'I knew it was all just hot air. Love is not locking someone in a room!'

'There are many different forms of love, and I am teaching you mine,' came the reply. 'You need to learn that people have feelings. Did you not think I would be hurt when I discovered your ruse for Miss Austen and Miss Fitzroy to leave behind my back?'

'I ... I am sorry. But it was not personal,' I said, trying to appeal to his common sense, if he had any. 'Lucy wished to leave forthwith, so Jane had to go with her.'

'Oh, did she now? Well, no matter. It is actually better this way. We can do what we like now. Smithy doesn't care, and Father, well ... Even if he finds out, he'll forget about it. And Maurice is discreet, of course—he has had to be over the years.' He laughed softly, and the sound chilled my bones. 'Until later, my love.' There was the sound of a kiss being blown and then footsteps heading down the hallway.

'Mr Hart! *Dorian!*' I pounded frantically on the door, but there was no reply.

I went back over to the bed and sat down dully. Part of me was in denial that this was happening. The other part was extremely aware that I was in real danger of being compromised. And I did not want to be a ruined woman, let alone the mistress of a castle that was full of secrets and lies!

Yes, my life with Max was a little staid, but his love was steady and true—a love that I could trust to last the distance. I loved him too much to ever want to be without him; and I wanted to go home and resume being his wife, his Fliss, without my reputation being sullied.

Determination rose in me. I was not going to let Mr Hart win—not without putting up a fight at least.

* * *

It was well into the afternoon before I heard the key turn in the lock and footsteps enter my room. Curled up on my side, facing the wall with my eyes shut tight, I was feigning sleep. But every muscle was poised and ready.

'Felicity.' There was a light tap on my shoulder. I did not stir. Then my shoulder was grasped and squeezed.

I faked a yawn and rolled over to find Mr Hart sitting on the side of the bed, cheeks flushed from riding and his dark hair dishevelled. His shirt was unbuttoned at the neck, and a light sweat bathed his chest. It was the same rugged look I had noted when we stopped on the road to Hartmoor. It was only a few days ago, but it felt like months. Little did I know at the time that our acquaintance would descend into this.

My eyes flicked to his hands. He was holding a tray laden with a plate of cheese sandwiches; a bowl of raspberries; and a small jug of cream.

'What is this?'

'A picnic, dearest,' he said, placing the tray on the bed.

'How romantic,' I said witheringly, and he inclined his head.

'Indeed, and what I have planned for you afterwards is even more so ...' he replied with a smug smirk, which made my toes curl in alarm.

Carefully, I sat up and gave the door a quick glance. It was slightly ajar, as if he had given it a half-hearted kick with his boot, and it hadn't quite shut properly. *Should I try to make a run for it?* But he was quick, and I doubted I could make it without him catching me, so I picked up one of the sandwiches with a shaky hand. 'How was your ride?' I asked conversationally and took a bite.

'Very pleasant, my love,' he replied jovially, picking up the other sandwich. 'I took the path that runs around the perimeter of the castle and which leads to the stream. If you like, we can go for a ride tomorrow. There is room enough on my horse, as I think I told you once before. If I remember correctly, we had stopped on the roadside when we were travelling to Hartmoor.'

I almost choked on my mouthful of sandwich. How odd that he had been thinking of that encounter then too, like he had read my mind.

'If I had known then what my host was really like, I would not have stepped back into the carriage,' I replied, unable to resist a barb.

'Ouch,' he said with a mock flinch. 'I was hoping that when I returned, I would find you more amiable. But I see you are still determined to vex me. Very well then.'

He finished his sandwich, brushed the crumbs off his breeches, and picked up the jug of cream. Without warning, he reached across and poured it liberally over my décolletage.

I gasped as the icy cream soaked my cleavage and dripped coldly down my ribcage within the confines of my bodice.

'W-what are you doing?'

But he simply smiled and pushed me back on the pillow and proceeded to lap at my creamy bosom with relish. I struggled to get up, but he had me pinned with those strong arms of his—how strong they were, I was now finding out. I kicked my legs in desperation. 'Stop it!'

But he laughed at my puny efforts. 'Stop? Oh no, I am just getting started.'

He grabbed a handful of raspberries out of the bowl and tucked them one by one into the top of my dress. Then more cream was poured over and, to my shock, he sunk his teeth into the ripe raspberries with a growl. It was a new dress too, pale-green silk with tiny yellow embroidered flowers around the neckline. Max had greatly admired it when I first wore it. But Mr Hart was ruining the flowers entirely with his brutish behaviour. My blood was starting to boil.

'Mmm, raspberries, cream, and a pert bosom—I think this might be my new favourite dessert,' he said, raising his head and licking his lips; his mouth and chin were smeared with raspberry juice. 'But I am being rude. I have not offered you some.'

'I do not want any!'

'Ah, but I see the problem,' he said, continuing as if I had not spoken. He stared at the fruity mess he'd made on my neckline. 'Perhaps you would feel more comfortable if you removed your dirty dress. Then we could really have some fun.' His eyes danced with mischief.

'No, I think not. I am quite comfortable as I am.'

'Come now, Felicity. You are not so prim and proper as you make out ... Didn't you say you are "well versed" in the bedroom?'

I pursed my lips, and he chuckled. 'So stubborn. I do love your fiery nature. Well, if you will not remove your dress, I will gladly do it for you.'

He placed his hands on either side of my shoulders so he was bracketing me, then lowered his head and tugged at the neckline of my dress with his teeth. *Oh Lord!*

'I ... I thought you were going to change your ways. Be a better man for me ...' I tried to buy myself some time by reasoning with him. But from the guttural sounds he was making in his throat as he twisted his head this way and that like a savage dog, he did not seem to be in a fit state to reason with.

My heart knocked against my ribcage as the material started to slowly rip down the middle, exposing my chemise.

With a delighted grunt, he pawed at it eagerly with one hand to expose my breasts. But he was so intent on the prize that he did not notice he had left himself vulnerable, and I was sliding my hand into my pocket.

I brought the letter opener slowly up to Mr Hart's throat and pressed it in firmly.

'Stop that *right now*!' I hissed.

The pawing ceased the moment the cold sharp tip jutted against his skin. I felt him swallow, but he did not move, and his hot breath washed in slow waves against my bosom.

'Let me go *or else*.' I agitated the letter opener against his jugular, and he laughed, but nervously.

'You would not.'

'Try me,' I said through gritted teeth. 'I grew up in the country, and I have spent enough time at the Austens' to know exactly how they cull their pigs. Plus I have enough rage right now not to care what happens to you.'

I dug the letter opener in harder, and he flinched.

'All right, all right,' Mr Hart said hastily. 'I will stop.' He withdrew slowly to the end of the bed and crouched there like a gargoyle.

But when he saw what I was holding in my hand, he burst into laughter. 'My god, I thought you had a knife! "Killed by a letter opener", that would have been even better than Royden's demise!'

I said nothing but kept brandishing it in front of me so he knew I meant business.

But Mr Hart looked entertained rather than scared. 'If I really wanted to, I could knock that paltry weapon out of your hand and take you here and now. But I do admire your spirit.' He wiped his mouth thoughtfully with his sleeve and smiled at me disarmingly.

I kept the letter opener aloft, my heart thumping in my chest. I knew that look. Whatever he was planning next, I had to keep my wits about me as he was a fast mover. But his next words were something altogether surprising.

'As you are feeling so playful, Felicity, and since I am a generous host, I will make you a deal,' he said. 'You have ten minutes to try to escape the castle, and then I am coming after you. If you manage to get out, I will let you go. However, if I catch you, you agree to be mine and submit willingly to whatever I wish to do to you.'

What other choice did I have? I was in a precarious situation, and at least he was giving me some chance of escape.

'Deal,' I said. Swiftly, I leapt off the bed and was out the door before he had time to react.

'Run fast, little mouse!' he called out laughingly after me.

Chapter 21

Sprinting down the stairs, I had a sinking feeling that Mr Hart had engineered it so it would be impossible for me to escape. Sure enough, the main door in the foyer was locked tightly, and there was no key. My plan to greet the mail coach with my letter was foiled from the start, even if I had not fallen asleep.

There was nothing for it but to try the back entrance while I still had time. I raced into the kitchen, ignoring Mrs Webber at the sink, and down the stone hallway. The back door was missing its giant iron key too, and I already knew it was locked before I tried the handle and discovered that it was. Mr Hart had been toying with me for his own amusement. He knew there was no escape, but he thought it would be fun to see me try.

A wave of panic washed over me, and I fought back a sob. My peaceful, uneventful life in Derbyshire—where I was safe and had a husband who truly loved me—had never looked so good as it did at that moment.

Feeling hysteria threatening, I ran back to the foyer and looked around wildly. I was about to enter the parlour and attempt to squeeze through one of the small windows when I saw Mr Hart slowly descending the stairs, taking his time.

He paused on the bottom step and leaned against the banister with an amused expression. 'Looking for these, little mouse?' He dangled two iron keys from his finger, looking pleased with himself.

Grabbing a nearby antique vase from a table, I hefted it at him. It hit the banister and exploded into shards of china, causing him to jerk back in shock. 'Do not call me that!' I yelled.

I did not wait around to see if blood had been drawn but raced off to the kitchen. Mrs Webber, now chopping a cucumber swiftly on the bench, glanced up, startled. 'Mrs Fitzroy, I thought I saw you running off just now. Can I help you?'

'Where is Maurice?' I whisper-gasped.

She gestured with her chin to the dungeon. 'Down there, collecting potatoes.'

Her eyes dropped to the juice-stained ruined neckline of my dress and drove back up again to rest on my untamed hair. But I had neither the time nor inclination to explain my appearance.

'Please do not tell Mr Hart where I am,' I begged. I needed to tell Maurice what was happening and to enquire if he had a spare key.

She nodded and, to my surprise, crossed the kitchen and opened the small window above the sink.

'I'll tell him you went through there,' she said, tapping her nose. I doubted he would believe I could squeeze through it but it might buy me some time.

'Thank you,' I said gratefully and slipped through the dungeon door and padded softly down the steps into the musty space.

Maurice was stooped over a tray of potatoes, picking out the good ones and dropping the rotten into a wooden bucket by the light of a lantern. The scene was medieval, and I felt like I had been transported back three hundred years.

He looked up and started when I emerged out of the darkness, my boots rustling the strewn straw.

'Maurice, please help me,' I said in a low voice. 'Jane and Lucinda have taken the mail coach to the inn, but Mr Hart ... H-he is keeping me here against my will. I tried to get out, but he has locked both doors and taken the keys.'

Maurice's kind brown eyes widened in the lamplight, taking in my disorderly appearance.

Alarm flickered across his face, but then his jaw tightened. 'I thought he had stopped all that ...' he murmured despondently.

'I assure you he has not,' I whispered. 'He is behaving

most wickedly with me ... and with his father.'

Maurice looked bewildered. 'With his father?' he echoed.

I glanced behind, fearing that Mr Hart had descended quietly without my knowledge and was even now reaching out to grab me.

'I do not have time to go into detail. But he is planning to steal the castle off his brother and marry any woman with a big-enough dowry to keep him in the lifestyle he is accustomed to and then ruin her. I found out about his plan, and now he is trying to ruin me too.'

Maurice looked suitably shocked. 'Master Dorian has always had a wayward streak, but I did not expect this of him. His father's mental state is steadily getting worse. I have been trying to set him straight about which brother is which. But that lawyer, Mr Smith-Withers, keeps visiting him too. He must be trying to undo my work ... Oh, I cannot believe Master Dorian would do this to his own father!'

'Shh. Yes, I am afraid he is. He is trying to get him to sign a new will ... But back to my problem, which is quite pressing. Do you happen to have a spare key?' I was starting to feel like I was running out time.

Maurice shook his head, and I almost groaned aloud. I was doomed!

'But there is another way ...'

He took the lantern and shuffled over to a rectangle of stone in the wall that had one of the prisoners' brass rings in it. He twisted the ring, then tugged on it sharply. There was a soft grating noise, and stone pulled out and swung open on some kind of hinge to reveal a narrow gaping space behind it.

'You can climb in here.' The opening was barely big enough to fit my head and shoulders, and I gulped at the thought of being shut up in the walls and no one ever finding me.

'I ... I do not want to die alone in a hole,' I said fearfully. How had my life been reduced to this? Being ravaged or dying in a hole!

'It is not a hole,' said Maurice. 'It starts off like that, but it widens out into a tunnel, which runs between the castle and the inn.'

'Are you sure?'

Maurice nodded. 'Apparently it does. The innkeeper told me about it one day when he and I were having an ale. He said his great-great-grandfather built it to rescue some prisoners. I came back here and immediately tested it out, and lo and behold.'

'B-but this was not on Mr Hart's tour.'

'No, his family does not seem to know about it. And I was sworn to secrecy, so I have never told anyone. I assume the innkeeper was telling the truth, even though he'd had quite a lot of ale by that stage. Yet why would he make up a story like that?'

We stared at the hole together in silence.

'So you have not been in there?' I asked.

'No, I cannot with my back.' He lifted one of his lopsided shoulders helplessly. 'Otherwise, I would go with you.'

There was a creaking noise at the top of the stairs as the door opened, and I stiffened in horror. 'Oh, Felicityyyy!' Mr Hart's voice sing-songed. 'Are you down there?'

Oh no!

'Go, quickly now,' urged Maurice in a low voice. 'I will say I am collecting potatoes for supper and have not seen you.'

All my fears of being walled up in the castle paled in comparison to being caught by Mr Hart. Frantically, I inserted myself into the hole feet first and wriggled down until only my head remained. But at the last minute, I remembered my note to Maurice.

I drew it out of my pocket and thrust it silently at him.

'Godspeed, Mrs Fitzroy,' he whispered, taking it from my hand. But before I could say 'Thank you so much. How can I ever repay you?' and 'Which way exactly is the inn?' Maurice had swung the stone back into place, and I was left in total darkness, surrounded on all sides by thick stone. My fate now rested upon a drunken innkeeper telling the truth!

After listening for a few moments and hearing nothing but my own breathing, I felt behind me with my toes, and there was only empty space beyond. So I inched slowly backwards using my forearms to support me. This seemed to go forever, and I gathered that I was making my way underneath the walls of the castle. But there was not much space, and I grew hot, and it was hard to breathe, making me wonder if I was going to run out of air.

Just when I thought I could not bear it a moment longer, my feet and ankles left solid ground and poked out into the open. Gingerly, I wriggled back still further, unsure of what was beneath me and how far down it went. It could be some kind of pit. Eventually, my legs were hanging down at a right angle from my waist. I felt about with my toes, but they were dangling in mid-air. There was nothing for it—I was going to have to jump and trust that there was solid ground to catch me and that I did not break an ankle when I landed.

Of course, this was easier said than done, and I spent quite a long time talking myself into doing it. But I had no other choice—it was either that or stay here and die. Cursing Mr Hart with all my might, I pushed off from the ledge with a scream and fell on my backside in a heap a little way below, my elbows stinging from being rubbed raw. But the pain was nothing. The innkeeper had been telling the truth!

Eagerly scrambling to my feet, I felt all around in the pitch blackness, my fingers touching rough stone walls on either side. It seemed to be a narrow passage about the same size as the one that led from my bedroom to Mr Hart's art studio. I did not think about the direction I was going but stumbled along it, keeping one hand on the wall for reassurance. The passage twisted and turned. At one point, it went down for so long that I felt like I was heading into the bowels of the earth, and I almost lost the will to live. Icy water dripped onto my head and down the back of my neck, and I realised I must be under the famous stream that Mr Hart was always rattling on about. This gave me some hope that I was heading in the right direction, though I had no reason to believe I was!

After stopping for a rest and wiping some of the refreshing icy drips over my hot face, I continued on. Soon after that, to my relief, the passage started sloping upwards—indeed so much upwards that I was forced to scrabble at the stones in front of me for purchase, then ripped my nails and wailed like an undead creature from the pain!

The only things that kept me going were my burning

hatred of Mr Hart for putting me in this position (the smell of stale cream wafting up from my dress was a stark reminder!) and desperation to see my darling Max again.

I was relentlessly forcing myself upward when my head cracked against a wooden ceiling, and the pain jolted me out of my dry-mouthed stupor. There was nowhere else to go. This was the end of the passage. Feeling the smooth texture of the wood above, I assumed I must be now under the inn. But how would I get out? Maurice had been vague on the details.

'Help!' I croaked. 'Let me out!'

Fearing that I was now going to be trapped under the floorboards, a new surge of energy rushed through me. I screamed at the top of my lungs and banged with my fists like a madwoman.

Suddenly, the ceiling split above my head and became a trapdoor. There were exclamations and hands grasping at me and voices saying urgently 'Get her out!' I looked up to see Jane and Lucinda peering down at me with expressions of amazement. As I was pulled up out of the hole into the light and warmth, and into their arms, I sobbed with relief.

'You do not need to send the burly men to search for me, Jane. I am here! I am well! I am safe!' I cried. Then I fainted clean away from sheer exhaustion and knew no more.

Chapter 22

After I woke up from my fainting episode in Jane's room and had my face and hands carefully washed by Lucinda, I was extremely tired, so they said I should sleep. When I woke again in the early evening, Jane brought me a dish of hot stew. She said she had spoken to the innkeeper, and he had kindly arranged for a carriage to pick us up at noon the next day. We needed to return to Bath forthwith in case Mr Hart and Mr Smith-Withers came looking for us, and in any case, we were all eager to leave.

It was only when we were in the carriage and safely on the road that I told them exactly what had happened and how Maurice had helped me escape. And I explained more fully to Lucinda about Mr Hart's diabolical plan to marry her for her money. The information did not at first seem to register. But then after several minutes of silence, she turned away from us and pressed her forehead to the window, tears rolling down her cheeks.

Jane bit her lip and whispered to me, 'What should we do?'

'We must comfort her as best we can,' I whispered back.

'She is in shock and rightly so.'

Thankfully, there were no hold-ups on the road (and we required no comfort stops). So a few hours later, we were on the outskirts of Bath.

Lucinda had not spoken for the majority of the journey but sat pale and withdrawn, her eyes closed and hands clasped tightly in her lap. What she was thinking, I could not begin to guess. *She will recover in time*, I thought. *It could have been so much worse.*

I was still reconciling with how close I came to being ruined by Mr Hart myself—it did not bear thinking about. But at least I had managed to extricate my niece (and myself!) from his clutches. Now all that remained was to count our blessings that he was out of our lives.

* * *

Elizabeth was overjoyed we had come back early as she had exhausted the social circuit and said she had 'found no company worth having' apart from her own and Edward's.

Of course, she wished to hear all about our trip to Hartmoor—the events of which we had to downplay quite considerably, especially our abrupt leave-taking from the castle. Besides that, my fingers were injured and my nails ripped to shreds—I had to wear gloves indoors and say I had chilblains!

Lucinda was still reticent, so at least I did not have to worry about her saying anything. Elizabeth put her silence down to feeling Mr Hart's absence acutely and kept reassuring her that he would write and call soonest to resume their acquaintance and perhaps even propose! This caused the blood to drain from Lucinda's already-pale face and her hands to shake. It was hindering her recovery, so I had to put a stop to it. I took Elizabeth aside to have a private word in her bedroom.

'I know you are only trying to reassure Lucy. But please, I beg of you, do not speak to her any more about Mr Hart proposing. There will be nothing of the sort taking place.'

Elizabeth's forehead wrinkled in concern. 'Oh no, what has happened? Has there been a falling-out between them?'

'He made it clear that he has set his sights on another. Lucy has taken it rather badly ...'

Elizabeth murmured her condolences for Lucinda's sake, then patted my hand excitedly. 'Do not tell me, for I have already guessed, and my feelings are always right on these matters. It is Jane who Mr Hart has set his sights on. I could detect an affinity between them as they both enjoy writing ... and she so admired his art ...'

I shifted uncomfortably at this line of thinking. *Blast, I had to put her straight before she started telling Jane's family to expect an engagement!*

'It is not Jane he is interested in. It is me,' I said bluntly.

Elizabeth's mouth fell open. 'Oh dear!'

'Yes, and it has been most uncomfortable and the main reason we left the castle early,' I said somewhat irritably. The wounds on my fingers were starting to scab over and itching unbearably in my gloves. I longed to scratch at them but could not as I wanted them to heal by the time I returned home. 'So if you could please not mention his name again, I would be grateful as we all wish to forget about him,' I continued.

'Yes, of course,' Elizabeth said hurriedly. 'Oh, you poor thing! How awkward. And it goes without saying that your husband must never know of his sordid affection. You can trust me. I will be as silent as the grave and not tell a soul, not even Edward.' She twisted her fingers by the side of her mouth to resemble a key turning in a lock.

'Thank you,' I said, hoping that I could trust her. Her nature did incline towards gossip after all.

But telling Elizabeth had the advantage of her understanding why we wished to lie low for the last week of our stay and not visit the pump room or partake in any other social events. Every time Edward queried if we wished to go out or suggested we go to the theatre, Elizabeth neatly circumvented it by saying it was much nicer to stay in and all be together.

She would also sit next to Lucinda and occupy her with some idle chat or encourage her to do some plain embroidery, which, to my relief, did seem to help distract her from her woes. Towards the end of the week, she even giggled at an amusing incident Elizabeth told us about one of her children. Upon hearing that, Jane and I exchanged rather tearful glances. *Thank goodness, our girl was on the mend!*

***

The afternoon before we were due to leave, I was packed and all ready to go. I had received a letter from Max yesterday morning, and what he had written was so funny and endearing and full of expectation at seeing me again that I could hardly sit still. I wished to be in a carriage and heading towards Derbyshire this instant!

To that effect, I was not breaking my journey in Steventon but catching a public stagecoach north without delay. However, a short letter from Harriet had arrived in the afternoon. She said she had arrived at Ashbury, apologised profusely for the lateness of her reply and gracious was something happening with Papa and Aunt! She would keep her eyes peeled!

It had been so long ago that I had written to her about Papa and Aunt, and so much else had happened meanwhile, that my concerns about them now seemed laughable. Why should they not be together if they wished? Life was too short not to be with the person you loved and they had both been widowed at a young age.

Harriet finished her letter saying she was very much looking forward to seeing me, and as I had a strong desire to see her too, it could not be helped; my reunion with my husband would have to be delayed.

So I had spent this morning writing to Max, informing him that I would be travelling to Steventon with Jane and then staying at Ashbury for two weeks and how torn I was at wanting to see Harriet but also yearning to see him too. But once that was done, there was nothing else to do but sit in the drawing room with Jane and Lucinda and feel a bit bored and sorry for myself.

Elizabeth and Edward had gone to the pump room after lunch, but I had declined Edward's invitation to accompany them. Elizabeth had given me a knowing look and whispered, 'I shall report back if I see or hear anything.'

I was reduced to plucking lint from the cushion buttons while the other two read when Mrs Bromley entered the room and announced that a Mr Hart was at the door and wished to call on us.

Lucinda's head whipped up from her book at his name, and she seemed to shrink into herself. A slow horror crept over me, and I was instantly back in the dungeon, hearing his voice sing-songing down the stairs. 'Oh, Felicityyyy ...'

Jane, seeing that Lucinda and I looked on the verge of fainting, spoke firmly to the housekeeper. 'We do not wish to receive him. Please tell him we have gone out.'

Mrs Bromley raised her eyebrows but said, 'Very well, Miss Austen.' Then she went off to convey the message.

'Shall I creep to the window and see if he goes away?' asked Jane.

'No, do not,' I said nervously. 'He may catch sight of you and try to force his way in. He is obviously back in Bath. But what gall that man has to call on us! Thank goodness we are leaving tomorrow.'

I glanced at Lucinda, but she had hidden her face behind her book. Mrs Bromley reappeared, I assumed to tell us that Mr Hart had left. However, she had a different message.

'The gentleman says that if by any chance I was mistaken and that you *were* in to tell you that his name is Harrington, and he is the brother of the other Mr Hart.'

'Oh!' said Jane, then looked at me enquiringly. I, in turn, looked at Lucinda.

'Lucy? Are you all right with us receiving his brother?' I asked her.

She shrugged her shoulders, so I nodded at Jane, thinking, *This should be interesting.*

'Please tell him that you have searched more thoroughly, and we are in fact in and will receive him,' said Jane.

The corner of Mrs Bromley's mouth quirked. 'Very well, Miss Austen,' she repeated, and I imagined her rolling her eyes as she left the room.

We waited in some anticipation, and she showed a tall dark-haired man into the drawing room. Immediately, I saw the resemblance. Harrington was handsome, but not as much as his brother. He had thinner hair, a longer nose, and a stouter middle, as if he enjoyed a pint of ale or three. Nor was he as confident. He bowed to us awkwardly after Jane had made the introductions, and when he was seated, he seemed ill at ease in our company.

'Please do forgive my intrusion. But I received a letter from my butler of late, outlining certain serious events that have taken place at my home, Hartmoor Castle,' he said with a grave expression.

'And how did you come to connect us with these "serious events", sir?' asked Jane.

'When I arrived from London to ... rectify matters, my butler told me your names, Miss Austen, and that your party was staying in lodgings in Bath. It was not too difficult to discover your whereabouts ... After organising my affairs, I came straightaway to apologise profusely for any grievous harm that my brother, Dorian, may have caused you and your friends.'

He glanced at Lucinda, who, at the mention of Hartmoor Castle, had withdrawn behind her book again so her face could not be glimpsed.

'Can you tell us where you normally reside and what you do for a living, Mr Hart?' asked Jane smoothly, neither confirming nor denying that his brother had caused us grievous harm but attempting to find out more information before we trusted him.

'In London,' he said. 'I am an accountant.' He sounded faintly apologetic, as if we would throw him out for having a profession.

'Ah, I do some bookkeeping for my father, and it always pleases me when the figures balance,' said Jane.

Mr Hart smiled, his eyes crinkling. 'It is rather pleasing, isn't it?' Before they could launch into a discussion about taxes, I spoke up.

'So Maurice told you about your brother's plan to inherit Hartmoor?'

Mr Hart nodded soberly. 'Indeed. But I have since removed Father and Maurice to my lodgings in London, where they will be safe from Dorian and his friend. My footman is under strict instructions not to permit them entry. You may think my action extreme, but owing to my past history with my brother, I have deemed it wise to do so.'

'I think you had better tell us the whole story,' said Jane, her eyes shining with interest. 'Shall I ring for tea?'

Ooh, be careful, Mr Harrington Hart, I thought. *If you do not watch out, you may find yourself in a novel!*

Between sips from his cup of tea, Mr Hart relayed how he had journeyed from London to Hartmoor as soon as he had received Maurice's letter about his father.

'It was a shock to me as I have not had contact with Dorian for a couple of years, not since the business with my fiancée when I resolved to cut ties with him.'

A flash of pain crossed his features, and he stared into his teacup, lost in thought.

'Your fiancée, Mr Hart?' prompted Jane.

I frowned at her. 'You do not have to tell us if you do not want to,' I told him.

'But you will find us sympathetic listeners if you do, and sometimes it can help to unburden yourself,' countered Jane, raising her eyebrows at me. 'Please, do help yourself to another biscuit.'

'Thank you.' Mr Hart took a biscuit from the plate and dunked it into his teacup. 'These are rather good.'

Suitably groomed by Jane to tell his story, he proceeded stiltedly, as if reciting a list of facts to a courtroom. Apparently, he had met a certain young lady called Rose Bishop at a ball in London. He had begun courting her. Soon, their relationship progressed to the point where he proposed, and Rose accepted.

'I loved her,' he said, and he spoke the words so emphatically that I had no doubt that he was sincere. 'I suppose we were opposites as I tend towards seriousness, and Rose was vivacious. But she said that she liked that about me—that we complemented each other, if that makes sense?'

'It is the same with my husband and me, Mr Hart,' I said reassuringly. 'So yes, it does make perfect sense.' Indeed, Max had become much less serious since marrying me and had a silly side that at times surpassed my own!

'But please, continue with your story,' I said, noticing that his jaw had clenched.

'Ah, this part is difficult, so forgive me if I stumble upon my words.'

We nodded encouragingly.

'I saw my future clearly with Rose. She was pretty, kind, easy to talk to. And she made me laugh. We discussed many things, including having children—she wanted four. I invited her to visit the castle and meet my father, which she immediately agreed to. She had a chaperone, of course—her governess, Miss Price, who was a young widow and her dear companion.

'At first, everything was very pleasant, and we were all having a lovely time.' Mr Hart took a deep breath, and I sensed a large 'but' coming. 'But', he continued, 'my brother, Dorian, arrived unexpectedly from Bath.'

Uh-oh, I thought.

'He had been evicted from his accommodation for not paying the rent and had no money. At that point, my father had been giving him an allowance, so he had come home to try to get it increased. I do not know if he was successful, but they had several meetings during that time. I was not paying full attention as I was solely focused on Rose, making sure she was looked after and suitably entertained. Of course, with Dorian there, it was impossible to spend much time alone with her. He likes to be the centre of attention, you see.'

'Yes, we know,' remarked Jane. Lucinda did not respond, but I sensed she was listening to every word.

'A week after he arrived, Rose began to act differently. S-she and Dorian would walk off together and talk and laugh, leaving me to converse with Miss Price. I did not mind at first as I wanted Rose and Dorian to get along, but it soon became obvious from her manner and her remarks that s-she ...' He took a breath. 'Forgive me, that she liked him very much indeed.'

His voice was tinged with pain, and it was evident that it was not a pleasant memory for him to recall. It was difficult enough to hear!

Mr Hart cleared his throat. 'The day before we were due to return to London, she came to me and said that she no longer wished to be engaged. When I asked her why, she said that she loved Dorian and wanted to marry him instead,' he said flatly.

'Oh no! You must have been devastated!' exclaimed Jane.

'I was,' he replied sorrowfully. 'But I could not claim to be deluded because I had seen their relationship developing before my very eyes. So there was nothing to do but release her from our engagement and give her my blessing. I know it must seem strange that I did not fight for her ...'

'Not at all. You loved her and wanted her to be happy even if it was not with you. Was that the case?' I asked.

He nodded. 'Yes. And my brother too as he had been unable to settle at any particular profession after Eton. I had thought he might go into law, but he seemed more interested in spending money and going to parties ... and I thought marrying would be good for him, that he would settle down ...

'The last I saw of Rose was her being handed into a carriage, with her governess, bound for London to make arrangements for the wedding. My father gave my brother a generous stipend to set them up in Marylebone, but ...'

'Let me guess,' I said wryly. 'The marriage did not take place?'

'It did not,' he replied. 'Though Dorian pretended for six months that it had. He said it had been a quiet affair with only her family as he assumed Father and I would not want to attend. During this time, he wrote to Father several times, saying he needed more money. It was always for Rose, to pay for her dresses or accessories or some such excuse. My father dutifully paid him, but I doubt she ever saw a penny of it.'

'And what of Rose now?' asked Jane. 'Where is she?'

Mr Hart's hand shook, and his teacup rattled in its saucer. He placed it carefully on the side table and composed himself.

'In Scotland with relatives, I believe. She fled from her lodgings with my brother one night after an argument, whereupon he admitted he was never going to marry her—in fact, that he did not even love her. However, by that time, it was too late. She was already ... corrupted.' Mr Hart's mouth pinched shut, and he shuddered.

'Gracious,' Jane whispered.

Indeed, we all knew what that meant. Rose was lost, and her chances of making a good match were practically nil, thanks to Dorian Hart. I was not surprised. After his attempted raspberry-and-cream seduction with me, I could believe him capable of anything.

'Can you not rescue Rose from her fate?' Lucinda spoke softly, but her voice was clear and firm. She had lowered her book and was gazing at Mr Hart unflinchingly.

He inclined his head, acknowledging her. 'I tried, Miss Fitzroy. Believe me, I did. Immediately after I heard their engagement was broken off, I wrote enquiring after her health and intimated that I still cared for her. But she replied with a curt, dismissive letter, telling me never to write to her again as she despised anyone by the name of Hart. Any letter I sent after that was returned unopened. I feared that visiting her would only reopen the wound he had caused since she has tarred me with the same brush.'

Lucinda nodded, seemingly satisfied with his answer.

'We were initially told by Mr Smith-Withers that your brother was recovering from a broken heart, that he had been cruelly separated last year from a girl he loved, Cecilia Spencer. But I assume that was also a lie?' she asked.

I hadn't told Lucinda the truth about Dory and Ceci as I had not wanted to burden her further, but it looked like she had figured it out for herself.

'Correct, Miss Fitzroy.'

'Does your brother even stay in Royal Crescent when in Bath?' she asked.

'No, I believe he stays in cheap lodgings with Mr Smith-Withers in Monmouth Street.'

My ears pricked up at that. I had seen him walking along that very street the morning we had gone to the baths! It appeared I was right to wonder about it.

'His fine clothes are not his own nor his shiny carriage. He gives the impression of being a fine gentleman. But in fact, he is destitute and borrows everything from Mr Smith-Withers, who, by the way, is not our family lawyer. Insufferable man. *He* is only hanging around because, as you ladies have cleverly deduced, my brother's new plan—since my father refuses to give him any more money—is to marry a young woman with a large dowry and continue doing as he pleases. And he has promised Mr Smith-Withers a cut of it. But if I were him, I would get that in writing.'

Lucinda chuckled at his wry humour. Mr Hart smiled at her, causing a faint blush to appear, and she quickly lowered her eyes. Jane and I glanced at each other in surprise. Indeed, Lucinda was sitting up straighter; and her book was lying in her lap, forgotten.

Wonders will never cease, I thought, watching Mr Hart haltingly enquire about Lucinda's family and her shy reply.

Perhaps Mr Hart's brother was the suitable gentleman that Lucinda was meant to attract all along? If so, it had taken a very roundabout way of getting there. And it was a pity if they were to marry as she would have a scoundrel for a brother-in-law.

Chapter 23

At the conclusion of Mr Hart's visit, he asked if he might write to Lucinda when she returned to York. She agreed, and I gave my approval too. There was no need to have the same reaction as Rose and despise anyone with the Hart name—that would be cruel. Besides, we had all liked his honesty and openness when speaking of his broken heart. His pain had been clear for everyone to see. He would have to have been an excellent actor to fake that.

It was also clear that Mr Hart was a far superior man to his brother as he had taken a profession so that he was not a burden to his father. We had all been impressed that he had chosen to lower his social standing rather than project a false image like his brother.

Of course, we had not a jot of proof that he was any better than him. But I, having spent a month in the company of a dastardly rake, now considered myself an excellent judge of character in that regard.

Plus his visit had aided in Lucinda's recovery, so for that, I was grateful. And if he did write to her, Seraphina would be pleased that her daughter's trip to Bath had not been completely in vain and that she might have a son-in-law in the near future (though she would probably rail against him being an accountant).

Indeed, Lucinda could tell her mother all about him as Seraphina was coming to collect her at Steventon in the family carriage.

And it was here that I parted ways with my niece the next day. I hugged her tightly, trying not to cry, and was reluctant to let her out of my sight. But I had to. Seraphina was impatient to get on the road and reach their inn before nightfall.

'Goodbye, Aunty Fliss,' Lucinda murmured. 'It has been a most interesting and ... educational trip. I think I will be busy for quite some time updating my journal when I get home.'

Her mouth quirked, and I smiled at her, relieved that she had regained her sense of humour despite everything that had occurred.

'Write to me when I am back in Derbyshire in a couple of weeks,' I urged, and she promised me she would.

Jane and I stood arm in arm, waving to the carriage, until it rounded the bend in the road and was lost to sight.

'Well', I said, wiping my eyes with my handkerchief, 'I don't know about you, but I could murder a strong cup of tea and some cake. Will you come with me to Ashbury to see Harriet and Evie? Or are your parents expecting you?'

'Oh, they can wait a few more hours, I'm sure. And I am longing to stretch my legs after the carriage ride.'

'Very well.'

We made arrangements for our luggage to be delivered and set off on our familiar route across the fields, chatting about what kind of cake we hoped there would be and wondering how much baby Evie had grown.

The mile-and-a-half walk encouraged our appetites, so we were starving by the time we reached Ashbury and ran up the front steps. The house looked as grand and wonderful as it always did, and I marvelled that Harriet was its mistress. I rapped on the front door with the knocker, eager to see her.

'She is probably running to the door right now,' I said over my shoulder to Jane. But when I turned back, it wasn't Harriet standing in the entranceway.

My mouth dropped open.

'Hello, my love,' said Max, his voice gruff with emotion. 'Harriet wrote and said she'd asked you to stay, and I travelled down forthwith as I could not wait a second longer to see you. So here I am.'

I burst into tears and flung myself into his arms, and he held me tightly. Oh, I never wanted him to let me go!

***

Our two-week visit to Ashbury whizzed by in a flash. Soon, Max and I were back at home in Derbyshire, and I was picking up the threads of my old life. Six weeks ago, I had been restless and eager to seek out excitement. But now that I had had a taste of it (and almost lost my husband and home in the process), I was quite content to live quietly and appreciate every moment, especially when it came to Max's abundant kisses and cuddles.

The only inkblot on my happiness was that I had not told him about certain *things* that had happened at the castle—namely that Mr Hart had professed his feelings and then tried to seduce me.

When we were at Ashbury, I had given him a watered-down version of the tale—that we had been fooled by Mr Hart in Bath, but he had shown his true nature whilst at Hartmoor. However, the details of how this had come about, I glossed over, saying vaguely that it had become 'obvious' to me by his manner and speech (here, I mentioned his distasteful reading of *Teaching Molly* in the parlour to back it up). But there was such a lot I had to leave out that he only glimpsed the peak of a buried mountain.

Fortunately, Max accepted what I told him without

question and said he was grateful that he had married such a smart woman. He added that Seraphina should not have sent Lucinda to Bath as it was such a disreputable place, and what had she been thinking?

To that, I replied that something good might still come out of it and mentioned how Mr Harrington Hart had called on us the day before to apologise for his brother. I told him the story of the man's stolen fiancée and Harrington's request to write to Lucinda before he left. Max joked that it would be a satisfying end to the story if he did end up marrying her as it would be recompense for his blackguard brother stealing Rose.

The next night, Ashbury's cook had presented us with a raspberry tart and a side jug of cream for dessert—both of which I wholeheartedly declined.

***

One night, a couple of months later, I was perusing a letter from Jane on the parlour sofa whilst Max read a book in his armchair. Shortly after, I became tired and told Max I was going up to bed, and he said he would be up soon. I had walked into the entranceway to ascend the stairs when there came a loud rapping at the front door.

I thought it was a messenger, though it was very late for

that, and waited to see if Bertram would appear. He did not, and the rapping came again. Grumbling to myself, I strode over and unlocked the door.

Standing there were Seraphina and Lucinda, the latter's upper arm being gripped by the former.

I blinked at them in bewilderment, and over their shoulders, I saw a driver unloading their trunks from the carriage. Seraphina pushed past me, dragging Lucinda with her, who seemed to be in some sort of dazed state and could hardly walk.

'Ah, hello. Max didn't mention you were staying,' I said, staring at Seraphina. Her face was a vibrant shade of pink like she had steadily been building up steam in the two-day carriage ride from York. 'Would you like some tea or—'

'Her monthlies have stopped!' Seraphina hissed at me and shook Lucinda's arm, somewhat viciously, to rouse her. The girl's head lolled, and I could see her eyes were red and swollen.

'What do you mean? Has she caught something from the baths?'

'Don't be naive, Felicity. You know perfectly well what it means.'

As Seraphina's insinuation sunk in, I gaped at Lucinda; and she hung her head, a flush creeping into her cheeks.

'Not ... not Harrington?' I said in disbelief.

Surely we hadn't been wrong about him!

Lucinda shook her head slightly, and it was then I realised there was only one other person it could have been. The room expanded and then contracted to a pinpoint, and I felt like I might faint. I gripped the sideboard for support, waves of nausea washing over me.

'Dorian,' I whispered, and Lucinda gave a slight nod.

I felt like screaming 'But I locked you in!' Yet Lucinda's odd silent behaviour before we left the castle and her disinclination to say goodbye to Mr Hart now made perfect chilling sense. He had somehow traversed her moat under my watchful eye, and she had been too ashamed to tell us, hoping that it was all a bad dream and would go away—like I wished it would now. But unfortunately, it was all too real, and her mother was livid.

'I left my precious child in your charge, *and now I find out she's pregnant!*' screeched Seraphina, causing me to take a hurried step backwards. 'Make no mistake, I blame you entirely, Felicity. What have you got to say for yourself?'

There was only one thing I could say.

'Oh *hell!*'

To be continued …

Keep Reading

Will Felicity be able to brazen her way out of this one?

Will her husband ever let her go away again?

And most importantly, can she trust Jane to keep the whole sorry mess out of her books?

Find out what happens in *Trusting Miss Austen*

(book 3 in the Miss Austen series)

***

Thank you for reading *Visiting Miss Austen,* I hope you enjoyed it as much as I did writing it! If so, I'd be thrilled if you left a review or star rating on Amazon and/or Goodreads. Your feedback truly makes a difference and helps this indie author's journey immensely.

Also by Angela

Amusing Miss Austen

POX

Brontë Lovers

The Holly Project

You Had Me at Ice Cream

I'll Meet You in Florence

The House of Dating Disasters

My Double Life

Travel & Mayhem

3 Book Rom-Com Collection

All books available on Amazon and Kindle Unlimited

Acknowledgements

I'm so grateful for having a team of people to help me on the publishing journey. Thank you to my beta readers—Katharen Martin, Sarah Williamson, and Joanna Woollcombe-Gosson—for your insights and encouraging comments. Big thanks also to my diligent copy editor, Peachy Yap, and to My Lan Khuc Valle for your gorgeous cover art.

Check out the *Visiting Miss Austen* Spotify playlist at

➜   angelapearse.pub/book-spotify-playlists

Join my mailing list for new releases,
offers, and bookish news!

➜   angelapearse.pub

About the Author

ANGELA PEARSE writes quirky romantic comedies that capture the humour of everyday life. A freelance editor with an MA in English, she enjoys travelling, hiking, cooking, binge-watching Netflix, and reading copious amounts of chick lit. Originally from New Zealand, Angela currently lives in Edinburgh with her partner. Visit angelapearse.pub.